# Sins
## *of the*
# Son

Martin J. Woods

**Outskirts Press, Inc.**
**Denver, Colorado**

Outskirts Press, Inc.
http://www.outskirtspress.com

ISBN: 978-1-4327-6749-5

Outskirts Press and the "OP" logo are trademarks belonging to Outskirts Press, Inc.

PRINTED IN THE UNITED STATES OF AMERICA

# Chapter One

The story was like so many others in the newspaper every day. "Gold's Lake Man Dies in Car Crash." In fact, it wasn't even the kind of story that Joe Mann would normally read. He'd usually scan the death and mayhem section for a name in case he recognized it, allowing no more then two seconds tops. But this time a name did stand out.

It was amazing how quickly the brain could recognize a familiar name from the past, Joe thought, even if it had been many years since he had had a thought about that name

This name stood out for its ugliness. Edward Kutz. It also stood out in Joe's mind for another reason. Ed Kutz was the man who forty years earlier had killed two policemen in the basement of an empty house on Locust Lane in Gold's Lake and he was the main character of a book Joe's father had written thirty years ago about the killings.

Joe didn't know how to react to this.

Could it be the same guy? It had to be, he thought. Why was a New Jersey paper reporting on a car accident in Gold's Lake, New York? Was it that slow a news day in New Jersey? There should have been a grisly rape or a bloody murder closer then Gold's Lake.

Joe would later learn that it was the horrific nature of the accident that gave it at least regional appeal. The car tried to pass a truck on the right and ended up crashing into a telephone pole. The immediate crash probably would not have killed the man, but the telephone pole snapped twenty feet up from the impact and fell straight down like a spear on top of the car, over the driver's side, and drove the driver's head into his abdomen. The car also burst into flames before emergency people arrived. Joe was pretty sure this was the same guy who killed those policemen that his father had written about.

Back in the 50's and 60's, the police, as a public service, would check on people's houses who were away for many weeks or months to make sure the furnace was still working and that a pipe hadn't burst and was pouring water everywhere. They'd check to see that nobody was living there or a window hadn't been broken. On this particular humid June day, on the only house on Locust Lane, they would find that someone had taken up residence in the house.

Two experienced policemen, Bill Hollar and George Allen, were chatting mindlessly about whatever popped into their heads. They had been working together for so many years, the banter came easily. They were both overweight, bored with their jobs and in their mid forties, but they were honest and decent. The key to the house had been dropped off at the police station when the owners left for vacation. So Bill and George pulled their black and white police car to a stop on the dirt driveway and walked up onto the wooded porch. The lawn was overgrown as were the bushes and plantings around the house. Bill and George knew it wasn't the case, but the house looked deserted. Bill reached into his pocket, fumbled for the key, stuck it in the key hole, lifted up on the whole door to get the key all the way in and put his shoulder into the door to open it. The humidity was making everything stick.

They walked through the door and stepped over a monstrous pile of mail, mostly junk.

George scratched out a quick note on his pad and pinned it to the door to tell the post office to stop delivery. The house was dark and the air was stagnant with the shades drawn, and all the chairs were covered with white sheets. Mouse traps were in every corner with a dead mouse in each. One unfortunate mouse had been unlucky enough to only get his leg caught in the trap. There was evidence that he had dragged the trap around with him for a while before succumbing to starvation or exhaustion.

The ones that got their necks snapped and died instantly were the lucky ones, George thought.

For some reason, when checking these empty homes, Bill and George always checked the inside of the house before the outside, despite the official procedure rules and their chief's admonishment.

He's such a worrier, thought Bill, with a smile, and such a nit-picker. "Who cares?" Bill said under his breath, not meaning for anyone to hear. Inside first or outside was fine, as long as they both got inspected, he thought.

The house was dusty. These people must have left a long time ago, or they weren't very neat. The dust on the floor was thick enough to leave footprints, and if Bill and George had stopped talking long enough to see the obvious prints coming up from the basement to the refrigerator and back, they might have made it home that night to see theirs wives and kids.

There was only one light fixture in the kitchen. It was a swag fixture with a plastic round cover that looked like a flying saucer, a vintage 1940's piece. Only one out of three bulbs was still was working, and that one was flickering. Bill reached to re-screw the bulb so it would burn evenly and he singed his fingers.

"Jimminee," he said.

At the request of his priest, he had developed the annoying habit of substituting moronic words for cuss words since his baby daughter had been born a year ago. "Jesus Christ!" was now "Cheese and Crackers!" "Crap!" was "Crud!" "Holy shit!" was "Great day in the morning." Bill had been involved with his church, St Tim's, as long as he could remember and on more then one occasion had let a cuss word slip out while speaking to the congregation at church while reading announcements or to the kids he taught at his Sunday school class.

One Sunday morning a few months back, the priest, Father Moore, had pulled Bill aside and warned him about his foul language. That day Bill had to address a bunch of Sunday school eighth graders and their parents about their upcoming confirmation. Father Moore stood right up front, but off to the side. Bill, who liked to open his class with a funny story, told a story about getting dog dirt on his shoe that morning and getting it all over the gas pedal in his car. He used the word "poop" to his class and then leaned over to Father Moore and whispered, "Aren't you glad I didn't say 'Shit'?" loud enough for the whole class and their parents to hear. Even the priest had to laugh.

Bill picked up a cloth napkin from the kitchen table and grabbed the bulb to tighten it. Perhaps the poor light quality was why they didn't see the footprints of maybe it was a combination of the dim light and the even dimmer conversation. As they headed to the basement door, Bill mentioned that he had an in grown hair on the bottom of his scrotum.

"I'm not your damn wife," George said, feigning annoyance. "I could care less about your ball sac and what you have growing out of it."

Bill smiled, clearly pleased that he had gotten a rise out of George. Both men headed down the stairs.

The basement was completely dark except for the ray of late day sunshine that reflected on the barren basement floor. The coolness of the basement was welcome relief to the humidity of the day. Another mouse trap with a deceased rodent lay in the light. The stairs were the original builder stairs with treads, but no risers.

The two men kept jabbering. Perhaps if they had employed their sense of hearing they would have heard the shuffling below. Only as they neared the bottom did they start to feel that they weren't alone.

Fear overtook them and they both clumsily starting reaching for their guns. In their panic, all the color drained from their faces. There was no order to halt or to identify whoever was down there.

Then came three flashes in the dark dank basement. The last thing Bill Hollar and George Allen saw was the split second frame of a tall man with matter-of-fact eyes pointing a gun.

The first bullet hit George in the side of the forehead and broke away a big piece of skull and left it hanging as if on a hinge. He didn't fall back right away. He stood there confused and startled for a second. He was likely dead already when the second bullet hit him in the chest. Bill got hit in the neck with the third shot and went down.

"Cheese and Crackers!" he thought.

Joe reread the article about the crash.

It had to be the same guy because of the guy's age, location and the ugly name, but the writer of the article made no mention of the crime for which Ed Kutz had been in prison for the last forty years. Joe had figured Kutz was long dead or that he would never get out of prison, but he obviously did if he died in a car crash. It stood to reason that the writer of the article was some young beat reporter assigned to a city desk that covered the shootings, robberies, house fires and car cashes. He would have gotten 98 percent of his story from the police blotter and never did any real investigating.

It was the last line of the article that would send Joe on an adventure that would consume the next few months of his life.

It said that the car that Kutz had been driving was a Porsche Turbo Carrera, a $100,000 plus car.

Joe thought back to what his father had told him about the murder of those two policemen. The killer had been a young kid, early twenties, with intense dead eyes. In anticipation of writing a book, Joe's father sat through the trial and thought that Ed Kutz's face was completely expressionless, his eyes cold and dead. He thought that happiness, sadness, fear, disappointment and loathing all looked the same on his face.

When he was spared the death penalty at the end of his trial because he hadn't planned on killing the two policemen, claiming that they scared him and that rather than identify themselves, they just reached for their guns, Kutz's expression never changed. Joe's father kept referring to Kutz's face as haunting and hard to get out of his head. In fact, in later years, when Joe would think of bad people in general, he'd always assign them Ed's face in his imagination, just as his father had described it to him.

Joe had been fascinated by his dad's book. It had been written when Joe was in the sixth grade and getting exceptional grades in writing himself. The book generated local press and the schools wanted Joe's father, Cal, to come in and speak. The local library had a signed copy on display. To the young boy, his dad was famous.

The book had been written in a make shift office in a garage on the property he grew up in. It had been started in the attic of the house, but the sounds of the family being a family always caused him to explode in anger because he couldn't concentrate. Joe's mom, always trying to be the peace maker, had the office built as a birthday present for her husband, but in truth it was really to get him out of the house more often.

Joe remembered his father sitting out there by himself toiling away at his book and he remembered how happy his father was when he found out his book would be published. His father was so seldom happy that Joe had thought there must be some magic in writing a book. When his father had brought the first bound copy home, Joe had never seen such a broad smile on his face.

Meanwhile, the more Joe excelled in writing at school, the more his teachers told him he would follow in his father's footsteps.

The book had done well. It won the Edgar Allen Poe Award for young adult mysteries in 1974. It made his father a substantial amount of money and continued to do so for years until it was taken out of print. Joe's family had money, but most of it came from an inheritance his mom had gotten. It was always a source of tension between them and caused more then one physical altercation. He was a man's man and having to depend on his wife to be successful never sat well with him. It was just one of the many dogs chasing him through the woods of his mind.

Joe's father considered himself an Ernest Hemingway type at heart. An adventurer, a womanizer, a world traveler, a connoisseur of everything fine, a lover and a fighter, a dare devil, but in fact he was a husband and father in a sleepy town on the outskirts of New York city where he traveled everyday to a job he hated and to a boss he hated as well. His image of himself was not consistent with reality and he tended to take it out on the people who loved him the most.

Joe had read the book and was fascinated. On the inside cover it said it was based on true events. Joe wanted to know what was true and what was made up. He constantly pestered his father about the book, maybe because it was the one topic that Joe could bring up without incurring his father's wrath.

Something always seemed to be bothering Joe's father. His mood could turn dark in a flash. Back in the fifties, driving home from work with a beer in one's hand was a common thing. Joe's father, Cal, had at least one every day. It wasn't until many years later, when Joe grew to be an adult and a father himself and had started to drink beer, did he realize that beer had the same effect on him. He became moody and combative and very easily offended. Joe was aware enough to realize how beer affected him and stopped drinking it.

This was not the last time Joe would see a connection between himself and his father. In fact, the older Joe got, the more connections he saw and some of them were not good at all.

Joe had gotten married himself in 1993, four years after his father had died of lung cancer, alone and scared. After a year of marriage he and his wife Barbara had their first child and then had two more, quickly, after that. It was a tough adjustment, but they managed. Having little kids around made everything lighter, and although it was stressful, they managed it well and they managed it together. They didn't have a lot of money because Joe was getting his own landscaping design business going, but that didn't seem to matter very much back then. Two a.m. feedings and diaper changes were all consuming. Although Barbara and Joe didn't always agree, they did definitely agree that they loved their children.

Joe sat staring at the newspaper and the story of the crash. It instantly brought back a flood of memories of his father. As he got older, Joe loved talking to his father about the book, but by that time the topic of the book no longer made Cal happy. He had planned to write so many more and be a celebrated author, but the drudgery of writing another book overwhelmed him. He'd much rather live on the glory of the awards he won than go out and do it again.

And doing it again had its risks. If he failed, it could mean he wasn't a real talent and had just gotten lucky. Those dogs chasing him through the woods might start to bark again, claiming that he was a hack and would always need his wife's money to support them. A few beers with some admirers would erase all those thoughts.

One cold mid-winter day, about a year before Cal died, the effects of the lung cancer already easily apparent and Cal confined to his bed, Joe stopped by to see him in his tiny, poorly furnished apartment. Just watching him get out of bed to walk the few feet to the toilet was almost more then Joe could bear. He'd take three steps and have to stop and hold himself up to catch his breath.

Once he had gotten back in bed and regained his breath, he asked if Joe had heard that the old Wrin house on Locust Lane had been broken into. It surprised Joe at first. His father hadn't started a conversation about the book in years. Maybe Cal knew he was dying and wanted one more ride through his glory years, or maybe he thought there was more to the story.

"The Wrin house? Really?" Joe asked. "I thought that place had been torn down years ago."

Cal explained that the house had been boarded up and never lived in again. In fact, it was in the last area of town that hadn't been developed.

"Someone broke in through the same basement window that

Ed Kutz had climbed through forty years ago," Joe's dad said.

Joe thought it was mildly interesting, but he was more interested in how his father could have known this. He lived in New Jersey and the house was in Gold's Lake. Most of the people who were around during the murders were long gone. Joe thought ninety-nine out of a hundred people in Gold's Lake would have no idea that the murders had ever taken place. Cal handed Joe the letter he'd received that day.

It was a handwritten letter, most definitely from a woman's hand, three pages long, both sides. It was from a childhood friend of Joe's father named Robbie, short for Roberta. They'd grown up on the same street in Gold's Lake and she'd always had a secret crush on Cal although Joe believed that Cal never acted on it.

Odd, Joe thought, because his father had had so many flings in his life, plenty of them while being married to Joe's mother. Robbie must not be very attractive if my father never tried to bag her.

She had never moved out of her childhood home and had never married or even had a boyfriend as far at Cal knew. Was she pining away for Cal? He liked to think so.

*Dear Cal,*

*How are you? I hope that nagging cough you mentioned in your last letter is all cleared up.*

Cal hadn't mentioned his cancer to her.

*Something was stirring at the old Wrin place last week. Someone cut away the thick brush around the basement window and climbed in. The same window. I was walking my dog as I do everyday by the house and noticed the broken window. It was me who called the police to investigate. Two policemen drove up. I met them and showed them the window. They didn't seem to care about the crime and they had NO idea what had taken place there. I explained it, but they acted like I was senile. I guess that's how I might have seemed. I assume that by now they have checked out my story or maybe not. They looked to be about the same age as officers Holler and Allen were. It brought me back, but at the same time made me sad for the time gone by.*

The letter went on to rehash the killings and Cal's subsequent book. She mentioned a few more acquaintances from their youth who had passed away. Cal found Robbie's letters getting sadder with the passing years, not because of the news they contained, but because her world was getting smaller and smaller every day.

But Cal still had a soft spot for her and kept up the pen pal relationship. She had been very helpful when Cal wrote his book. She had done research for him and had pulled old photographs for him. It was the most useful she had ever felt.

Joe put the letter down, but didn't think much of it. Cal started to speak in his labored breath. He was so skinny it was hard for Joe to look at him. This man, who had always seemed so powerful and often scary to Joe, was pathetically frail.

"There was a robbery at a Country Club jewelry show outside of Gold's Lake two weeks prior to the Hollar and Allens killings. I think they're connected," Cal said.

"How?" Joe asked.

"I don't know," Cal said, "but crime was a non issue in that region in the sixties except for that two week period, and the robbery was never solved. The take was huge, and it included a rare diamond necklace. It was robbed by two men, one short and one tall."

Then the coughing started and Cal couldn't get it under control. The coughs were so forceful that they made Joe think his father might burst a blood vessel in his head. It was painful to watch. After about ten minutes the coughs stopped, but Cal was so exhausted, he dared not speak for fear that the coughing fit would return.

Joe kept looking at the article of the crash.

How did Ed Kutz get the money to own a Porsche after spending forty years in prison? Did someone leave him the money?

As well as Joe could remember, the Kutz family was small and had forgotten about him years ago. None of them were well to do at all. The conversation he had with his father before the coughing attack came back to him.

What if Ed Kutz robbed the country club and stashed what he had stolen in the Wrin's basement and then waited for almost forty years to go claim it? Weren't there two people involved in the country club robbery, he thought. Did the other safeguard Ed's share all those years?

The story intrigued Joe. He began to wonder if he would he finish the story that his father had started. Joe had always compared himself to his father, both his good attributes and his bad, and Joe considered what it would be like if he were as successful with his own book as his father had been with his.

Joe started to think of little else. He couldn't understand why the story intrigued him so much. Maybe it made him feel closer to his dead, flawed father. Maybe he could gain some understanding as to why his father behaved the way he did. Each day Joe was feeling more and more compelled to investigate the story. It no longer felt like a choice, but a duty he had to fulfill. And maybe in the process he might learn to forgive his father and to understand himself.

Joe's relationship with his wife Barbara was on the rocks. They just weren't firing on all cylinders. Their days were filled with work and caring for their kids and not much else. The life they knew before kids was a distant memory. All their discussions revolved around them, and as far as Joe could see down the road, things weren't going to change. It was as if romance, flirting and sneaky sex were never a part of their past. He loved her, but he was bored and his restlessness was becoming all-consuming. He internalized things that bothered him and they festered. He feared he might do something to sabotage the relationship. He was acting like his father and he knew it. He had to get away, for his kids and for his marriage, but mostly for himself.

Why couldn't he be happy with what he had? He had an enviable life. Why couldn't he be happy in the moment? Was this his father's curse?

Joe's father had moved out after twenty years of marriage and had taken up with a nasty woman that Joe loathed. Had he left Joe's mother for a hot young sex pot, at least that would have made some sense, but his new lady was neither nice nor warm nor attractive. Joe thought she was just convenient and willing. Nothing was better about Cal's life after leaving. In fact, when he got cancer, she threw him out.

Joe never asked his father what caused him to stray. It would have been easier to understand if Cal had met his once in a lifetime passion after he had married Joe's mom and just couldn't deny the force of nature. But that wasn't it. He had had many affairs and none were particularly meaningful. He had screwed around every chance he got. It was what his father did to prove to himself that he was a man.

Joe didn't have to ask his father why. The answer had been coming into focus as Joe got older and was becoming a family man himself.

Despite his insight, Joe felt like he was on a train picking up speed and chugging down the track inexorably toward the same conclusion that ruined his father's life. He had the lens of history to look through, however, and he remembered well the day his father moved out. Joe had been lying on the threadbare carpet in his living room watching his black and white TV when his father left the house. He left a note on the kitchen table which said simply "Goodbye."

Joe got up when he heard his mother come home from her school board meeting. She walked over to the note on the table, said "Good," and then walked into her laundry room and locked the door. With those few words, twenty years of marriage were over.

Joe was killing his own marriage. He felt that if he didn't get away, his marriage would die and he didn't want that. He loved his wife and his children. So where did this urge to sabotage his marriage come from? Sure, it would have been easy to blame it on genetics, but Joe knew that was a cop out.

Granted these feelings didn't come up very often, but they seemed to be coming up more and more. He would let little things bother him until they consumed him. He'd sulk around for days, not even sure why he was mad. Barbara would simply let these dark periods run their course. But even she was getting worried about their frequency.

Didn't he think he was worthy of the love of a terrific women? He would soon find out that his wife felt the same way. Talking about his feelings wasn't his strong suit, so when he confronted his wife about heading away to Gold's Lake for a few weeks, he stuttered like a high school boy asking a girl on a date for the first time.

To his shame and astonishment, his wife walked up to him, kissed him on the forehead and said, "Just come back to us."

Was it a mid life crisis? Maybe, Joe thought. Were his forty-seven years catching up to him? Was the gray hair clouding his thinking? Whatever it was, he had to get it straightened out.

As he started packing, he really wasn't sure if he was going to Gold's Lake for his marriage or because of unresolved issues with his father or to shed light on a car crash and a forty year old double homicide. Or, he quietly began to think, to write his own book. Whatever it was, he was going. He walked into his kids' rooms after they were asleep and kissed them each. He left a note on the table for his wife that simply read "Goodbye."

# Chapter Two

J oe gassed up his 2003 Ford Explorer and headed up the New York State thruway. He'd thrown some clothes together and not much else.

He had bought a pile of legal size lined paper and some pencils. He felt stupid and laughed at himself because it felt silly to act like a writer when he really wasn't one. Yet.

Another thought pulled at Joe, too. He'd never been the kind of guy to follow things through. He'd start with all sorts of gusto and good intentions, work hard for a couple weeks, and then stop once the excitement was gone. He started the piano and flute and had given them both up. He'd done better with the guitar, but wasn't working that hard at it recently. Only with his landscaping business had he followed through from his first day there, when the company was still owned by Frank Emerson, until he assumed the business, became the owner, and built it up into a specialty design outfit three times its original size.

Frank Emerson had stipulated that if Joe was to assume the business, he had to hire Frank's grandson and share ownership with him. The boy turned out to be an eager learner and very capable. With Joe's help he moved up through the ranks and now, as the junior partner, was able to run the company and keep it expanding. Joe could usually do most of his work from home, call in to his partner, and try to stay out of the office or the field because his presence would confuse the employees about who was running the show. Joe would smile to himself when he realized he had to stay out of the office so as not to undermine his partner's authority there and so everything would run smoothly and profitably. A perfect situation.

And it reinforced Joe's thought that being great at something was just too much work. Maybe I learned that from my father, he now thought, as he drove north along the thruway. Maybe, like him, I'll never do anything worthwhile enough to offset all my other faults in life.

Joe's negative side took over.

Who am I kidding? I'm not a journalist. I'm not an investigative reporter and I never follow through. I'll probably just spend a few days working on this and then head back home in no better shape than when I left. Perhaps I'll be in worse shape. I'll have another failure to add to my name. Like my father.

But Joe's father had finished something. He'd written a critically acclaimed book that won awards and made a lot of money. If they were so much alike, Joe should be able to write a book too. What if he couldn't? Would that mean he wasn't as good as his father? What other doubts of his father's would be visited on him?

In some ways Joe knew he was better than his father. Joe had never stepped out on his wife. When Cal died about five years ago, Joe found piles of letters from old girlfriends which Cal had kept. It blew Joe's mind that he would keep the evidence of these affairs, but Joe had concluded that his father dealt with self loathing issues and needed these letters to prove that he was lovable or worthy or something.

No, Joe had never stepped out, but that isn't to say he hadn't been tempted, despite a healthy sex life with Barbara. If faced with the perfect situation, might he? He didn't know the answer to that, but at times he was worried that he would fail the test if ever confronted. Was he really any better than his father?

That question can't be answered yet, Joe concluded.

The Explorer was moving at a steady seventy-five miles an hour in the left lane. The farther Joe got away from his home, the lighter he felt. Years of worry felt like they were draining away, even if it was only for a short time. He plugged in a Bruce Springsteen mix CD he'd made. The CD kicked on in the middle of "Racing in the Streets."

*"My baby and me,*
*we're going to ride to the sea*
*and wash these sins off our hands"*

Joe knew he had sins to atone for, but Barbara loved him. Was that the sin he was punishing her for? For loving him? The thought made him feel miserable and made him want to turn around and try to explain to her why he couldn't give her the love that she wanted and that he wanted so much to be able to give.

On the seat next to him, Joe had the notes his father had used to write his book. They were all handwritten in pencil and some were so faded he couldn't make them out. There were copies of documents from library archives and scraps from newspapers. They were a large sloppy pile of papers. Joe was glad he had his lap top. He thought that the first couple of days he would start organizing the file and in the process bring himself up to speed on the story.

A tattered copy of his father's book lay there also. A picture on the opened inside cover stared back at Joe. He was about the same age as his father had been when he had written the book. He hadn't read the book in years and had forgotten a lot of it. He also had a copy of the last letter Robbie had written his father. He wondered if she even knew Cal was dead. Maybe he should have called her to warn her that he was coming up and tell her that he would want to see her.

The ride could have been done in five hours, but Joe took seven. He was not on a schedule. No one was waiting for him in Gold's Lake. No one would send out an APB if he didn't show up. He started going slower as he got closer. The question of where to start was nagging at him.

Cal had told Joe that Gold's Lake was one of the largest townships geographically in that part of the state. It took more than half an hour to drive from one end of the town's land to the other. As he began to approach Gold's Lake, Joe could see that the area he was now driving through was mostly a thick wooded swampy terrain unsuitable for any kind of building. The highway brushed the north side of the town, but the center of the town remained invisible while the leaves were still on the trees. All that could be seen was part of the blue mirrored surface of the lake off in the distance, reflecting the world. And all we troubled souls in it, Joe thought, still humming along to Bruce.

Over the years Gold's Lake's town council had been dominated by those who would vote down any proposal to clear some of the trees so that the lake and the town would be visible from the highway and more tourists would visit the town. The town council supported Gold's Lake's anonymity and consequently the center of town had maintained an old world charm increasingly hard to find in northern New York State after the Olympics had been held in Lake Placid and the once rural area had changed to a popular tourist haunt.

The town had had one short lived moment of fame when a local Gold's Lake boy won a gold medal for speed skating in the Olympics and afterward opened a high end Italian restaurant in the center of town. For a while tourists came and the municipal buildings near the restaurant were cleaned up and began to exhibit what the tourists would call "character" after having merely appeared old and run down for so many years before. But the conservative town council continued to vote down any significant downtown re-development, and eventually the tourists stopped coming, the Italian restaurant closed, and the gold medal winner moved to California. Life in Gold's Lake returned to its isolated existence. Once again the town council had had its way.

As Joe pulled off the thruway, he wondered if Gold's Lake even had a visitor center. He thought not and decided the town hall seemed like a safe place to start his inquiry. Maybe someone would take pity on him and show him around. As he reached the end of the exit ramp, directly in front of him was the sign for the town hall. How accommodating, he thought.

Joe drove into the town and past the old brick police station and what looked to have been an old early 1900's grammar school now converted to a library. It sat on a rise a hundred feet off the street and was a hulking two story red brick building with massive oak front doors and cathedral style, double hung windows. Joe pictured Cal years earlier climbing up the stone steps to do his research on the murders.

Down the street the town hall looked like its granite façade had been power washed within the last few years, but the paint on the four majestic columns in front was a dull, grayish white and was chipped and peeling from top to bottom. Joe parked out front and by habit started to reach into his pocket for change when he realized there were no parking meters anywhere along the main street.

After visiting the town hall, Joe felt he now had his bearings. He also had left with Robbie's address. He got back in his Explorer and headed east on Gold's Lake Road past the Gold's Lake Inn. It's been redone since my childhood, Joe thought. He vaguely remembered his father taking him and his brother up to Gold's Lake in the summer to see his father's home town. They stopped briefly by the inn, he remembered, but he was sure they hadn't eaten there.

My dad was always too cheap. We probably brought PBJ sandwiches with apple juice for lunch. We did stop by the cemetery, though, where Cal's father was buried.

Joe had never met his grandfather because he'd died long before Joe was born. Joe remembered his father not seeming the least bit upset or emotional when he was standing at his father's grave for the first time in twenty years. It could have been anybody's grave site. It was almost as if his father had gone to the grave to see if he'd feel anything. He didn't. We just moved on, Joe remembered.

Joe's father had grown up at the base of nearby White Head Mountain and had always been an excellent snow skier. He'd taken Joe and his brother skiing many times during their childhood. Cal was a graceful skier, but not a particularly fast skier. Being the cheapskate he was, he wanted to get the maximum distance out of every trip down the mountain. He also used to make sure they were the first ones on the mountain and the last ones off. Getting the most ski runs down the mountain for his money was important to Cal.

As Joe cruised the streets of Gold's Lake, he saw the signs for White Head Mountain. He remembered that family trip they'd taken and the one thing his dad did spend money on was a summer trip on the chair lift up the mountain. At the time Joe thought it was fun, but he had wondered about the look on his father's face that day.

Cal had spent an unhappy childhood there. He had an abusive father and an apathetic mother. It was in this town, some fifty-five years ago, where Cal had stood on his front steps, clad in army fatigues, with a crew cut and a duffle bag over his shoulder. As he was getting ready to head for basic training to join the fight in Europe against the Nazis, Italians and Germans, a woman he didn't recognize appeared on his front steps.

"I'm your real mother," she said.

Cal told Joe that at first he had never questioned that the woman who raised him might not be his birth mother. He had wondered why she was so aloof and cold, but he just thought that was the way she was. The woman who had raised him denied the other woman's claims then and just sent Cal on his way off to war.

At first Cal thought she was crazy and put the episode out of his head, but as time crept by, the event kept coming back to him.

Who was this woman, he thought. Why would she say something like that? Why would she come on the day I was heading off to war? How did she even know I was heading off to war?

The answers to those questions were what gave validity to what she had said. Was she afraid that Cal would be killed in the war and that she would lose her chance to reconnect with her child? If she was in fact his biological mom, wouldn't that be a natural desire, to make amends before it was too late. Cal broached the subject with both his mother and father, but both dismissed the woman as a loon. Cal did, however, remember her name and had repeated it to Joe. Funk. Mary Funk.

Why was his supposedly natural mother so cold to him? That natural bond seemed to be missing. Cal noticed it and people and friends noticed it as well. She wasn't outwardly mean to the boy, but she didn't seem to like him very much.

So Cal's life went on with the nagging question: Was that woman he had seen for a few minutes really his mother?

It had seemed impossible, but then it seemed, well, maybe. Cal had told Joe that he knew nothing of his birth. Was it a long delivery? Was it easy? Hard? Was he a pretty baby, Cal had wondered. Was he born at night? In the morning? Did he breast feed?

Cal knew none of it.

During the war Cal was stationed in Alaska. Even though the Russians were on the Americans' side in the war, it was an uneasy alliance. No one knew where Stalin's ambitions would take him. The U.S. wanted to make sure Alaska was protected and that there was a secure jumping off point if America had to attack them. After boot camp at Fort Dix, Cal was sent to Alaska, where he served out the duration of the war, mostly in absolute boredom. Although Cal felt like he was being punished by being sent to Alaska, he was well respected by his superiors there. There was a real fear that Alaska could be a target and the government wanted quality people there to defend it if it was attacked.

After six months Cal was praying that Alaska would be attacked, not only to interrupt the boredom, but so that he would have some stories to tell about his heroism in battle or so that he would have a scar or two to show. He wanted to use his training. Despite ghastly body counts and stories of hand to hand combat, starvation, prison camps, torture, and mass killings, he still wanted to go into battle. He made several requests to be sent to Europe or the Pacific, but to no avail. He would sit out the war.

Although Cal was never allowed to join the real war, he did get a project. He was put in charge of developing an airstrip in Alaska, four hundred miles due north of Anchorage. The challenges were numerous because there were no roads in or out of the area selected. He had to bring all the supplies across rivers, once they had frozen, into a town that didn't exist yet. A whole community had to be built around the airstrip because people would have to live there to maintain the strip. A system of government would have to be developed and it all fell to him.

Cal did not have any particular credentials to be put in charge of this task, but the others in his unit had even less, and his superiors recognized that Cal had far more native ability and spunk than his platoon mates. It was war time. The job had to be done. Cal was put in charge.

Cal attacked the challenge with all the gusto he could muster. It momentarily made him forget his bitterness about being left out of the war. Cal brought the job in under budget and had it done earlier than expected. He worked days and nights and weekends. He proved he could lead people effectively and get things done. He hoped that if he did a good job on this task, he would get sent to Europe.

By all accounts, Cal did an exceptional job at such a young age. He was praised by all who saw him, but they were too few. Unfortunately, the attention of the armed forces was on Europe and the Pacific and his accomplishment went almost completely ignored in those places. Once the project was completed, he was sent back to his unit and to complete boredom. The euphoria of his accomplishment faded and his bitterness returned.

When Cal returned home, he felt as if his father was disappointed that Cal never saw combat. He wouldn't be able to brag to his friends about his son, the war hero. At times Cal even felt that his father might have been happier if he'd been able to tell his friends that his son died charging up a hill or had been shot down in a plane. His father never said that he was glad he was safely home and his mother only gave him an awkward hug when he walked in the door. Neither of them ever asked him a single question about his time in the war or where he'd been or what he'd been doing. It was almost as if they were embarrassed by him.

Both of Cal's parents eventually died in the nineteen fifties, shortly after he was married. His father wasn't the kind of man you asked a question a second time and Cal and his father just weren't close.

His father was a big thick man who liked to drink, but he wasn't a nice drunk. Some people get lovable when they drink. Cal's father got nasty, especially on beer. His father was a hitter and a taskmaster who believed kids should be quiet and obedient and nothing else. The only time Cal's father took any real interest in him was when he brought home a less then stellar report card. Cal remembered getting whopped by his father's belt and wondering, what do you care how I do in school?

As a boy Cal worked with his father on the streets of Gold's Lake in his newspaper stand. Cal enjoyed it because his father was always a lot nicer to him in public than he was in private.

In the late 1980's, when Cal's cancer made him so weak he could no longer work, he needed something to work on. With the question of who his real mother had been still nagging at him and with his own death staring him in the face, he decided to create his family tree.

It was a big project. Cal thought that maybe he would find the inspiration for another book during the project, but what he really wanted to know before he died was if that woman he met on his front steps all those years ago was his real mother and if so, why did she leave him.

The project took him from Germany to Ellis Island and on to the archives of New York City. On days he felt good he would go and do the investigation himself. On most days, however, he would write and request items by mail.

A big break came when he found the boat manifests that showed when his great grandfather had come to America. Cal was proud that he'd gotten good enough at this type of investigation that he was able to pull the copy of the actual manifest that showed when his ancestor had come over. He was really enjoying himself, but there was a feeling of dread. He wasn't sure if he wanted to find out the truth about this other woman or not. If the woman who raised him was not his mother, then that would explain why she found him so unlovable and why he didn't love her very much. However, if it turned out she was his real mother, then maybe he wasn't worthy of love. He began pulling for the other woman.

What would he do if he found out that the visitor was his real mother? He would go visit her grave, he thought. Maybe he'd look up her family and find out if he had any brothers or sisters or nieces or nephews that he didn't know about.

The answer came rather swiftly and without much fanfare. Cal had requested a marriage certificate for his father from the Gold's Lake Office of Records. It seemed like the easiest way to find out if the woman he thought was his mother was or was not. It took about a month to come in the mail. Cal didn't open it right away. He just kind of held it and twirled it around in his hands as if he wasn't sure if he would open it, file it or simply throw it away. Maybe not knowing was better than knowing.

After about an hour he sat down in his sparsely furnished kitchen in his rented apartment and slit the envelope open with a butter knife. It read, "In 1908, Calvin Mann married 19 year old Mary

Funk in a ceremony in the back of the Catholic church because he was Catholic and she wasn't."

Cal just stared at it. He really didn't know what to feel. He had met his real mother so briefly and had dismissed her as if she were crazy. Relieved at having some understanding as to why his own stepmother was so apathetic toward him, a new wave of feelings came over him. Why did my mother leave me, he wondered. He was so young when she left, he had absolutely no memory of her. She must have left when I was one or two years old, he figured.

With nothing to do but sit in his apartment, too sick to do much of anything, Cal obsessed over the question of why. Who could he ask? Everybody who knew his father or his biological mother would be long dead and even if they were still alive, he wouldn't know who they were or where to find them. He didn't have the energy to travel to Gold's Lake and go door to door looking for someone who might not even exist.

He started to investigate Mary Funk. Maybe he could find a relative of hers and they could shed some light on what happened. Maybe he could find out where she was buried and backtrack from there. It now became necessary to complete his family tree. But how does one go about finding someone with so little information, he worried. All he had was a name.

On the certificate it listed the best man and the bridesmaid. A woman named Ann Sloan had apparently been friendly with Mary Funk many years ago. Cal called several Sloans in the Gold's Lake area and found, without too much trouble, the son of Ann Sloan. They spoke on the phone for a while. He was a man in his sixties who spoke slowly and haltingly, as if he'd had a stroke. When he mentioned Mary Funk to him, Cal expected not a flicker of a memory would be ignited.

There was a long pause and then he said, "Yes, I remember Mary." His mother and Mary had remained close until she was chased away. "Out west, I think," he said.

Cal had so many questions he didn't know where to start. He hoped he had found the fountain that was going to give him all the answers.

"Out west? Where? Chased? What do you mean by that?" Cal's flurry of questions seemed to startle the man. His memory was so vague that he couldn't offer Cal very much and he sensed Cal's disappointment.

"I'm sorry," he said. "I was young and didn't pay much attention."

Cal apologized for getting him so excited and tried to calm him down.

"Is there anything else you can tell me? I think she might be my real mother and I'd like to find out some more information about her." The conversation went on for a few more minutes, but it was pretty clear that the man was not healthy and his memory was not good. Cal sensed that he had gotten as much information as he was going to get.

"Well, thank you very much," Cal said. "If you think of anything else that might help me, here is my number."

Cal gave him the number and was preparing to say goodbye when the man said something else in what seemed like a more lucid moment.

"One thing is for sure, she was an abused woman. One of my clearest memories from my childhood is of her coming to our house with a huge knot on her forehead and a bloody nose."

And then the man abruptly hung up as if he didn't like thinking about that memory and he could shut it down by hanging up the phone.

Cal immediately got a pad of paper and wrote down everything the man had said. This was an old habit from his writing days. *Moved out. West. Chased away. Abused.* Maybe Cal's mother left him because she was being abused. Maybe she feared for her life. While this was obviously sad news, it was also a possible explanation of why she left him. If he never found out anything further, there would be the lingering possibility that she left because she had no choice. Maybe it wasn't because he was unlovable.

A week went by and all Cal did was think about that phone call and what he would do next. He was really no closer to finding out what happened to her than he was before. Well, maybe a little closer, he thought. He did know she was "out west." But what did that mean? Western New York or the western United States? Cal decided that it must be the western U.S. and formulated a game plan. He would find out the name and address of every "Funk" west of the Mississippi and send them a postcard asking if they knew anything about Mary Funk.

Before the Internet, getting this kind of information was not easy, but Cal had the time so he did it right. He did a tremendous amount of phone work and got what he thought was a fairly comprehensive list of all the Funks in the western US. There had to be a connection to his mother with one of them.

The post card he sent said simply, *My name if Calvin Mann. I grew up in Gold's Lake and have recently found out that my real mother's name was Mary Funk. I'm trying to find out what became of her. She married my father, John Ernst Mann, in 1908 and they divorced when I was very young. If you have any information, please call me.*

Cal thought this was a long shot, but he was still excited. He felt useful again. This whole family tree endeavor had given him energy. He wasn't dwelling on the cancer that was ravaging his body. He wasn't dwelling on the fact that he was dying.

Two weeks had passed since his post cards had gone out. He was a little disappointed that he hadn't heard anything yet, but he was still hopeful. He really didn't have a next move so this one had to work, he thought. Maybe when the spring comes, I'll see how my energy level is and I'll make a trip to Gold's Lake if I have to.

But it turned out he wouldn't be going to Gold's Lake. He would be going to Arizona. The phone rang early one gray rainy Monday. He got up slowly out of his recliner, tossed away the blanket that he always had over him these days, and headed to the phone in the kitchen.

"Hello," he said in a crackly voice that hadn't spoken yet that day.

"Hello," he said again after clearing his throat.

"Is this Calvin Mann?" A shaky old lady's voice said on the other end.

"Yes, it is," Cal said.

"Well, I'm Mary Funk. I'm your mother."

# Chapter Three

Joe found a small hotel on the outskirts of town to settle into. It wasn't very nice and the lobby smelled of old cigarettes, beer and God knows what else. The place looked like it should have been remodeled twenty years ago. But Joe didn't care. He really had no idea how long he was staying or for that matter what he was even doing there. What would he tell people if they asked what he was here for? To investigate a forty year old murder that was long solved? Maybe he should tell them the truth: that he was running from a perfectly good marriage for reasons he couldn't understand and that he needed to get away from his wife until he could grow up.

Maybe not.

Joe wanted to be up and out of there early that morning. He had been a worker all his life. If he didn't have a full day of work ahead of him in the morning, he was out of sorts. He'd worked since he was ten. By the time he'd finished high school, he'd delivered papers, cut grass, shoveled snow, pumped gas and even babysat. Then he started at Frank Emerson's landscaping business, and it wasn't long before Frank was telling his friends, "Joe's the hardest working guy I've ever hired. He works even harder than I do."

In Joe's family it was understood that you made your own money or you went without.

Now that Joe was less busy at work and hardly ever in the office, that drive to remain busy had helped propel him into taking on this new adventure of researching the murders and perhaps writing a follow up book to Cal's. Especially since he'd seen that newspaper article, he'd find himself sitting in his office at home, staring out the window for an hour or two at a time, going over the facts as he knew them about Ed Kutz.

After he woke, he sat for a moment on the edge of his bed. There was a noticeable depression in the mattress. Any support had long ago gone slack. He reached over and grabbed one of his yellow lined note pads and a hotel issued pen and started to make a list of what he would do that day. He wrote that he would go to the site of the accident first.

Why, he thought to himself. Well, I guess that's where this whole hair brained trip started.

It seemed like as good a place as any to start. He wrote that he would try to make contact with Robbie, and then he would go to the town hall to see what he could find out about Ed Kutz.

Maybe find out where Ed was living since his release from jail.

Maybe go to a bar and get drunk.

"Maybe pack my shit up and drive the hell back home," he said to himself, sitting on the edge of the bed looking into the mirror

Joe tore the sheet of paper off the pad and put it in the file with everything else. He wrapped an oversize rubber band around it and headed for the door.

The accident happened on Route 100, west of the center of town. Joe approached the long straight flat stretch of road that just begged you to drive fast. It would have been virtually impossible for me to go slow on this road in a Porsche, Joe thought.

Joe had no idea where the accident took place on a road that was many miles long.

Well, I got the time, he thought. Let's just drive up the road and maybe I'll see it.

It didn't take long to find the spot. It was about a mile up on the right side of the road. A new telephone pole had been sistered to the old one. It was obviously a temporary repair because the old one with its jagged edges was still there. The part that had snapped off and had driven Ed Kutz's head into his chest was gone. The grass around the pole was all dead from the fire after the crash.

What a mess this must have been, Joe thought.

He looked up and noticed that the vinyl siding on the two houses closest to the accident was melted and almost dripping off. The fire must have been intense. He hoped Ed was dead before the inferno started.

With nothing much left to see, Joe drove further on Route 100, intending to turn around at the gas station at the corner about a quarter mile up the road. Joe pulled into the gas station's lot and swung around to head in the other direction and almost ran into the burnt out, crushed Porsche.

There was no doubt that this was the car.

But why would it still be here? It's been a month since the crash. And why in such a public place?

Joe could see the service station had a fenced in area in the back where they stored other crashed cars. Joe walked up to the car. He suddenly felt a chill as if he had never thought he would be this close to Ed Kutz and his father's proudest achievement. Everything became much more real to him than Joe ever thought it would be. He walked over to the car and peered in the window on the driver's side. It must have been a very hot fire. The seat cushions had been burnt off completely, revealing the springs. Nothing was left of the interior of the car. Joe couldn't help but wonder what was left of Ed when they pulled him out.

Was he just ashes? Did they clean him up with a broom or a dust buster? Did they find his teeth? His bones? Was he steaming like a Thanksgiving turkey after being in the oven at 475 degrees for eight hours? How would he have tasted with sweet potatoes?

Joe always resorted to a gallows humor in the face of death. He didn't know why, but he always had. Maybe it was a defense mechanism to keep from crying. In his house growing up, you just didn't cry. His farther forbade it. If you did cry, you were likely to be degraded as a sissy and beaten. Men don't cry. If you don't cry for a long enough time, you can't cry at all. Joe couldn't remember the last time he had cried. He thought it was funny that when a very old person would pass away, people would act as if it was unexpected. Joe had a very low tolerance for hypocrisy. Even at a funeral he had to bite his tongue not to point it out. People who knew him well and knew what a nice person he was couldn't reconcile this behavior. If they had known more about his father and grandfather, they might have understood.

After staring at the car for ten minutes, Joe wandered into the office. An old man who had been watching him look at the car was standing over the register. He had a long unkempt gray beard and was wearing an old coat with a Knights of Columbus patch on the sleeve. The coat looked to be as old as he was and much dirtier, as if he had used it to wipe oil on for the last thirty years.

"Yah wanna buy a Porsche?" the old man said with a wry smile. "I'll give it to yah cheap. Nobody else will give you that kind of deal on a Porsche," he laughed.

Joe smiled back. He liked him at once because they both shared the same sense of humor surrounding death.

"What happened? I guess that driver died?"

"He's dead alright. If the crash didn't kill him, then the telephone pole did. And if he managed to still be breathing, the fire took care of that. It just wasn't his day. His maker wanted him that day and wasn't gonna take no for an answer."

"Who was he?" Joe asked, pretending not to know so he could see if he could squeeze some information out of the grizzly guy without showing his hand.

"Don't know. I don't think he was from around here."

"What was his name?" Joe asked.

"I can't remember," the man said, "but the newspaper article is right behind you on the wall next to the thermostat."

Joe turned to read the article. It was a much longer article than the one he had seen back in New Jersey. Ed's name appeared in the second paragraph. It said he had recently moved to Gold's Lake. There was no mention of the crime for which he had spent forty years in prison.

"Ed Kutz," Joe exclaimed, still pretending not to know much about him or the accident.

"Isn't that the same name as the guy who murdered those cops all those years ago?"

Instantly Joe knew he'd made a mistake. His approach had been clumsy and amateurish.

The man behind the counter stopped talking and stared at him. It was obvious to them both that Joe was too young to have remembered the killings. The old man knew he was being used. At the same time that he had realized that he was being manipulated, Joe thought he saw a glint of a memory come back to him.

He might have remembered that was the same name, but he

didn't say anything. Joe saw he was angry at his approach.

"I'm sorry," Joe said. "I wasn't sure if it was the same guy or not and I didn't want to sound foolish if it wasn't."

"I knew George Allen and his family," the old man said. "If that son of a bitch who killed him was out of prison, I'd have known about it. It must have been someone else."

Joe could see by the look on the old man's face that he wasn't sure if what he was saying were true. A car pulled up to the pumps out front and even though it was self serve, the old man excused himself to go help the customer. He was no longer interested in the conversation.

As Joe walked back to this car, he passed the charred Porsche. He noticed the hole in the roof where the telephone pole had come through. It occurred to Joe that maybe the killings weren't as far removed from the town's consciousness as he had assumed. There had been real anger in the gas station owner's face. Joe got the feeling he'd laid bare old wounds. Maybe the papers didn't mention the fact that the guy who died in the car was the murderer of the policemen because they didn't want to bring up such an awful time. Maybe dredging it up wasn't a good idea for Joe either. Joe wondered if he were in way over his head before he really had even gotten started. The thought of abandoning his quest and going home occurred to him, but it be would be just another stop and would start to add to his already faltering self esteem.

I'll just quietly look into it and then head on out, Joe decided.

Feeling like a novice detective, Joe thought he'd lay low for awhile so he headed to the Gold's Lake public library to do some research on the murders and on the trial. He would see if he could find something on the country club robbery that had happened a few weeks prior to the murders to see if there had been a connection.

When Joe climbed up the stairs and went into the old brick building in the center of town, it was so quiet he was afraid it was closed and the front door had been left unlocked by accident. He poked his head around the corner and saw a small, older woman with more wrinkles on her face then he could count. Despite her age she was wide-eyed, energetic looking and had a happy disposition. She was almost giddy to see someone in there, Joe thought, or maybe she was happy and friendly to everyone.

"What can I do you for? I'm Corra and I've been here since before you were born."

Joe wondered if that was her standard greeting or did he look like that much of an out-of-towner that she felt the need to introduce herself.

"Well, I need to do some research," Joe said.

"You've come to the right place," Corra said. "What are we researching today?"

The way she said "we" meant exactly that. She was going to help. She had a way of saying things that told you she was in charge and you wouldn't want to disappoint an old lady. Joe really didn't want to have to explain what he was doing there since he really didn't know himself.

"Well, I'm just kinda looking around."

"This ain't a car dealership. People who come to research have a project in mind. Now what's yours?"

Joe was trapped. He simply could find no way out of this, given her approach. Somehow he felt if didn't allow her to help, it would be rude.

"Well, I'm looking into a couple of crimes from years ago."

"Why you doing that?" she asked with a quizzical look on her face.

"It's a long story," Joe responded.

"I got time," she said and motioned to Joe to sit in a chair. She pulled up a chair, turned it around backward and straddled it.

Joe said, "I barely know you and I haven't told anybody in the world why I'm here, but I guess I kinda need to tell someone so I may as well tell you. There was a murder here of two policemen about forty years ago," Joe said, watching to see her reaction after the gas station owner had responded so darkly.

"Know all about it," Corra said. "George Allen and Bill Hollar. You passed Allen/Hollar ball field on the way over here today. I was a young lady then, but I remember it well."

Joe was again surprised. These forty year old murders were still pretty close to the surface with most of the older people around here.

"You see, my father wrote a book about the murders and before he died, he thought there might be more to the story. I'm here to look into it."

"Your dad wrote *The Basement Killer*?"

"Yes, ma'am."

"I remember that book. He put Gold's Lake on the map for a little while. Some people weren't too happy with his portrayal of our little town as a backwater hick town. We had an Olympics gold medal winner from here, you know."

Joe suddenly felt as if he needed to defend his father, but he refrained.

"My dad was from here. He grew up and had a rough life with his parents. I guess his unhappiness with his upbringing came through in the book. Actually he spoke fairly kindly of the town itself to me, growing up," Joe added.

"Now why in the world after all this time would you be following up on the story?"

Joe told her about the car accident. Corra knew about the accident, but she didn't know that the driver had killed those policemen.

"Are you sure?" Corra asked.

"Yeah, I think so," he said.

"I didn't know he got out of prison. Well, I'm glad I didn't know because I would have been scared out of my wits. Those killings terrified this town. Even after he was caught in another house, people thought he might not have acted alone. I never locked my doors a day in my life prior to those murders, but I have ever since and I still do today."

Joe suddenly jumped in. "That's what I think. That he didn't act alone. I think that a country club robbery two weeks before was somehow connected."

When Corra heard that, there was no hint of a recollection.

"Country club robbery?"

"Yes, it happened in Harding, a town a few miles from here."

"I know Harding," Corra said, "but I don't remember the country club getting robbed. In fact, it isn't even there any more."

Joe had formed a scenario about the two crimes in his head on his way up to Gold's Lake. When a big story happens and then an earth shaking story happens, nobody would remember the smaller of the two. It had been completely overshadowed by the deaths of Gold's Lake's finest. Corra's reaction told Joe that he was probably right.

"Maybe we could start our research by seeing what you have about the country club," Joe said.

Joe was now glad to have told Corra and to have someone to talk to.

"The murders happened in June of '67, right?" Corra asked.

Joe nodded.

"So the country club was robbed sometime in the beginning of the month. We didn't start putting newspapers articles on microfiche until '69 so we are going to have to go to the tombs."

The tombs were aptly named. It was an area in the sub-basement of the library where there were rows and rows of file cabinets. It was dark and dusty and it smelled like moldy plaster.

"No one comes down here very much," said Corra. "In fact, most people don't know it's here. The *Gold's Lake Gazette* went out of business and donated all the contents of the newspaper morgue to the library. It seemed like a good idea at the time. Before the computer and microfiche they used to get about twenty copies of the day's newspaper. They cut every article out and cross-referenced it with every name and topic in the article. A small article on a boat accident could be filed five times. It'll be a great way for you to do research because the reporters used them to check facts. Every article doesn't have to be independently checked."

Joe was thrilled. His research was going to be easier then he anticipated.

"Let's look up the country club robbery," Joe said.

They both started toward the "H's," but suddenly Joe felt an urge to go straight to the "K's" and look up Ed Kutz. Oddly enough, the drawer with the Kutz file was open. He walked over to it and pulled it out. It was a big file that told Joe this was a big story back then. Many of the articles had yellowed and become frail and were quite literally falling apart.

Gingerly Joe thumbed through them. Almost every article had notes in the margins and Joe recognized the handwriting instantly. It was the handwriting of a Catholic schoolboy who had had his hands slapped with a ruler by nuns if it wasn't neat enough. It was the handwriting of a man who had been educated by Jesuits in high school and college. It was the handwriting of Joe's father.

Joe had come to Gold's Lake as much to find himself as to investigate this case. Some days his biggest concern was that he was in danger of becoming his father, yet here he was retracing his father's footsteps, in his dad's home town, to follow up on a book his dad wrote.

Maybe one has to go to the source to really understand a person, he thought. Maybe this would help. Maybe not.

Joe knew he was getting ahead of himself, but he lifted the entire Kutz file out of the file cabinet and took it over to a small barren room with dirty scuffed up walls and two broken chairs. Corra followed behind him carrying a much smaller file with a heading that read "Harding Country Club."

They sat down and started looking through the files. No one had ever heard of Ed Kutz prior to the murders, so his file started with an article about the murders and then about the manhunt that eventually trapped him in another empty house and then the court proceedings that followed.

As Joe started reading, two scenarios started to come into his mind. The scene of the robbery itself and then, superimposed over that, the scene of his father poring over these same articles and trying to put the story fully together with his imagination. Joe realized he was again finding himself following closely in his father's footsteps as he, too, sitting in the musty basement, tried to imagine every detail of those events so he could understand every aspect of the robbery and of the murders that followed.

What seemed like an open and shut case that should have ended with the death penalty or at least life imprisonment ended with a compromise because of incompetence by the prosecutor and his predilection for screwing his young summer teenage assistants. He was the kind of smarmy guy that most adults can see through in five minutes, but a young girl would be duped.

His hair was slicked back and an overwhelming smell of cologne arrived long before he did and stayed long after he left. He wore cheap imitations of high end suits, but never bothered to polish his shoes. The summer of the trial, about a year after the murders, right as everything was coming to a head in the trial, a huge burly man in farmer's overalls walked into the court room while the trial was in full session, reached across the divider and started choking the prosecutor. He had walked in calmly, but with definite intent. He headed straight for the prosecution table and had grabbed the prosecutor by the neck.

At first people thought it was a criminal the prosecutor had put in jail or maybe a friend of Kutz come to break him out. The court room guard, not a big man himself, awoke from his near slumber and jumped on the burly man's back, but the big man didn't seem to notice. He just went on choking. Realizing he was having very little effect, the guard jumped off and grabbed his night stick clumsily out of his belt. He was quoted later in the article that in retrospect he wished he had done that first.

He took a mighty swing and hit the man on the shoulder, but still the big man wouldn't let go. The guard didn't want to do it, but the next swing was right to the back of the man's large head. The guard was ready to run if this didn't bring him down, in case the man turned his attention on him.

The court room was quiet. Everyone was too stunned to react. The billy club made contact with the big man's head with the sound of a watermelon hitting the pavement after being dropped from a two story roof. Still the man didn't let go immediately. The guard thought about hitting him again, but was afraid he might literally split the man's head in two.

The big man finally let go of the prosecutor. He slowly turned around and felt the back of his head to see if it was bleeding. It was. He took one step toward the guard and then both his knees started to wobble. Everybody knew he was about to go down, but they didn't know where he was going to fall. He wobbled to the left, wobbled to the right, and then, to add insult to injury, fell on the prosecutor and drove his nose into the marble floor.

The big man was moaning on the cool marble, trying to pick himself up to go at the prosecutor again. The guard, now kneeling on the man's back trying to pin his hands behind his back, said, "Relax, buddy. You're not going anywhere but to the hospital and then to jail. What the hell were you thinking?"

"That son of a bitch got my sixteen year old daughter pregnant," the big man said.

His words hung in the air like a stinky cigar. The sympathy for the prosecutor vanished instantly from the gallery in the room. The lady holding a handkerchief to his bloody, mangled nose let go suddenly as if she was touching something disgusting. The guard didn't seem sure if he should arrest the man. The judge had bravely retreated to his chambers when the commotion started and was peeking his head back in through a large oak door, afraid the big man was coming after him next.

"What should I do?" the guard asked him.

"Get him the hell out of here," responded the judge.

Per the articles Joe was reading through, the court adjourned for the day for obvious reasons and the next time that prosecutor would see the inside of a court room was for his own arraignment on statutory rape. But the crime and the trial had taken a toll on the town. There was absolutely no appetite for granting a mistrial and retrying the case.

The next day the judge got together with Kutz's lawyer to make a deal. They both agreed that there was more than enough evidence to convict him in a retrial, but the judge thought the best thing for everybody was to put it behind them for the good of the town. So the day after the big man attacked the prosecutor, a deal was struck to have Ed Kutz serve forty-five years to life in a prison about thirty miles away in Plattsburg. The idea was that Ed Kutz would never get out of prison and that the townspeople could get on with their lives and never have to think of that awful time again.

Joe was shaking his head after reading the story of the prosecutor. He mentioned the story to Corra, but she didn't recall it. That made Joe worry that what she told him might not be as accurate as he had hoped. Corra remained busy looking into the country club robbery when a buzzer from upstairs started to ring. Someone else had just come into the library, so she went upstairs, but promised to be right back. She was clearly enjoying this project.

Joe spent the next hour looking into the country club robbery. Indeed it was big news for awhile but literally stopped the day of the murders. In the first article Joe came across about the robbery, someone had circled, in pencil, the words "dead eyes."

It had been early June and there was a high society party at the Harding Country Club. There was also a jewelry show where a noted designer from New York City was going to show her wares and hopefully sell a lot to a group of very rich people. It was a black tie affair meant to raise money for a local hospital wing. The hospital was already too big for the area, but it gave these rich people a chance to get out and be seen.

The event was held in a very large room festooned with exotic plants and an all male wait staff dressed in Tuxedos. There were two waiters for every table of six and they stood ready to refill the wine glasses if they got below one quarter empty.

Joe could picture them standing at attention with a bottle of wine held awkwardly in front. Everybody was probably standing around making small talk. A harp was being played in the corner so as not to drown out any of the boring conversations that were going on. When two men entered the room, no one seemed to notice. They were far too caught up wallowing in their fake goodness and philanthropy. The maître d' seemed annoyed when he saw the intruders, as if they were hired help that should only enter through the back door. He put both hands up as he walked toward the men.

"You can't be in..."

Before he got the words out of his mouth, the smaller of the two men punched him viciously, square in the face, sending him crashing into a table, upending chairs and sending three guests to the floor with him. The place went silent as the taller of the men pulled out a gun and motioned everybody to the back of the room. A few people on the far end of the room tried to exit through the side doors only to find they'd been nailed shut from the outside.

As if in union, the crowd moved as far back into the corner of the room as possible. The harp player sat at her harp as if she wasn't sure if he meant for her to move as well. She thought maybe she would be excused because she wasn't a guest, but hired help. The smaller man grabbed her by the hair and pushed her toward the back of the room.

He then pulled a short club out of his overcoat as if to say, "I'm as likely to use this as I am my fist, like I did to the maitre d'."

He was menacing enough without the club. The guests understood his message clearly.

"Empty your pockets onto the tables in front of you. If I find you have not put everything on the table, I will break your leg with this club."

He said it so matter-of-factly that no one doubted that he was totally serious and might be disappointed if he didn't get to break someone's legs that night.

As Joe continued through the articles, he could envision the scene inside the country club unfold. Men frantically emptied their pockets as women took off their jewelry. Wallets and watches, rings and necklaces were dropping to the floor all over. One woman in the back of the room tried to take her diamond necklace off and hide it within her ample chest. Her husband looked at her bug-eyed and reached between her two flabby breasts and grabbed the necklace. The little man walked straight toward them, guests parting as he walked, and when he got to him, he smiled and tapped him lightly on the legs with his club, having witnessed the exchange.

The small man ordered two of the waiters to start gathering everything up. He produced a canvas bag from under his coat and handed it to the men. After pulling the club and a bag out from his coat, the people wondered what other surprises he might he have under there.

The smaller of the two men made no effort to try to hide his appearance while most of the bigger man's face was covered up either by hair, glasses or a cap. He didn't seem to be worried about having people behind him or about being outnumbered two hundred to one, although his accomplice had a gun. He'd done this before and he liked doing it. He didn't seem in the least bit nervous or uncomfortable and didn't seem to be in a hurry.

The maître d' was still unconscious on the floor where he had been dropped. A member of the wait staff was still with him despite being ordered to the back of the room. For some reason, the two men let him stay. The little man walked over to the jewelry designer who had dutifully taken off her personal jewelry, but closed the trunk carrying all the expensive jewelry she had meant to sell. The little man smiled at her as if the two of them were sharing a secret only they were privy to. He just stared at her, slapping the stick into the palm of his hand menacingly.

His eyes said, "If I have to ask you to put the jewelry into a bag, I'm going to break your legs with this stick."

She quickly changed her mind and opened the truck. Inside there were thirty to forty pieces of jewelry. All the rocks were big. Unless it was costume jewelry, the stuff was going to be worth a lot of money. And from the looks of that crowd, the small man knew this wasn't costume.

The men left the country club in no particular hurry, but they did stop long enough to slide the club the little man had been carrying through the handles on the door to make sure it remained shut. By the time the patrons got the door opened, the men were gone. The men in their tuxedos and the women in their gowns stood outside the Harding Country Club without their jewelry and money, wondering which way the men had gone.

All did not go well for the tall and short man as they made their way on foot away from the country club through a wooded area. The taller of the two was carrying the sack, which was heavier and larger then he would have imagined. He actually thought about stopping to unload the empty wallets so he wouldn't have to carry them. As they emerged from the woods onto a main road, they saw a police car coming right for them.

In retrospect, the men realized that the policeman couldn't possibly have gotten there so quickly and that it was just a coincidence, but in that second they panicked. The short man made a left, heading for the police car, while the taller man with the loot and the gun went in the other direction. When the smaller man realized his partner, money and jewels were no longer with him, he considered turning around, but he didn't want to arouse the policeman's suspicion.

The smaller man just kept on walking, his head looking down, his collar up to obscure his face, his hands buried deeply in his pockets. The taller man had walked about ten yards when he abruptly made a hard right into the wooded area. As soon as he was out if sight, he started to run and he didn't stop until he got to the house on Locust Lane.

When the news of the robbery broke the next day, the policeman that passed the two men put the events together and realized that he had seen the men, but had been unaware of their crimes.

Joe had gotten more information than he ever thought he would from that day in the library. Corra had spent about an hour upstairs helping her customer while Joe read each article, made notes on his note pad, and marveled every time he came across his father's handwriting. He put everything back into the files and returned them to their drawers. Joe thanked Corra and said he would be back to continue the investigation, but he wasn't sure if he was telling her the truth.

"I may not be back," he said to himself.

# Chapter Four

J oe was full of energy and excitement. Going back to the ciga-
rette smell of the motel to watch old reruns of lousy sitcoms was
completely unappealing. He had had a good day and wasn't ready
for it to end yet. He knew there was a tavern about two doors down
from the motel, and he decided to go sit at the bar, get something
to drink and have dinner. He liked doing that because people were
much more likely to talk to you sitting alone at a bar than sitting
alone at a table.

The place was not very crowded for a Thursday night, which
made Joe want to leave and go find some place that had more people to choose from. He wanted some human interaction. But he
was already inside so he wandered up to the bar thinking that he
could have a quick drink and then head for greener pastures. It was
the kind of bar that Joe loved, however. It was old and dark, with
a lot of character, the look a place only gets from longevity. The
stale beer odor went perfectly with the yellowed out pictures on
the walls and the names carved into the tables. Locals came there to
drink and get drunk.

They didn't get a lot of tourists in here, Joe thought.

There were about five people in the whole place. One guy at the
other end of the bar with a long grisly old beard looked to be asleep.

Another man asked for a double Jack and water and promptly put the glass to his lips and just left it there. He didn't appear to be drinking much. It looked more like he was marinating his lips. He didn't drink it fast, but he kept it to his lips until it was completely drained.

Joe pulled up a stool at the opposite end of the bar from the sleeping, gray bearded drunk. There was a newspaper sitting there. One seemed a little less creepy if he was alone, but reading something at the bar, Joe thought. He'd only been there a moment when the bartender emerged from the kitchen carrying a case of fresh glasses. She promptly put them down and approached Joe.

When Joe would look back on meeting her, he had to agree that he wasn't blown away by her beauty. She was okay, he thought back then. She was well endowed and in good shape. She was a strawberry blonde with a few light freckles. Joe could imagine that as a little girl she hated the freckles, but now they were what made her interesting to look at.

She was attractive, but not the kind of girl that men went to war over, Joe said to himself. In the weeks that followed this would always strike Joe as odd, because within a week he would be totally infatuated with her.

She wore jeans that fit her small body well and she wore a green shirt that showed her figure, but still left a little to the imagination. She had the short sleeves rolled up almost to her shoulders and had her hair pulled back in a pony tail.

She said "Hi" and asked Joe if he wanted a drink. He asked for a Gimlet and she brought him a Gibson. He knew that she'd made the wrong drink as she was walking it over to him.

He looked up and just shook his head. She stopped in her tracks as if to say, "What'd I do?"

"That's not a Gimlet. It's a Gibson," Joe said. Feigning fake disappointment for getting the drink wrong, she dejectedly turned around to make another. She tossed the drink into the sink and started making a Gimlet.

"Its just vodka and Rose's lime juice," Joe said.

"I know what it is. I just had a temporary brain fart."

She made the correct drink and brought it over. "Don't worry. I didn't spit in it," she said with a smile.

Joe, feeling like a bit of a jerk, apologized and said, "Can I start over? I'm Joe."

"Melissa," she said. "You're not from here. Where you from?"

"How do you know I'm not from here?"

"Why don't you answer my question? Are you running from something?"

"Not really. How'd you know I'm not from around here?"

"Because I know most everyone who comes in and I haven't seen you before."

"Fair enough. I'm from New Jersey." Joe knew what the next question would be.

"Why are you are here in our sleepy little town?"

In anticipation he'd already started to say, "I'm doing a research paper on the economy for a newspaper." He felt badly almost immediately about lying, but thought, what's the harm? I'll probably never see her again after tonight.

The night wore on. A few more regulars came into the bar. She would serve them, but kept making her way back to Joe. Probably because everybody else was paired up and Joe was alone. A good bartender takes care of her patrons. Around ten, the bar was completely empty except for Joe. Everything was cleaned up so Melissa came over and sat on a beer cooler opposite Joe.

"So what's your story?" Joe asked.

"I have no story. I wake up. I come here to work. I go home to my cat. That's my story."

"Nobody's story is that boring," Joe said. "Boyfriends? Kids? A husband?"

A look came over Melissa as if she'd answered this question a million times and just couldn't get around it.

"Can't we just talk about the weather or something easy like that?"

"So there is a story," Joe said. "Tell me and then I'll tell you why I'm really here."

Intrigued, Melissa said, "So you're a liar. Yes, there was a husband. He was a mountain climber. He went out one day and didn't come back. They found him about a week later at the base of a mountain. He'd broken his neck and died instantly. That was four years ago. But thanks for making me bring that back up," she said with a wry smile.

"I feel like a jerk," Joe said.

"Don't feel like a jerk for making me tell that story. But you can feel like a jerk for lying to me. Let's go. Your turn."

Joe told her the story of why he was in Gold's Lake, leaving out the problems he was having with his wife.

"Is that the truth?" Melissa asked.

"Well, most of it," Joe said. "Gimlets make me forget details."

"Details like your wife?" she asked.

"How do you know I'm married?"

"I didn't until now, but since you left out your love life, I kind of guessed."

"Are you disappointed?" Joe asked with a smile.

"Oh, no. Not me. I'm done with men."

"Why? Have you had a rough time on the dating scene?

"I haven't dated at all," she said, "and I don't plan to."

Joe felt like he'd gotten more personal than he should have so he left it there.

"That's enough for one night," she said. "I'm throwing you out."

Joe said good bye and headed back to his motel, but sleep would not come easily that night. He had learned a lot that day about the accident, about Ed Kutz, about the Harding Country Club, but the thing that would stay on his mind all night and keep him staring a the ceiling was the strawberry blond bartender, Melissa.

# *Chapter Five*

Joe had always been faithful to his wife in as much as he'd never had sex with any other woman since he had married. He did have a few missteps when they were dating, but Barbara had never had an inkling that Joe would be the kind to step out. At the time he wasn't sure if she was the one he'd marry, so he wanted to keep his options open. At least that's what he told himself.

Those dating infidelities, while great at the time, had weighed on his mind, though he wasn't sure why. He now asked himself, what had he been feeling? Was it guilt for being dishonest? He didn't think so. Was it guilt that there were never any repercussions? Was he feeling badly because even after all these years his wife still believed that from the first time they slept together till today, he'd never been with another? Over time he had stopped thinking about them. What seemed like conquests worthy of bragging about had now become trysts he wished he'd never had.

While he'd always been physically faithful since his marriage to Barbara, he still lusted after other women. Never overtly, but he always wondered: if the perfect situation presented itself, would he step out? If he met someone and there was no chance he would get caught, would he? Were these the kind of internal conversations his father had had, as well, he wondered, prior to his long list of affairs?

And was getting caught the only thing stopping him? What about the vow he had taken? What about the woman he truly loved? He was afraid that he knew the answer to that, but he didn't often dwell on it.

Why were these questions coming up today, Joe wondered.

Was he really in Gold's Lake to test his fidelity to his wife? Was he trying to find out if he were as much like his father as he feared he might be? These questions swirled through his mind. He suddenly felt as if there were an urgency to answering them. While he didn't know the answers to all of them, though, there was one question he could answer. He was going to see Melissa again at the bar that night.

The day was not the nice September morning Joe had hoped for before he stepped outside the motel. It was overcast and misty. There was a rawness to it that made Joe want to go back inside and get back into bed. He stood at his own doorway facing out, looking out over his small access road to a two lane highway clogged with absolute strangers. He could go left or right, east or west, up or down. No one would care. The town felt foreign to him and he had an urge to drive home, to New Jersey, to his home, to his wife, away from Gold's Lake, Ed Kutz and dead policemen. The urge surprised him because he had had a fruitful first day.

He forced himself to his car and drove to a coffee house across the highway, a minute away. He sat down and reviewed his notes. He thought about going back to the library. In fact, that was his plan as he left the coffee house, but something suddenly changed. He had an urge to go and see where this whole thing started. He had to go to Locust Lane.

The house was almost exactly as his father had described it. He had undoubtedly been here to detail it so well, from the style of the

railing on the front porch to the slope of roof. He had wanted to give an accurate description of the place where George Allen and Bill Hollar met their end. But Joe's father couldn't have described the state of disrepair the house was currently in. It was a mess.

Windows were broken and had been boarded up, which told Joe someone was looking after it somewhat. But that was the only sign. The vegetation had grown and died year after year and now to approach the house, except up the driveway, was very difficult. The shingles on the roof appeared to have few of the granules that they came with. Several shingles could be seen strewn around the property. Interestingly, there was a pile of broken shingles on the broken steps to the porch. Joe wondered if maybe Robbie was looking after the house in some bizarre tribute to the policemen or to Cal.

The house had been a starter home for Brian and Susie Wrin. He had been a vacuum salesman and Susie had apparently come from money, although no one would know that judging by the way they lived. Neither of them liked the cold weather and they spent as much time as they could in their vacation home in West Virginia, where they eventually retired.

After the murders they tried to sell the Locust Lane house through a local broker, but there were no takers. The "For Sale" sign sat out in the front yard for years until it was completely overtaken by weeds. At one point they tried to give the house to the town just so they could stop paying property taxes, but considering what had happened there, the town didn't want it either. Finally the Wrins died of old age. They had had no children and the house had been sitting in limbo ever since.

The shades were drawn on the windows without boards on them. There was no evidence that paint had ever been on the shiplap siding except on the underside of the bead board porch ceiling. The weather had washed it away so completely that one might wonder if it were ever the blue house Joe's father had described. Joe sat in his car, wondering if this was the same vantage point his dad viewed it from. Joe made notes, then put his pad down and exited the car. The mist was growing thicker, but now it felt appropriate as Joe prepared to examine this grim place.

Joe had to leave a wide berth around the house due to the overgrowth. As he walked around the house, there was a clear path leading up to the basement window in the back. The bushes had been flattened and hacked down. They had started to grow back, but there was no doubt someone had been there. Joe followed the path with some difficulty to the window. The window was smaller then he imagined.

One would really have to flatten out on his belly to crawl through there, Joe imagined.

The window had been boarded up, but not very well. Someone had nailed it to the foundation with the wrong kind of nail so it easily came away from the window when Joe pulled it. The angle was not conducive to getting a good view of the basement and without any sun, Joe couldn't see anything. Still it was sobering. Two men, about Joe's age, had been gunned down on the very floor he was looking at. Even though it had been forty years ago, the fact remained.

Joe wasn't sure when he had arrived at Locust Lane that he would go in. He hadn't brought any tools to gain entrance, but now he knew he had to go in. He thought about going to a hardware store to get a pry bar or a screw gun to remove a board from a window. He decided not to, afraid if he left, he would lose his nerve and not go back.

He went around the front of the house to his car to get a small flashlight he hoped would still work. He retrieved it from the glove box and headed for the porch. He stood by the front door, took a deep breath and turned the knob. It was locked or simply rusted shut. Joe put his shoulder into the door as George Allen and Bill Hollar had done forty years earlier, shortly before their deaths. There was definitely some give to it. He leaned into it again. He knew that with enough of a push he could get in even though it meant breaking up the interior door jam.

Joe was intent. He was going in. He put all his weight into the next push and the door jam split and the door opened. It stopped only half way because of a big swell in the hardwood floor that had gotten wet from a leak in the roof. Joe turned his body sideways and went in. He stood by the door letting his eyes adjust to the darkness.

Is this what the two policemen had seen when they walked in? Joe thought not.

All the furniture had been pushed to one side. There were dozens of empty Black Label beer cans strewn everywhere.

Evidence of teenagers trying to prove their manhood, Joe thought.

He imagined kids thirteen or fourteen years old daring each other to go into the house, having heard the stories passed down over the years about what happened there. Joe wondered if they knew the real story or if it had been too embellished over the years. He wondered if they really knew the kind of horror that went on. He wondered if maybe they'd read his father's book. Maybe it was still required reading in the local schools. Maybe they had to sleep in the basement overnight to prove their worthiness to join some kind of gang or cult.

While some of the furniture was still there, few personal items were still in the house. Joe figured that the Wrins, the older couple who owned the home, found out what happened, returned one time to get their stuff and never returned again. This was the way it had been sitting ever since, until Joe cautiously took a few steps in. He worried there might be weak floor boards that could give and send him plummeting to the basement floor. The smell of must and mold was overwhelming. Joe turned to a window with a shade drawn and tried to pull it up. Instead of it coiling up, the shade simply disintegrated in his hand. Instantly he wished he hadn't done it.

Now a passerby familiar with the house might notice the difference, he worried.

With a little bit of light shining through the dirty window, Joe had a better look at his surroundings. What struck him instantly was how well his father had described them in his book. There was no doubt Cal had been in the house. The time line had always been a little fuzzy in Joe's mind. Exactly when was his father here? Was it during the trial? Was it years after? Did he get permission to go inside or did he break in as Joe had done? Perhaps Cal had known of this house as a child in Gold's Lake and had been in for a cool drink or had known the children of the neighbors. In Joe's memory, this house was so close to exactly as he had imagined it that it seemed like an actual memory.

Impossible, he thought. I've never been here.

Or had he? Did his father bring him along to collect information for his book when he was three or four years old? Had the years jumbled up his memory so he couldn't tell what he had read and what was real? As Joe walked deeper into the house, he felt like he knew what was around each corner. He knew exactly where the refrigerator was. Maybe there were pictures that his father had shown him from a file somewhere, although they weren't in the file that Joe had with him. His memory was so vivid it actually started to unnerve him.

If I'd been here before and just can't remember it, what else am I forgetting, he wondered.

Joe stood in the kitchen looking at the appliances, the worn out linoleum floor and the faded red countertops. There was a variety of dead insects all over the counters, but mostly in the sink. He reached for the sink faucet to wash them down and then laughed to himself when no water came out. Even if the water company had forgotten to shut the water off, Joe doubted the pipes would hold anyway after so many years of sitting idle. The wall surfaces were covered with an old floral wall paper, but the color was completely gone, a testament to its age. Joe lingered there for moment, knowing what he had to do next. He felt he knew exactly where the basement door was, but was almost afraid to look. He turned slowly toward the hallway, made a sharp left, and there it was.

Damn. How did I know that, he thought. It struck him that his own reality again seemed to be merging with his father's from so many years earlier.

He reached for the door knob and turned it. Surprisingly, it worked, as if it had recently been oiled. He trained his flashlight down the stairs. The beam of the light was weak. It only made it half way down the staircase. It occurred to Joe to head back out to the hardware store and buy the biggest flashlight he could buy so he wouldn't have to walk in a dark, seemingly unfamiliar basement with a crappy light. It would make good sense to do that.

Meanwhile, every fiber in his being was saying, "Get your ass out of here."

What if the stairs had rotted? "I could fall through to the basement floor and no one would know where I was. And if I did get rescued, I'd have a hard time explaining why I was there," he said out loud under his breath.

Joe hadn't felt fear like this since he was a child. It was the foolish, unreasonable fear that a child feels, not a grown man, Joe hissed at himself.

"Stop being a friggin' coward," he told himself.

Joe had let fear control him before in his life and had always lived to regret it. Whether it was not asking a girl to the prom or backing down from a fight, these episodes always weighed on his mind. Getting the shit kicked out of him would not be nearly as bad as the shame he felt for years for having backed down. As a boy he had sworn that would never happen again.

The same voice that caused him to miss going to the prom with Wendy Collins was urging him now to run away and never come back. Joe had a crush on Wendy for his whole high school career. For months he had wanted to ask her, but couldn't get up the nerve. When he finally did, she said she would have accepted, but had already agreed to go with someone else.

"You were wrong then and you're wrong now," the voice in Joe's head said.

"I'm going."

With that he started to head downstairs. He felt the presence of two dead policemen almost instantly as he made his way down.

This was the last thing they ever did. They were about my age, too, he thought.

Each of his steps caused the stairs to creak and bend under his weight, but there was no indication that they would break. Still, he proceeded slowly. He stopped half way down and shined the flashlight over the railing. His light was so weak he really couldn't see much. He could only make out that it was completely empty. He reached the bottom and just as had happened upstairs, he turned and knew exactly where the furnace was that Ed Kutz said he'd been hiding behind.

He stood at the bottom of the stairs for about a minute and a sobering realization came over him. At that point George and Bill would have already been lying on the cold dark basement floor as their life blood flowed out of them.

Joe shook the thought from his head. He pointed the flashlight around the perimeter of the room. His eyes were adjusting to the darkness. He started to walk around the basement, trying to imagine the scene all those years ago.

Why was Ed here? Was he alone?

In the trial transcripts, it said there was evidence that he been there several days. Any food wrappers or drink cartons would have been picked up and bagged as evidence long ago, Joe concluded. There was an old slop sink with a makeshift counter top against the wall opposite the furnace. Ed probably got water from there unless the vacationing homeowners had turned it off when they had left.

Joe's fear was starting to subside now that he'd confirmed that no one was down there. He felt a little silly that he had been scared at all. He kept walking around the perimeter of the basement until he reached the furnace. It was a big old cast iron furnace with asbestos insulation on the outside. It always amazed Joe how big they were, considering how small the newer ones were today.

The basement wasn't telling Joe anything he didn't already know.

The police had been through it hundred times, Joe thought, after the murders. What could they have missed? Nothing, Joe concluded, and started back up the stairs.

Half way up he stopped. Had he seen something that just hadn't registered yet? Was someone trying to tell him something? He started back down and walked over toward the furnace. He thought he might have noticed something that now caused him to want to go back over there. Maybe there was something his father had said to him about the country club robbery being related. If that were true, maybe, just maybe, Ed had been in the basement to hide what they had stolen. But where? And why wouldn't the police have found it?

Maybe there was a corrupt cop who found the stash from the country club and kept it for himself. If he'd tried to sell it locally, though, he would have been caught, Joe thought.

Because the basement was empty, Joe concluded that around or in the furnace was the only place to look. But then another thought hit him. If Ed Kutz had broken back into the house after getting out of jail, wouldn't he have found the stuff and taken it?

I'm too late, Joe thought.

Still, Joe wanted to find out where the loot could have been hidden. Subconsciously Joe had already made the mental leap that both the country club robbers had been in the basement. He scanned the furnace. There was an iron door on it, but it was welded shut and the weld did not appear new. Defeated, Joe started to turn to leave.

As he turned to head up the stairs a second time, a stone in the foundation caught his eye. It looked just like all the other river stones that made up the foundation, but this one seemed to stick out more and it had no mortar around it. It appeared to be bigger than most of them. He walked over to it and examined it like a bomb squad might look at a briefcase carelessly placed in a public place.

He put his hand on the stone and pushed down. To his astonishment it fell to the ground. It wasn't a big stone at all. What Joe saw sticking out of the wall was all there was to it. The other three quarters of the stone were no longer attached. Joe took his flashlight and pointed it into the hole left by the rock. It appeared to go back about two feet and it also appeared to have been dug down a bit.

As Joe contemplated sticking his hand into the dark forbidding hole, the same childish fear came streaming back to him. He steeled himself, rolled up his sleeve and stuck his arm into the hole up to his shoulder. He bypassed the cobwebs and felt around, grabbing handfuls of arid dirt.

"Nothing," he whispered.

He stuck his arm in further, but this time he directed it into the dug out area. He felt something. It wasn't a pile of old jewelry, as Joe had hoped. It was canvas sack. Joe pulled it out. Even as he pulled it out, he could tell it was falling apart. He brought it over to the window and examined it. Mice or bugs had chewed it so much it barely resembled a sack.

Despite there being nothing in the sack, Joe was delighted. His father had been right. He had been smarter than the police. He had put the final piece of the puzzle together on his death bed.

Joe suddenly felt bad that his father was no longer around for him to tell about it.

It was a ratty old dilapidated bag, but Joe was going to take it with him. He rolled it up into a ball to tuck inside his shirt when something sharp stuck him in the palm of his hand.

"Shit," he said.

He unrolled the sack and pointed his flashlight at it.

"What the hell was that?" He examined the sack again and saw nothing. Then he looked at his palm. It was bleeding.

"Well, I'm not imagining that," Joe thought, trying to prove to himself that he wasn't crazy.

He lay the sack down on the basement floor and shined the light all over it.

"Nothing. Did I drop whatever it was?" Joe said.

He flipped the bag over and there, at what used to be bottom of the bag, was a sharp gold pin with a pendant that resembled three flowers. On top of each stem sat a large, perfect diamond.

Joe just stood there and stared at it. He had never seen three diamonds so huge. How much might they be worth, he wondered.

And could this really be a piece of jewelry from a forty year old robbery that led to two murders and a book by my father? I'm not that smart. How could everybody else have missed this?

He thought of the article that first led him to Gold's Lake. No one else had the intimate knowledge of this crime and no one else was as interested because no one else had a father who had written a book about it. Joe stood with the pendant in his hand for two minutes just staring at it.

What next? Do I call the police? What good would that do? Is it a crime to keep it? The case has been closed for years.

Joe discounted the idea of calling the police right away. If he did that, everything would be out in the open and he didn't want that. He had to find out more about what happened to the rest of the pieces of jewelry. Did Ed Kutz come back into the basement after his release from prison and take them and sell them? Was he still involved with the short stocky guy from the country club robbery?

A million thoughts were running through his head when a little bit of dust fell from the rafters and then Joe heard foot steps above. He wondered if someone had called the police when they saw his car outside and the broken shade in the window.

"Shit. I knew I stayed down here too long," Joe whispered.

That childish fear was now at full throttle. Joe had to put a hand over his mouth to keep from screaming. His eyes darted around the basement. He knew there was no bulkhead door to escape from. He looked toward the window. Could he pull himself through? Even if he could get up that high, he didn't think he would be able to squeeze through. There was no way to get up the stairs and out of the house without being seen.

Joe slid behind the furnace and squatted down. The footsteps moved toward the basement door. It occurred to Joe that Ed Kutz was probably feeling the same way all those years earlier with the two policemen above.

Joe was on the verge of panic when he heard a yelp from a little dog. That's strange, he thought. Would a killer or the police actually bring a dog to kill him or arrest him?

It could just be a neighbor who happened by. But he'd still have a lot of explaining to do, so he just sat there quietly. But my car, he thought. What if the person called the police and they came? He had to head upstairs. If he stayed where he was, things could only get worse. If he walked up now, there was a possibility that he could talk his way free.

Joe started up the stairs with the pendant in his pocket. He walked slowly, each stair creaking as he went up. He got to the top stair and stuck his head out. As far as he could see, the kitchen and living room were empty. Was the person laying in wait to jump out on him? With his wimpy little dog?

Joe walked further. Still nothing. He made it to the front of the house and stared out. No one was in sight. Had he imagined it? Not likely.

His car was about thirty feet away. He could run to it and jump in and drive away. But the person walking above would already have his license plate. The police could be on their way. Not knowing if that was the case would be bad also. Joe walked cautiously out on to the front porch. Still no one.

# Chapter Six

As Joe walked down the wooden steps on to what had been the lawn, he heard a yelp, the sound a small dog would make. He looked around. There at the side of the house, obviously worried about who might be in the basement, stood a big boned older woman with Bozo the clown gray hair.

Joe had heard his father describe her that way. As usual, he had described her perfectly. There was no doubt that the person standing there was Robbie, his dad's childhood friend.

As soon as she made eye contact with Joe, she turned quickly to walk away, as if, at her advanced age and weight, she could outrun him. The pathetic little dog didn't offer much protection. Joe wanted to run after her, but feared causing her a heart attack, so he simply shouted, "Robbie?"

She stopped and turned around.

"Do I know you?" she said in a shaky voice.

"I don't think so," Joe said, but he was a little unsure of everything now, after how familiar to him the inside of the house had been. "I think you knew my father."

Robbie, relaxing a bit now, was walking toward Joe. Her cowardly little dog was still retreating. She wore thick glasses and she moved even closer to get a better look.

When she was about two feet way, she said, "My lord, your Cal's boy, Joe."

"Yes," Joe said. "It's good to finally meet you."

"Oh, we've met before," Robbie said. "You were about two or three years old. Your dad brought you here when he was working on his book. In fact, we sat on these very steps over thirty-five years ago."

Joe was stunned. So he had been here, and most likely inside the house. How could his father not have told him?

Robbie's fear had completely melted. Now she wrapped Joe in a hug as if her own child had returned home after many years away.

"It's so good to see you again," she said.

Joe wanted to return the greeting, but had no memory of her. He figured he'd have remembered that hair before he'd remembered the inside of the house. The two stood in an awkward embrace for what seemed like an eternity to Joe. Then they broke and Robbie invited him to have a seat on the porch steps. Joe sat carefully to avoid a rusty nail poking up from the tread.

"What in the world are you doing inside this nasty old evil house?" she asked him.

Joe didn't know where to start. So much had gone on with him being in Gold's Lake at this house that he wasn't really sure. He decided to tell her the short version about being there to do some research to write a sequel to his dad's book.

Each time Joe mentioned his father, Robbie's eyes lit up. Even as an old lady, Joe could see she saw her relationship with Cal as more than friends. They sat and talked, mostly about her days growing up in Gold's Lake hanging out with her very best friend, Cal Mann. Her version and her father's versions of their relationship were very different. Cal had described her as big, unattractive, but very friendly.

She talked about Cal as if he were the love of her life.

Joe was getting more comfortable with Robbie so he decided to tell her more about his father's theory about the country club and the car accident. Nothing he said seemed to come as a surprise to Robbie. It was almost as if she'd already thought about the theory, but had discounted it.

"But none of the jewelry or cash were ever recovered and they searched that basement carefully," she said.

"That's because they didn't know the cases were related, so they didn't look very hard. I believed all along that they were related, so I looked harder."

"Well, did you find anything?" Robbie asked, her eyes wide.

Joe knew this question was coming and he also knew he was not prepared to tell her the truth just yet, but he did want to keep her engaged so he pulled out the tattered burlap bag and said, "I found this inside the stone foundation behind a big rock. I think it's what's left of the bag they used to collect the wallets, purses and jewelry at The Harding Country Club."

Robbie felt the bag. She wasn't convinced, but she sure wasn't discounting it either.

"Maybe it was there since the building was built. Maybe the original builders left the bag," she offered.

She turned the bag over.

"No," she said, refuting her own statement. "This bag is from the old Mill Hardware and Feed down on West Main. It closed up a year ago when Home Depot came into town and undersold them right out of business."

"How do you know?" Joe asked.

She spread the bag out and the faded picture of a windmill was on the front of it.

"That store wasn't in business until the forties, long after this house was built."

It occurred to Joe that the sight of a middle aged man and a big old woman with crazy hair sitting on the front steps of a long abandoned and dilapidated house would make an odd scene if someone passed by. But since the house was mostly obscured by trees and brush, the chance of someone seeing them wasn't likely.

Robbie seemed to be trying to compute too much at one time. Having the love of her life's son with her after so many years made her very happy. It seemed to Joe it was almost as if she had a part of Cal again, and to think that the story of the murders at the Wrin house was coming to life again was almost too much. She had simply set out to walk her dog as she had for years, and also several dogs before this one, and events turned so suddenly.

Joe found out that Robbie's life was the same thing day after day. All she really had was her routine. She'd retired as a bookkeeper for a small manufacturing firm that had long since vanished. She still lived in the house that she grew up in. She had lived there with her mother and her aunt until they had both passed away within two months of each other. There were days when she had no human contact. Rarely did anyone ever come to visit, although she used to have some friends, old single or widowed biddies like herself, who had since passed on.

She would have the same thing for breakfast every day. She'd walk her dog at long established intervals that she rarely deviated from. She'd always check on the Wrin house. She'd watch her soaps. She'd clean her house, which was immaculate to begin with, eat her dinner and go to bed. She'd learned to live her life devoid of excitement.

But today was different and she was happy for it. She wanted to talk about Cal, but Joe wanted to talk about the murders and what the burlap sack might mean. He wanted to tell her about the broach, but dared not until he could process its implications. He was antsy sitting there. He wanted to leave for fear that someone else might take an interest in the house. What if the cops showed up and frisked him and found the broach?

Robbie had been deep in thought for a minute and then she started to speak again.

# Chapter Seven

"Your father and I grew up next door to each other. We were best friends. We were each other's only friends. Cal's dad wasn't a nice man. He beat Cal regularly for nothing. And when Cal wasn't being beaten, he was working around the yard, in the house or at the newspaper stand. He had very little free time to make friends. But we really didn't need any other friends. We'd walk to and from school each day. We'd help each other with homework. I was really good at math and Cal was really good at English. He loved to read. I think it was his way of escaping the unpleasantness of his home."

"What about his mom?" Joe asked.

"You mean his stepmom, don't you?"

Obviously Cal had not told Robbie about his discovery concerning his real mother.

"She was a dark, unhappy, unfriendly woman. She got beaten sometimes also, once in the backyard where I could see. Cal's dad hit her with a broken broom handle. The saddest thing about it was that she didn't make a sound. It was as if she was used to being beaten."

This was not a memory Robbie was very keen on reliving so she went back to Cal.

"As Cal got bigger, he learned to avoid his dad. His dad would come home drunk and Cal would make himself scarce. Cal's dad was a big man with a sizable belly. By the time Cal was twelve, he could outrun him."

"Did Cal ever stand up to him?" Joe asked. He suddenly felt protective of his father, and that feeling surprised him.

"Yes, once. In some ways it marked a new beginning for him and in some ways it marked the end. Cal was about sixteen. He was sweeping the front steps of his house and his father came home drunk. Immediately he started yelling about Cal's bike not being put away. It didn't seem to matter that Cal wasn't done with it yet. His dad went inside to get another beer, but came back out and started yelling about something else. Cal didn't respond. He just kept on sweeping. This enraged his father. He put his beer down and started walking down the porch stairs, taking off his belt, heading toward Cal. Still Cal didn't react. As his father approached, he reared back and swung the belt, buckle side up. Cal deftly dodged the belt, took the broom with both hands, held it horizontally, and jammed it right into his father's face. Blood immediately poured from his father's nose as he stumbled backward and tried to maintain his balance. But the beer, the rage, the shock, and the force of the broom sent him sprawling backwards. He tried to catch himself, but his arm got stuck underneath him awkwardly. Cal heard the snap."

"There was no doubt what it was. He had broken his father's arm and most probably his nose. His father sat a moment and stared at Cal. Cal would have gratefully taken the worst beating of his life just to erase the memory of that look on his father's face. He instantly regretted standing up to his father, despite imagining this confrontation a million times as he was being beaten. Cal felt sick to his stomach."

"Cal started to walk away, not sure if he'd ever return. Part of him wanted to help his father up. He looked back to see his father stand up with great difficulty because he didn't have his right arm to help him stand. As his father walked toward the house, his arm hung limply at his side and his forearm was at an unnatural angle."

Robbie stopped talking and stared. She enjoyed speaking about the old days, but this was obviously upsetting her. Joe sensed it and decided he didn't want her to start crying only a few minutes after they met. It was starting to rain.

"Why don't I come by tomorrow and we can talk more about it?" Joe said.

"That would be fine," Robbie said. She seemed like she might enjoy the night to contemplate the day's events.

They exchanged information and set a time to meet. Then Joe got back in his Explorer, and Robbie started to head in the opposite direction with her little rat dog, now damp from the light rain.

As Joe drove away, he picked up his cell phone and called the Gold's Lake public library.

"Hello." It seemed like a strange greeting for the public library, but Joe knew it was Corra immediately.

"Corra. It's Joe from yesterday."

"Who?" she asked.

"You know. Joe. The guy who is looking into the murders at the Wrin house from all those years ago."

"Oh, Joe. Why didn't you say so?"

Joe realized Corra's hearing wasn't what it once had been.

"Can you look into something for me?" he asked her.

"Of course, sweetheart," she said.

"Did any of the articles on the country club robbery say anything about what the robbers carried everything away in?"

"You mean like a bag or a box?" Corra asked

"Yes, exactly," Joe said

"Well, I don't know, but I can check."

"Will you and can you call me back at this number?"

Joe gave her the number, but was not at all comfortable that she got it correctly. He figured that if he didn't hear from her by five today, he would go there first thing in the morning.

Joe's head was swimming. He had learned so much in his short visit to the Wrin house. He felt he had to get back to his motel room to write everything down and just to think about what he had learned. As he approached his motel, he changed his mind and stopped at the coffeehouse across the street. The thought of being cloistered in a boring motel room didn't appeal to him.

He found a round table and ordered a large black coffee, forgetting how sensitive he was to caffeine. Any caffeine after noon meant he'd be awake all night.

He took out his pad and started to write furiously. He wanted to capture every detail before he forgot something. In a short time he had filled five legal size, lined yellow pieces of paper.

As he turned to the next page, his cell phone rang. It was Corra. Joe immediately felt badly for doubting her.

"They used a burlap sack," she said. "I found a copy of the police report and several of the guests mentioned the sack."

"Were there any markings on it?" he asked excitedly.

"Not that anybody mentioned," Corra said, "but I'll keep looking."

Joe thanked her and hung up. On one hand he was happy because he found out it was a burlap sack, but on the other hand he was disappointed because he wanted concrete proof that he had the right bag. There was little doubt in Joe's mind that this was the same bag, but a little more confirmation wouldn't have hurt.

Joe made some more notes, including what he just learned from Corra. Then in big letters he wrote, "What should I do with the broach?"

He stopped writing and started to stare out the window. The broach was proof as far he was concerned that his father had been right all along and that the house had been used to store the goods from the heist. The murders were the biggest crime in this area, maybe ever, and he had information that no one else had except Ed Kutz and the short guy, if he were still alive. Was he breaking the law if he didn't report the broach to the police because it concerned murders as well the robbery? While the murders were solved, the robbery never was. The statute of limitations was certainly up, so Joe felt he was safe there.

Patrons were moving about the coffee shop as oblivious to Joe as he was to them. The bell on the door sounded every time someone went in or out. Joe kept staring out the window, lost in thought, when he noticed a figure standing at his table. Joe awoke from his staring to see Melissa standing at there.

"Hey. How are you?" Joe asked, standing to greet her.

Joe felt his face get all flushed and then felt worse because he thought she must notice it too. He felt like a high school boy talking to a pretty girl for the first time.

Melissa explained that she came in to the coffee shop everyday before her shift across the street at the restaurant. Her restaurant served coffee, but she said it tasted musty so she never drank it. Instead she stopped here. It pissed her boss off, but she didn't care. She was a good looking, affable, hard working dependable thirty-five year old who a lot of the patrons came in specifically to see. She gave old, out of shape men a chance to talk with a pretty girl, and the owner knew it. Half his revenue was from customers loyal to her. If she were to go to a restaurant across town, they'd all follow her.

Joe knew she was constantly being hit on by patrons, young and old. She had a way of making people feel like they were a close friend after only meeting her once of twice.

"So how's the big secret investigation going, liar?" she asked mockingly.

"Liar is kind of harsh, don't you think?" he responded.

They both laughed a little and Joe invited her to sit,

"Can't do it. I have to get to work."

"Then I'll come in later."

"Well, don't expect me to babysit you again. I only do that for first timers. On your second visit I consider you a regular."

With that she bought her coffee and left. Though the exchange had been brief and she rejected his offer to sit, he felt like they had connected again and she would be disappointed if he didn't show up at her restaurant.

Joe was feeling good about himself and then he started to think of the nasty old men who sat at strip clubs and gave the girls dollar bills to sit on their lap. The girls pretended to like them for the cash, but some of the men were so pathetic they actually thought the girls had real affection for them.

Maybe that's her talent, Joe thought. Maybe making people think that she really cared about them is why she is such a good bartender. Maybe she's just a good salesperson for the bar.

That tempered Joe's good feeling a little, but he knew he was still going back to see her.

Joe watched her walk away to her car. It was a shiny, mint condition, jet black 1987 El Camino. At first the car didn't make sense and then Joe thought, well, it might make sense if your husband was a mountain climber who used to store his gear in the back of it. He imagined that she kept it in such perfect condition as a way of honoring her dead husband.

As the car pulled away, Joe could hear the guttural roar of the engine. As if knowing she was being watched, Melissa spun her wheels as she entered the highway, spewing dirt, dust and rock all over the parking lot.

Joe hoped she had done that for his benefit.

Joe left the coffee shop himself and headed back onto the highway to the next exit so he could get on the access road that led back to his motel. As the crow flies, his motel was about a half a mile from the coffee shop, but because there was a highway in between, he had to drive about a mile and a half to get there.

Joe had just gotten on the highway when a police car pulled out from the shoulder and got directly behind Joe's car. Joe figured the cop would put on his siren, pull around him and take off after someone else. But he just stayed there, uncomfortably close to Joe's car. Joe signaled that he was exiting the highway and the cop did too. The traffic light at the end of the ramp was green so Joe made a left without stopping. The cop did also. The police car was still close, and Joe considered pulling over to let him pass, but just then the cops lights went on.

Joe pulled over. Had someone reported his license to the police after seeing him at the Wrin house? Joe considered throwing the broach out the window, but decided against it.

The cop car sat behind him with its lights on, but the driver didn't get out. Joe was nervous. Sweat started to bead on his forehead and run down his face. He wasn't on the highway long enough to do anything wrong and he wasn't on the road long enough for the cop to run his plates. Was he speeding? This had to have some-thing to do with breaking into the Wrin house. Joe had the awful feeling the cop had been lying in wait for him.

After what seemed like an eternity, the police car door swung open. A heavy man, about five and half feet tall, emerged. Getting in and out of the car wasn't that easy for him due to his oversized belly. The officer appeared to be in his early forties and wore mirror sunglasses despite the overcast weather. He walked to Joe's car in big, lumbering steps. He was not in a hurry. His billy club and gun hung at his side.

"What's the hurry, boy?" he asked, a chaw of tobacco in his mouth.

"No hurry, officer. I'm just going home." Joe had decided to be as polite as he possibly could. He had a lot to hide.

"Where's home?"

"I'm staying across the street at the Crest View motel. I didn't realize I was speeding."

"That's what the speedometer's for. Maybe you should look at it once in a while."

Joe knew he wasn't speeding, but wasn't about to start arguing with a stolen broach in his pocket.

"Let me see your license and registration, will ya, boy?" It was much more of a demand than a request.

The use of the word "boy" annoyed Joe because this cop appeared to be younger than he was. It was obvious that this over-weight policeman used his position and authority as well as his ample gut to intimidate people.

Joe gave him the documentation he requested and the police-man went back to his car. He sat there for about five minutes. Joe was starting to get nervous that he was calling in reinforcements when he emerged.

He walked back up to Joe's window and asked, "What's your business in our little town?"

"I'm just visiting."

"Visiting who?"

Joe wondered why the cop would need or be entitled to this information.

"Well, no one, really. My father grew up here and I wanted to see it."

"What's your business with that smashed up car there on Route 100?"

Joe was stunned. How the hell did he know I was looking at the car wreck?

That gas station attendant must have told him. Maybe he did some checking after Joe told him Ed Kutz was in the car.

"No business, sir. I was just looking at it. I noticed it was a Porsche and I've always been interested in them."

Joe lied, but he couldn't tell him the truth although Joe was feeling that this cop knew more about him than he was letting on. Joe continued to be very polite, knowing that one misstep could get him arrested

The policeman took a leisurely stroll around Joe's car, peering into each window.

"Pop the back, will ya, boy?" the cop said from behind the vehicle.

Joe did as he was told. The cop poked around and then continued around the car, forgetting to close the rear door. He arrived back at Joe's window.

"How much longer do you think you're gonna be in town?"

"Just a few days."

"Ok. I'm just gonna let you off with a warning. We can't have out-of-towners speeding through our streets now, can we?

"No, sir."

Joe had a powerful urge to argue with the officer, but his better judgment prevailed. The policeman tossed Joe's license and registration back to him when he could just as easily have handed it to him. Joe noticed the name on the police uniform. It said "William Timothy" in brackets and below his name it said "Bull, Jr."

As Bull, Jr. walked back to his car, Joe thought, this guy is a menace. He's the type of guy you just want to stay as far away as you can from. But Joe also had a feeling that he would see this guy again.

Joe went back to his motel with his notes and pendant in tow. It was around four in the afternoon. He couldn't head over to see Melissa yet. It would look kind of desperate, so instead he got back in the SUV and headed to the center of town where he'd seen what looked like a high end jewelry store.

The store's name caught his eye when he'd first driven into town. Strongwaters' Jewelry. He wondered if it was an Indian name or a moonshiner's name. As it turned out, the store was started by the Strong family and the Waters family, both prominent families in town. He parked right out front and went in. On the window of the store it said "Established 1908."

The same year my grandparents got married, Joe thought to himself.

There were a few people casually shopping. The manager walked up to Joe in his fancy suit and asked if he could help him. Joe explained that he'd like to have a piece of jewelry appraised for insurance purposes. The manager directed him to the sales desk at the back of the store. Joe pulled out the pendant and showed it to the man.

Joe watched him for a reaction. The man grabbed his loop for further examination.

"I'd like to know its value," Joe said, "and anything else you might be able to tell me."

The man with the loop examined it for five minutes without saying a word or reacting in any way. Then he called over a much older man with a loop to take a look. Joe couldn't make out what they were saying.

After discussing it back and forth for a few minutes the older man broke away and approached Joe and said, "It's definitely one of ours. We don't usually get to see pieces this nice from that long ago. Was it your parents'?" the man asked.

Again Joe was unprepared for the question. He never dreamed they might recognize it. All he wanted to know was how much it was worth. He couldn't possibly tell them the truth, that he'd just taken it from an old abandoned house where two policemen had been murdered. They would have called the police immediately.

Joe decided to be vague to ward off any further questions.

"It's my wife's. I'm not sure where she got it."

Joe suddenly became self-conscious about having taken his wedding ring off back at the motel to try to fool Melissa. He folded his hand into a fist to hide his naked finger.

"Well, I can't put an exact value on it right now, but I can tell you it's worth at least fifty thousand dollars. Each of those diamonds is about a karat and half and the quality is nearly perfect. We rarely see them that clear these days."

Joe was clearly astonished. He tried to act nonplussed, but his bright red face belied his excitement.

The man took his loop off and said, "My uncle started this store and was well respected for the diamond jewelry he made. I can't be sure, but your piece sure looks like a piece he would have made."

Joe was getting nervous now.

What if they had records that could identify the piece? They might be able to trace it back to the person who bought it, and they would discover that it had been stolen."

In today's computer age they certainly could, but Joe doubted that they would have records going back that far.

"Is there anything else you can tell me about it? Do you keep any records?" Joe asked.

"Sure, we keep records, but a flood in the late sixties ruined them all. The diamonds are a classic pear shape cut that was very popular back then, but nobody uses that one any more. Some people think that makes them less valuable. I think it enhances their value. Can you leave this with me for a couple days?"

Joe didn't like that idea at all. What if they started showing it around and someone recognized it? What if the original owner was still alive or her heirs heard about it? It wasn't that Joe wanted to protect it for the money he could make by selling it. It was that if it was discovered to have been stolen at the country club, Joe would have to explain it, and that was something he simply wasn't prepared to do.

"How long would you have to keep it?" Joe asked.

"Just a couple days," the man said.

Joe was starting to panic. He was desperately trying to come up with a lie as to why he couldn't leave it there, but in the end he couldn't come up with a single reason, so he agreed to leave it.

"Could you have it done by Friday?" Joe asked.

"Certainly. Check in around lunch time."

Joe walked out feeling as though he'd made a big mistake. A fifty thousand dollar piece wasn't that common, even in this day. All kinds of scenarios started running through his head.

What if the original owner, from whom it had been stolen, had tried to get it back all those years ago? Maybe she posted pictures of it at every pawn shop in the area back then. Maybe there was a picture of it at the police station or the post office. It was obviously a highly regarded piece.

Intellectually, Joe knew this wasn't likely, but he also knew it was possible and that's what scared him. He was at least guilty of breaking and entering and of theft. He had come to Gold's Lake just to do some research and now he could be arrested. Joe walked out of the jewelry store fighting the urge to run in and grab it back.

He got in his car and started heading for the Oval Bar. He remembered reading that there were over two hundred people at the Harding Country Club fund raiser that night it got robbed. Maybe the piece of jewelry that he found in the remains of the burlap sack was just an average piece among all those rich people. Maybe it was low end. What if there had been fifty pendants of equal or greater value?

We'd be talking about real money. Ed Kutz could have sold two of them to buy the Porsche. The take from that robbery could have been huge.

If Ed Kutz had broken back in to the Wrin house to recover the stolen merchandise, he'd have to sell them to convert them to cash. How would he have done that? He probably didn't have any connections in the jewelry world since he'd been in jail for the last forty years. He didn't have a whole lot of friends to rely on. What if he had some prison connections who could set him up? Joe pulled his car over to think.

Ed showed an amazing amount of self restraint by leaving the loot in that house for forty years. He must have been tempted numerous times to have someone go and get it, but he also must have known he'd have been helpless if whoever he sent to recover it just took it all and fled. He also had to have worried that the house might be torn down or remodeled by a new owner. He bought the Porsche, so he had to have converted it somehow. Maybe he just pawned a couple of items to keep from raising any suspicions.

Joe continued to be lost in his thoughts.

If I had a bag of stolen property that I had to convert to cash, how would I do it without getting myself thrown into jail? I've got plenty of people I know in New Jersey, but I can't think of a single one that I would trust to tell that I had stolen merchandise I needed to fence.

Would I go to individual jewelry stores with one piece of jewelry and try to sell it? Would they ask questions? Would they want to see a receipt? Would they pay me cash so I didn't have to explain to the IRS where the money came from? The more Joe thought, the more the only conclusion he could come up with was a pawn shop.

Joe decided that his next move would be to check out the local pawn shops.

Joe put his car back into drive and pulled back onto the highway. He didn't really want to admit it, but his opinion of Ed Kutz was changing. Maybe his father had it wrong when he described Ed as a cold blooded, dead eyed murderer. Joe couldn't recall that his father ever actually interviewed Ed for the book. He'd seen him in the court room, but Joe didn't think he actually ever took the stand. He got most of his information about Ed from a discredited and disbarred prosecutor who was banging his underage assistants.

There was never a question as to whether or not Ed shot those two policemen, but why he did never came up. Joe knew that to really understand the events that took place in that basement all those years ago, he would have to find out more about Ed prior to the killings. How he would do that, he had no idea.

Joe turned his SUV onto the dirt access road toward his motel, just up the road from Melissa and the Oval bar. It was still too early to head to the bar without looking too much like an over anxious school boy, so Joe pulled up to the door of his motel room and went inside.

He'd been away from home for almost a week and hadn't spoken with his wife yet. It was customary that when he traveled without his family, he would call at least every other day. He had already called the house and left a message, but it was a weak attempt. He called at a time when he knew nobody would be at home. He could have called her on her cell phone, but instead he called home and left a message so he wouldn't have to answer any questions and she wouldn't try to read anything into his tone of voice. If he waited any longer, he ran the risk of upsetting her more than he already might have by taking this trip.

He sat on the edge of his bed with his cell phone in his hand. Would he explain everything that had happened so far? She knew the original story, but she never understood Joe's "obsession" -- her word -- with it. Would he tell her about the broach? About breaking into the house? About the burned out car? About meeting Robbie?

He decided that he would tell her everything, except about Melissa.

After one ring, Joe's wife answered the phone. They made awkward small talk for a few minutes before Joe asked to speak with his three children. They were really too young to carry on a conversation by phone, but Joe was happy to hear their voices. They made meaningless small talk for about a minute until his four year old decided that he'd had enough and went back to doing whatever he'd been doing before the call. Barbara picked up the phone again.

"So how's your little adventure going? Is it everything you

hoped it would be? Have you found out anything that you didn't know?"

Joe explained everything concerning the story in minute detail. He wanted his wife to know he was there and working hard. His story was that he was there for this story, and he was sticking to it. He didn't say anything about the problems they'd been having, but that never was their style. Whenever they had a problem in their marriage, rather than talk it out, they just kind of pretended it didn't exist and then each went about figuring it out on their own.

That had always worked before, so why change now?

Barbara tried to feign interest in Joe's story, but her mind seemed to be on the state of her family. Joe just kept talking and she kept saying, "Really?" and "How interesting."

They made some small talk about the kids until they reached another awkward moment in their conversation.

Rather than ask when he was coming back home to be a father and a husband, she asked, "So how much longer do you think this research is going to last?"

"Not too long, but I'm not sure. Every time I look into something, it leads to ten more questions."

"Okay," Barbara said. "We're fine here. The kids miss you. Just check in when you can. I love you."

"I love you, too" he replied.

He knew she loved him and he loved her, but that wasn't going to stop him from going to see Melissa, and his wedding ring would stay on the night stand.

Before leaving the motel Joe made few more calls related to his business. He checked in with his junior partner. There was nothing urgent that he needed to attend to, so Joe hung up, took a shower, got dressed and headed to the Oval Bar.

The bar was packed. It was Happy Hour and there wasn't a seat to be had. Melissa was behind the bar flinging drinks as quickly as she could. People five deep were shouting at her for drinks.

Despite being extremely busy, she looked up and spotted Joe almost as soon as he entered the bar. It was almost as if she'd been looking for him. She gave him a quick smile and went back to work. The manager of the restaurant joined her behind the bar to help with the rush, but he was making one drink to every five she made. He actually appeared to be slowing her down because she was moving fast and he was constantly in her way as she glided from one side of the bar to other.

Joe decided that he would sit back for awhile and let the rush subside before trying to get a drink when suddenly a hand reached through the crowd with a Vodka Gimlet.

Joe smiled at her, but she looked away quickly.

Am I that special or does she really like me, Joe wondered.

Joe stood against the back wall for about an hour and half while the rush went on. He liked the atmosphere and didn't mind one bit being by himself in the bar. On several occasions, Melissa had to come across the bar for one reason or another and each time she would pass right by Joe. He wasn't sure if he was imagining it or not, but each time she passed, she had gotten really close to him to the point of pushing her breast and her butt against him.

The bar is crowded, but not that crowded, he thought.

The crowd had started to thin out and only a handful of people remained. There was an overweight, dirty guy at the end of the bar with a tee shirt that had its sleeves ripped off. He was a big guy who looked like he may have been muscular at one time, but now was mostly just fat. He looked as if he had come directly from his landscaping job to the bar. He was there before

Joe got there and had been kind of loud and was now probably drunk.

"Ok, fella," Melissa said. "That's it for you. Hit the road."

"I'm not going anywhere. I'll have another drink," he said in a slurred voice.

It was clear that Melissa had handled this kind of guy before. She smiled and tried to calm him down.

"C'mon, bud. You're gonna get me fired."

He protested more, and the more he talked, the more drunk he appeared. She handed him his tab.

"I'll pay, but I'm not done drinking."

Melissa knew better then to argue with a drunk, but she was concerned about how he was getting home.

"You gotta ride, friend?"

"Yeah, it's that shitty pick up right there," he slurred, pointing nowhere in particular, but in the general direction of the parking lot out the front window. His tone was becoming increasingly belligerent.

Melissa didn't immediately respond. There was no way she could let this guy drive.

The drunk had a pile of his stuff on the bar: his wallet, cigarettes, a lighter and his pick-up keys. Melissa handed him the tab and then proceeded to walk around the bar to where he was sitting.

"You know, I may have overcharged you," she said to him. "Let me see that tab."

She learned over with one hand around his shoulder and the other hand calmly reached onto the bar to grab his keys.

She put the keys in her pocket and said, "Nope. I didn't make a mistake. Sorry."

She walked back around the bar, saw her manager and threw the keys to him. He caught them and put them in his pocket.

"We're closing up, fella. You got to go."

It was still an hour before they closed, but he was too drunk to tell time. He muttered about how they close too early and started searching his pockets for his keys. He looked all over the bar and below his seat. He walked out to his truck, came back in and checked his pockets again.

"Where the fuck are my keys?" he said under his breath.

In the drunken state he was in, it never occurred to him that Melissa had taken them. She pretended to help him look for them. After fifteen minutes or so, a cab pulled up outside. The manager had called the taxi company.

"Look, fella, when we find your keys, we'll drop the truck off to you. Just leave your address and it will be at your house in the morning."

He muttered something about having to be at work for eight o'clock. Joe wondered how much work his employer was going to get out of him as hung over as he was going to be. But Joe had seen that scenario played out a hundred times in his own business.

After searching for another ten minutes, the drunk agreed to take the cab. Melissa walked him to the cab, handed the driver twenty dollars from her tip jar, and a slip of paper with his address. It was obvious to Joe that she had done this many times before.

Melissa came back in. The bar was empty, save Joe.

"Very impressive," Joe said.

"I've had to deal with my share of violent drunks and let me tell you, nobody wins in that situation. I've found that outsmarting drunks isn't very hard. He must have been drinking before he got here because I only gave him a few."

Melissa told the manager that she was going to take off early so she could return the drunk's truck. He agreed and she packed up to leave.

"Don't make me throw you out, too," she said to Joe.

Joe took this as an invitation to meet her outside. He didn't want to look too obvious, so he calmly finished his drink and headed out a minute or two behind her. Just as he walked through the door, he saw Melissa getting ready to pull on to the access road to leave.

"Shit," Joe thought. Did I misread her signals? Had the game changed so much since he had been dating that he didn't now how to play it anymore? He ran up to the drunk's truck and tapped on the window.

"Do you want me to follow you to drive you home?"

"I can walk," she said.

"Don't be silly. I'll follow you."

"Now why would I get in a car with you? You could be a crazy killer."

"Well, you know my favorite drink," he said meekly, "so you know me a little."

"That's true. Plus, we have your credit card info in the bar. When I disappear, it shouldn't be hard for them to find you. Follow me."

Joe jumped into his Explorer.

# Chapter Eight

M elissa parked the truck in the street in front of the drunk's modest house and slipped the keys into the mail box.

Plastic kids' toys littered the yard. It made Joe sad to think that this guy was somebody's father. Melissa got into Joe's car and they quietly moved off down the road. It was late, but Joe wanted to go anywhere other than back to his motel alone. He was not ready to call it a night.

"Let's go get a drink," he said.

They pulled into one of the few places that stayed open later than the Oval Bar. It was called O'Brien's. They went inside where it was dark and the décor was from 1950 and in serious need of updating.

Melissa and Joe sat at the bar and the bartender appeared to know Melissa, but they didn't say much to each other. He put a Cape Cod in front of her without her having to ask, so Joe asked for the same thing.

Their conversation was easy. Too easy, in fact. They were talking like they'd known each other their whole lives. He updated her on his activities concerning the Wrin house and the murders. After a few drinks, he decided to tell her about the broach. Without seeing it, the story wasn't that impressive. Knowing that he probably shouldn't,

Joe told Melissa what the jeweler said it might be worth.

"So you are telling me you broke into someone's house and took something that could be worth fifty thousand dollars? Sounds like grand larceny to me. Had I known you were a felon, I wouldn't have let you pick me up," she said, half joking.

He explained that he wasn't in it for the money and in the end wouldn't keep the broach for its value. At least he didn't think he would.

Melissa was definitely intrigued.

They talked for another hour and then she said she was tired. They had each had three drinks plus what Joe had had at the Oval Bar. He was feeling pretty good and probably shouldn't have been driving, but he had other things on his mind.

It was worth risking the DUI, he thought.

Joe led her outside. The parking lot was empty and the highway was deserted. They walked side by side, but not too close, as they approached his car. He got his keys out and headed to her side of the car. He unlocked her door, but made no move to get out of the way so she could get in.

He smiled at her and she smiled back. Without saying a word he bent to kiss her. Not on the cheek, as if to say good bye, but a kiss to see how she would respond.

She responded by kissing back. They kissed for a moment and then Melissa seemed to get nervous that someone might be watching.

"We gotta go," she said.

They got into Joe's car. His interest was impossible to hide. As soon as both doors were locked, he leaned over and kissed her again. Then he pulled out of the parking lot and headed to her home.

When he arrived, he started kissing her again and he reached his hand up under her shirt. To his surprise she didn't try to stop him. While Joe had hoped for a good night kiss, feeling her warm skin for a moment, he thought, was a far more fulfilling way to say goodnight.

Joe woke up early the next morning, amazed by what had happened. He wondered how she was going too feel about it when they saw each other again. Had he gotten her drunk intentionally? She wasn't acting very drunk.

Joe kept going over the night before in fine detail. He wanted to relive every second of it. This kind of thing didn't happen to him very often. Well, not since he'd been married. How would she act when he saw her later, which he most certainly would. He knew it would be uncomfortable, but he couldn't wait to see her again.

Joe swung his legs over the side of the bed. His cell phone rang as he was rubbing the sleep out of his eyes. He fumbled around for the phone and as his eyes adjusted he made out that Barbara was calling.

He really wasn't ready to speak with her. He hadn't mentally prepared himself to deal with her in light of what had happened the night before. He was afraid the guilt would be obvious, even over the phone.

He let the phone go to voice mail.

Over the years their relationship had developed a certain tempo. They knew each other's habits, predilections, likes and dislikes. They intuitively knew how the other was feeling or what they were thinking. After meeting a new person, they could tell without even talking what the other thought of him or her.

So much of their relationship had become unspoken. Their sleep and bathroom schedules, comings and goings, had become very familiar. Some might think it boring. Others might think it comfortable. Joe was in the middle somewhere.

He never doubted his love for Barbara. He loved her and he was sure about it, but sex and love where separate in his mind. He hated the term "making love" when it was just sex. Every married couple understood the difference, he thought. There were definitely times when love and sex came together and it was very special, but there were many more times when it was just sex. Sex was not love.

Their marriage was a good one, but it wasn't exciting and Joe was afraid that exciting marriages didn't really exist. People married in a frenzy of newness and then that wore off and it was back to life as usual. Joe struggled with this constantly. It was almost as if, despite the fact that many people had warned him, he couldn't believe that boredom had settled into his marriage.

He had become afraid that excitement and marriage were mutually exclusive.

He hadn't been one of those guys who had screwed around a lot in high school or afterwards. He had been a one woman guy and would break up with a girl rather than cheat on her. His relationships were never one night stands. He felt if he became intimate with a girl that he should at least date her for a while.

A lot of his friends had no problems screwing a girl and then never calling her again. Joe just wasn't wired that way. The ultimate result of that, in his mind, was that his number of conquests was much lower than they otherwise should have been. And whether he liked to admit it or not, his number, around ten, bothered him because it could have been so much higher.

On a subconscious level -- and sometimes it wasn't so subconscious -- Joe would get angry at Barbara for no other reason than that she was stopping him from having sex with other women.

Joe was diligent about returning phone calls promptly, especially Barbara's, so if he didn't call her soon, it would make matters worse, he knew. They had spoken briefly the day before so this call was a little odd.

He sat on the edge of the bed and thought about what he would tell her. He'd stick to the investigation and not go in to any personal stuff, he thought. She didn't have to know anything about Melissa, the bar or what he'd done the night before. As far as she was concerned, he turned in early after reviewing his notes.

He dialed her phone and she answered on the first ring. It was if she'd been waiting with the phone in her hand.

"Good morning, babe," he said. "I was in the bathroom when you called earlier."

He lied, but so what?

They talked for awhile. Joe was listening more for what she didn't say than for what she was saying.

He told her all about the case and what had happened since the last time they talked. She was interested, but he felt what she really wanted to know was if he had gotten his head together and when he was coming back and would he be able to rejoin their marriage as a full participating member. They both felt the awkwardness in their conversation.

When things were going well between them, the conversation came incredibly easy. Easier than with anyone either of them had ever known.

"So are you working on the case all the time?" she asked.

"Pretty much. I'm learning so much during the day and then putting it together at night. There is a coffee shop across the street I've been eating at so I don't go crazy sitting in my nasty little motel room. I spoke to Corra from the library again. She's been a great help."

Joe figured a little misdirection wouldn't hurt. If Barbara thought he was hanging out with women eighty or older, she'd rest easier.

As far as Joe knew, Barbara thought the man she married was a good man who loved her, but she also probably knew he was restless. She was happy in their marriage, he thought, and she had no obvious complaints. In fact, it bothered him sometimes that she'd always compromise to accommodate him.

Doesn't she have a strong feeling about anything or have things she'd never compromise?

Only a man trying to sabotage a relationship would think this way, Joe suddenly thought.

Of course, he knew there were things that bothered her about him, but he also knew she just chose her battles carefully. She didn't like to fight because invariably she'd end up crying.

And Joe hated to see her cry.

Their phone conversation went on awkwardly for a few more minutes. They talked about the kids, their friends, the house and her family. When they reached the end of the conversation, he told her he loved her and would be home soon.

Barbara returned the "I love you," but Joe felt what she really wanted to know was exactly when he was coming home.

But she didn't ask, and he didn't offer.

He hung up the phone and was surprised that he didn't feel guilty for lying or for what he'd done the night before. He did feel badly that she was worried about him and their relationship. Still, he knew he loved her, and that their relationship wasn't in danger. At least, he hoped it wasn't.

He saw Barbara and Melissa as unrelated, and he wondered if

his father had felt that way when he stepped out, too.

After leaving the motel, Joe desperately wanted to go back to the jeweler, hoping that they'd have the appraisals done a day early, but he decided against it for fear of looking too anxious.

Instead, Joe headed back to the library to research local pawn shops. Corra was more than happy to help him and she already had a list of about fifteen shops, some as far as an hour away.

"You gonna tell me what you need pawn shops for?" Corra asked.

Again Joe hadn't anticipated her question. His mind had been preoccupied with Melissa. Corra noticed how uncomfortable he was with that question and withdrew it.

"If you want to tell me some day, you can."

Corra was smart. Withdrawing the question told Joe that he could trust her.

As Joe was making her swear to secrecy, she told him she considered her position at the library to be similar to that of a priest or a lawyer or even a doctor.

"If I go blabbing to everyone about what people are researching, they'd be afraid to ask me for help, so I keep it zipped," she said, pointing to her mouth.

Joe told her how he'd found the broach in the canvas bag and had given it to the jeweler to appraise. She sat stunned and amazed, obviously enjoying this to no end.

"Which jeweler did you bring it to?"

"Strongwaters'."

When Joe told her, her face went deadly serious.

"He's got the biggest friggin' mouth in town. If you want the world to know something, tell Walter Strong it's a secret. He's third generation. They should of drowned him at birth."

Joe felt a shiver go up his spine.

"Did you tell him it was a secret?" Corra asked.

"No, I didn't."

"Was it a nice piece?"

"It sure was."

"Well, all we can do is hope he does his job and that he doesn't show it to anybody that might recognize it."

Joe was feeling a little sick suddenly. The prospect of the cops hearing about this and putting all the pieces together wasn't sitting well with him. He knew he was being paranoid, but he couldn't help it.

They both sat thinking for a moment and then Corra sat up excitedly.

"I have a book about Strongwaters'."

"You have a book about a local jewelry store?" Joe asked, with a tidal wave of doubt in his voice.

"They put it together for their seventy-fifth anniversary. The founder was getting ready to die, so they put together a book about the store's history, its people and their most famous pieces of jewelry."

Corra headed for the back of the library and returned not sixty seconds later with the book in hand. She skipped the sections about the history of the store, its founders and its employees over the years, and opened up to the last section that had hundreds of pictures of jewelry they had made.

Joe pulled his chair next to Corra's so they could look at the pictures together.

Corra explained that Strongwaters' always made their own jewelry, but they also sold many other manufacturers' pieces. There was a good chance that the piece he found wasn't purchased there and if it had been, it could have been made by someone else.

Corra flipped through the black and white pictures until Joe spotted the broach he had found.

"That's it," he whispered in absolute awe.

It wasn't in color, but everything else was identical. It had the long gold stems and the three large pear shaped diamonds.

Underneath the picture it said "The Leeds Collection." There was a one paragraph description below the piece which explained how this piece had been designed by the youngest daughter of the founder, Walter Strong. It described the diamonds, the setting, and the gold, and the last line said that the piece had been so popular that Debra Strong-Leeds had been commissioned to make fifteen of the exact same broach in 1942.

Corra was feeling smug at having been able to indentify in mere seconds the piece Joe had found. Joe, on the other hand, was not sure what to think.

Corra suggested that he take the book with him to the pawn shops.

Joe agreed and reached out to take the book from her, but she pulled it back

"You'll need a library card first."


Joe spent the day going from pawn shop to pawn shop. Each had the same feel to it. It looked as though people, instead of renting a dumpster, had brought their stuff to a pawn shop. So much of the stuff was outdated electronics that nobody would ever want. Each shop had an old man behind the counter paying little attention to him, but Joe thought they were used to sleazy characters so they probably noticed everything.

At the first three stores Joe was hesitant to engage the shopkeepers in conversation. He would walk over to their jewelry case and look at it as though he was looking to buy something. Most of the jewelry was old and not very impressive.

Joe was not about to show the picture of the piece he had found just yet. What good would it do anyway since he already had that piece? What he wanted too know was, did anybody come into the store looking to sell pieces of jewelry like that lately.

He had been to the first three stores and really hadn't learned anything useful. But he hadn't asked any questions, either. As he got further outside of town, he decided that he would start asking questions. He quickly found out that pawn shop owners are not very talkative about who brought what in.

At the fifth store he decided to try a different tact. He would show the picture of the broach he had already found to ask if the owner had any other high end jewelry from the same era.

At stores six and seven, the owners were not inclined to give him any information at all. Joe thought that maybe they thought he was a cop.

At the eighth store, a chubby, kindly old man sat behind the counter with a jeweler's ring to his eye. Joe gave him the same story, but there was a weariness in Joe's voice that made the owner take sympathy.

"Tell me what you really want and then I'll let you know if I can help you."

Like Corra, Joe felt like he could trust this guy, so he told him most of the story, leaving out the parts that could get him in trouble or lead back to the country club robbery or the Wrin house.

He showed the old man the piece of jewelry in the book.

"Son, first of all, you are not going to find a piece that nice sitting in a case in a pawn shop. If I got that piece, I have several contacts I would call and they would scoop it up in five minutes and resell it. If someone brought it in here, I would offer about a third of what it is worth. And if he wanted cash, with no questions asked, I couldn't do that for him. Anything over six hundred bucks has to be reported. There is too much danger in doing that. There are some guys who would do it, but not me."

Joe was feeling more and more comfortable with this guy so he pressed him further.

"If you had to sell this piece quickly and maybe some others and you couldn't do it legitimately, what would you do?"

The old man smiled and said, "I wouldn't."

Disappointed, Joe said, "C'mon. I'm at a dead end here."

The old man took a deep breath, reached into his card file and handed Joe a card.

"If someone is trying to fence high end jewelry, this guy will know about it. But keep in mind he is not a nice man and neither are most of the other people in this business. They will chew you up and spit you out. They hate questions. Unless you are looking to buy, don't expect much help and also, if you ask questions about the seller, you can expect that he will find out you're asking."

Joe thanked him and started to head toward the door.

"Hey, kid. I'd appreciate your leaving my name out of any discussions you have with this guy. I don't need his kind of trouble. And you don't either."

Joe decided that he wouldn't check out the remaining pawn shops on his list. He figured he wasn't going to get any more information. He had the number of the man he needed, but the question was, should he call him?

It was getting late in the day. Joe had had enough. He headed back home and noticed the main door to the library was still open. He stopped out front and walked inside.

"What are you doing still open?" he asked Corra.

"I'm waiting for you. I want to hear what you found out today."

"Not much. Just that pawn shops probably aren't the way to go."

Joe showed her the card he had gotten along with the warning from the chubby pawnshop owner.

"So what are you gonna do?"

"I don't know yet. This guy scared me pretty good."

"What if I called him as a little old lady and said I was trying to find a piece of lost jewelry?"

"It could be dangerous for you, too," Joe said.

"Oh, who's gonna hurt a little old librarian?"

"I don't like it. Let's talk about it tomorrow."

Joe's day had been drudgery, but he had gotten far. His butt hurt from sitting in his car all day and he was tired of thinking about that broach. The thought of having a few drinks and dinner at Melissa's bar was on his mind, and whatever else the night might bring.

Joe drove back to his motel and parked right out in front of his door. He walked up to his door and put the key in the lock, but the door just swung open. He froze for a moment.

Did he leave it unlocked this morning? He didn't think so, but Melissa had been on his mind. He took a step into the room. The splintered wood from the door frame and the casing lay on the tacky orange shag carpet. Someone had forced the door open.

Once Joe was inside, the thought occurred to him that the person who broke in might still be there. He thought about running, but the apartment was small enough that he could see that nobody was there, unless they were in the bathroom. He walked slowly across the room. The bathroom door was half way open and he could see through the crack in the hinge side that nobody was hiding behind the door.

Joe walked over to the broken door and closed it. Despite the violent way it had been forced open, it closed properly. While the lock plate for the dead bolt was ripped off and lying on the floor, the dead bolt could still be turned to securely fit in the hole on the jam. Joe was glad for this because he wouldn't have to call the police and answer all their questions.

Nothing seemed to be missing, but everything had been rifled through. Luckily he had his entire file with him that day because he had left it in his truck the night before.

Joe sat on the bed. He was trembling. Thoughts started to fly through his head. Who could be interested in him? Had someone talked? Was it the jeweler? Had he shown the piece to someone who recognized it?

Corra was right not to have trusted that man, Joe muttered.

What about the guy at the pawn shop? Maybe he wasn't the nice old grandfatherly guy he pretended to be. But I never gave him my name or told him where I was staying. Could he have had me followed? No way

Who else had he told?

Robbie? He hadn't told her about the broach, or had he? He was starting to lose track of who he had told what. Maybe she didn't believe him when he said the burlap sack was empty.

What about Corra? Did she innocently mention something to someone she shouldn't have? She's old. Her memory might be slipping

Every person he had met since he arrived in Gold's Lake went through his head.

What about the gas station owner? He hadn't liked the fact that Joe conned him.

Slowly, Joe's thoughts arrived at Melissa. He had told her more than anyone. And since he was a little drunk last night, maybe he had said more then he should have. Maybe she had gotten him drunk to take advantage of him rather then the other way around.

The thought disturbed him.

"Please don't let that be what happened," Joe said aloud.

Joe didn't know what to do now. He was afraid to stay in and he was afraid to go out. He didn't know who to trust. He lay back on his bed and tried to think logically about who it could have been. He wasn't getting anywhere and eventually he fell asleep.

He awoke around three a.m., still dressed in his street clothes. He had the urge to head out to the Oval bar, but she would be gone. He took off his clothes and got into bed.

He spent the rest of the night staring at the ceiling and listening for noises outside his door.

Morning seemed to take forever to come. At first light he got up, got dressed and went to see the motel manager. He had to tell him that there had been a break in or otherwise they would come after him for damaging their property.

Joe asked the manager if he could wait for the police because Joe had an urgent meeting he couldn't miss. Lying was coming easier and easier to Joe. He explained that he had come home and found the door smashed in, but only a few dollars were missing.

That wasn't true either, but Joe felt that if the police thought the robbers were there for money, they wouldn't press him on what they may have really been after. The manager agreed and Joe left, not sure if he would return. He took almost all his possessions, especially everything that had to do with the murders or the country club robbery.

It was too early to go to the jewelry store and Melissa would still be asleep and probably be pissed at him for not calling or stopping into the restaurant. The library wouldn't be open yet either. He felt like he should stay away from most of these people anyway until he could find out who said what to whom.

He went to the coffee shop across from his motel and sat and waited for the police to arrive. He watched them come and spend a few minutes looking around. About fifteen minutes later a locksmith and a handyman pulled up and started working on the door.

It was another cold raw day, the kind of day Joe would have liked to have spent in bed. The wind was blowing a cold, hard misty rain against the window of the coffee shop. Joe was the only person in the shop, save the people who worked there.

He heard the door open and looked up, hoping to see Melissa, but it was a local businessman trying to stay dry and warm with an umbrella and a rain coat. He picked up a newspaper, got a cup of coffee and headed back out into the rain.

Joe was thinking more clearly now. He was sure that Melissa had not mentioned anything to anyone that would get him in trouble and he was pretty sure that Corra and the pawn shop guy were on the up and up.

He was very worried about the guy at Strongwaters' jewelers. He was going there as soon as possible to get the broach. It was 7:30 a.m. The store didn't open until 9 a.m.. He had to get the broach, but he was glad for the time to sit and recount everything that had happened so far.

He started to organize all his notes. Writing things down in lists always helped Joe in his school life and his business life. He made lists of everything he had learned so far, and he realized that he had forgotten to contact Robbie again like he said he would. He would have to call her today.

He also realized that he still knew precious little about Ed Kutz and his home life. Maybe he could ask Corra to find out whatever she could. If she couldn't find it, nobody could. He was pretty sure she wasn't the leak and even if she was, this was something he had to do. He would call her later in the day and give her that job.

The rain kept coming down and the door to the coffee shop kept opening. Joe would look up each time, hoping to see Melissa. Several times he got up and went to the window to look toward her restaurant to see if she was there yet. It was approaching 8:30. Joe packed up his stuff, threw his trash in the garbage and headed for his car. As he left the shop, he looked both ways to see if anyone was following him.

"You are getting paranoid, "Joe laughed to himself.

"I didn't imagine my door getting kicked in," he argued back.

He got in his car and threw his pile on the seat next to him. It suddenly occurred to him that maybe whoever broke into his motel room wasn't after his broach. Maybe he was after Joe's file. Maybe he wanted to know what Joe was snooping around about. Joe wouldn't be leaving that file lying around anymore.

He turned the car onto the highway. As he looked to his left, through the rain and mist, he saw Melissa's El Camino pulling into the Oval Bar. He had an urge to drive right over there and apologize for not calling, but it would look like he was spying on her if he drove over as soon as she arrived. He decided that he would go get the broach and then head over to the bar.

Joe pulled his car up to Strongwaters'. It was still a few minutes before 9:00 so he waited in his car. He could see the sales clerks uncovering the jewelry cases and putting the jewelry back in the window displays. Joe had learned years before that jewelers always locked most of their stock away in safes per the insurance company rules.

An elderly woman walked up to the front door and unlocked it, signifying the store's opening for the day. Joe got out of his car and walked in. He looked around to find Walter Strong, but he was nowhere in sight.

Joe walked around the store as if shopping for a gift. The same elderly salesman came up to him and asked him if he needed any help. He declined and kept looking. He wasn't sure, but he felt like everybody was staring at him. One clerk actually was staring at him from behind the repair counter with a phone up to his ear and Joe imagined that he was calling the police to tell them that the guy who robbed the Wrin house was back.

Joe began fighting the urge to sprint out of the store and jump into his car and leave town forever. As Joe headed toward the door, Walter Strong was on his way in. He closed his umbrella and took off his rain hat. He didn't notice Joe right away. He said hello to his staff and a few mumbled "Good morning" back to him. He went into his office and came back into the sales areas with a cup of coffee in his hand.

Joe walked up to him and asked him about his broach.

"Oh, yes. It's all done. Let me get it for you."

He handed Joe his broach in a small plastic bag along with the appraisal and the invoice for the appraisal. Joe paid him and thanked him and started to walk out.

"That's a very nice piece you've got there. Very nice workmanship."

"Thank you," Joe said.

He was expecting him to say more about the piece, but he

didn't. Immediately Joe found that odd. Didn't his guy know that his store had created it, that his aunt had actually created it?

Deciding to take a big chance, Joe asked, "Can you tell me anything about the history of the piece?"

Mr. Strong had nothing of substance to say to Joe, but mumbled some nonsense about the weight and the cut of the diamonds. Joe noticed one of the sales clerks rolled her eyes at his comments. He was not a well respected man.

Joe thanked him and turned to leave.

"By the way, young man, if you are interested in selling it, I might have a buyer for you."

Joe was dumbfounded.

I bring this piece in for a simple appraisal and this asshole is shopping it around? Is that even legal, Joe wondered. Joe could feel his face turning red with anger. He wanted to tell him what he thought of his offer, but he didn't need the attention so he said no, thanked him and left.

Once back in the car, still stunned, Joe opened the appraisal. It showed the weight of each diamond being a karat and a half, it commented on the clarity being very good, and it estimated its value for insurance purposes to be fifty-five thousand dollars. There was no editorializing on its quality or history.

Joe was disappointed that he didn't get more information, but he couldn't go back in and ask what he really wanted to know. Who was the original owner?

Joe backed his car out and started to head toward the Oval Bar. His mind was swimming. Who is this interested buyer? Is it part of the same group that the pawn shop owner had warned him about? Whoever it was, Joe was pretty sure there was a connection between Strong's shopping his piece of jewelry and whoever broke into his place.

Instead of heading directly to the Oval Bar, Joe turned toward the library. Corra's old, he thought. Old people don't sleep much. I'll bet she's there already.

He was right. The lights were on in the library, but the doors were still closed because of the rain. Joe went inside and said hello to Corra.

"You looked tired," she said.

"I am tired," Joe responded.

"Late night at the Oval Bar with the bartender?" she asked

"How do you now I've been at the Oval?" Joe asked.

"It's a small town," she said, "and I'm the librarian. I know everything. Including that your motel room was broken into last night."

After the shock of Corra mentioning him and the Oval bartender, Joe realized he continued to underestimate her. He would do well to stow the old people jokes and listen to what she had to say.

"Nothing's going on with any bartender," Joe insisted.

"Funny you would comment on that before you said anything about me knowing about your room."

Joe felt as if he had the word adulterer written across his forehead as he looked at Corra.

"Yeah, somebody bashed my door in, but didn't take anything."

"I heard some money was missing."

"Well, maybe."

"You think they were after the broach?"

"Well, I just found out that jerk Strong's been shopping my piece around. Said he found a buyer. I never said anything about selling it."

"That man has got shit for brains," Corra said.

That word coming out of her mouth was a surprise, but it summed him up in Joe's mind perfectly.

"He's been a dumb ass for as long as I've known him," Corra continued. "He was a lazy spoiled brat as a kid and he hasn't changed. He inherited that business, even though everyone knew he was too dense to run it. He went to gemological school three times and failed out every time. He's got a good manager, an elderly woman who really runs the place. When she retires, I give that place six months before they close their doors. He was a miserable disappointment to his father, who had no intention of ever letting him run the store, but his father got sick, Alzheimer's disease, and before he completely succumbed, he changed his will to leave the business to Dudley dumb ass."

"That kind of explains things a little for me. We are going to have to be much more careful going forward. With that in mind, I have a favor to ask you."

"Oh, boy! An assignment," Corra said. There was no hint of sarcasm in her voice. She was loving this. "But first I want to see the broach."

Joe showed her the broach. She was truly impressed. By the way she examined it, Joe guessed she had more knowledge of jewelry than Mr. Strong.

She handed the broach back to him.

"You better be careful with it," she said. "Hide it somewhere and not in your room. Now, what's my assignment?"

"I need you to find out as much information about Ed Kutz as you can. Where did he live? What was his home life and childhood like? Where'd he go to school? What'd his father do for living? Any information you could find out about him that would explain why he turned to a life of crime."

"I'm on it," Corra said.

Once again, her use of the vernacular surprised Joe.

Joe got back into his SUV and headed for the Oval Bar. He pulled in around back because if Corra already knew there was something going on with him and Melissa, others would know too. It's not out of the realm of possibility that I could run into someone I knew from New Jersey either, he suddenly thought.

It was still early. The restaurant wasn't officially open for the day yet. He went through the kitchen and into the bar area. He didn't know what he would say to the restaurant manager if he saw him, but he hadn't seen any other cars out front and he hoped Melissa was alone.

Melissa was squatting down in front of the beer coolers, putting the newer beers in the back and moving the older ones up front. Otherwise the ones in the back would never get used. Joe knew that from his teenage years working at a bar back in New Jersey,

"What does a guy have to do to get a beer around here?" Joe asked jokingly.

Melissa stood up. Joe had no idea how she would receive him. Would she be mad? Embarrassed? Annoyed?

"Well, you can wait til we open, fool," she said with a big friendly smile. "I was worried about you last night when you didn't show up. I thought maybe you'd had enough of our little town."

"No, no. I really wanted to come in, but a few things came up."

"I thought maybe you just stayed in bed all day. That's what I wanted to do since you kept me up so late."

Joe's first thought was, she sure isn't embarrassed.

They were comfortable almost immediately and they made small talk for a while.

People started coming into the restaurant and Melissa had to go and serve them.

She walked back by Joe and said, "Why don't you come back around eight tonight? I get off early."

"Sure," Joe said. "That sounds good."

He'd just been asked out on a date. He found that to be completely erotic.

On his way out of the bar, he turned back toward Melissa. She was watching him also and made no move to pretend she wasn't. She smiled and waved good-bye.

Joe drove away toward Robbie's house, but Melissa was all he could think of. He'd known her a very short time, but was completely smitten and to his mind, she was, too. This wasn't what he had wanted or what he had planned. Or was it?

Oh, God, what if she falls in love with me and wants me to leave my wife? What if she's a lunatic and decides to follow me back to New Jersey?

A few hours earlier Joe was worried that Melissa might be the leak. Now he was afraid she was madly in love with him. He laughed at himself.

"Get a hold of yourself, Romeo," he said out loud.

# Chapter Nine

Joe turned the car onto the dirt road that led to Robbie's. He'd called her earlier to tell her he was coming. She couldn't wait, although there was still nervousness in her voice.

In Joe's mind, the story had moved beyond what Robbie could tell him. He figured that at this point he knew more than she did. On the other hand, she had been very useful filling in the blanks about his father. He decided that he would tell her everything, as long as she promised to keep everything a secret. She lived alone. Who was she going to tell, anyway?

He parked the car and got out. It was a small house that needed a lot of repair. Her pathetic excuse for a dog was yipping out front, ready to run away if Joe or anyone else took one step toward it.

"Get lost, you weasel of a dog," Joe said quietly, in case Robbie was listening. He had always pretended to hate dogs and happily thought of himself, when he made these comments, as W.C. Fields, pretending to hate children.

The front door opened and Robbie stepped out.

"Come in, come in," she said.

The house looked as if nothing had been updated in fifty years. Everything was old and tired, but it was neat and clean.

Robbie offered Joe a drink, which he accepted. It was still early, but Joe's father had told him that if someone offers you a drink, you should probably accept it. People could take offense if you don't. Over the years Joe had found that his father had been right about that.

She invited him to sit down on the couch right next to him. Four bulging photo albums sat on the coffee table in front of them. Joe got the feeling that this was going to take awhile.

"There is so much I want to tell you about your dad. I thought that if I started with these photos, some questions might occur to you."

She opened up the first one. There were many photos of her family, her parents, cousins, aunts, and uncles. And there were a lot of pictures of Cal. The pictures belied the childhood that Robbie described and that Cal had described. Cal looked happy and carefree in almost every picture.

Joe had never seen pictures of his father as a young boy and they amazed him. The earliest pictures he had ever seen of his father were pictures of him in his army uniform. Joe figured he had never seen a picture of his father before the age of eighteen.

Robbie gave a running commentary on each picture, but Joe wasn't really listening. He was lost in the face of his father. Joe had never thought of him as an ordinary little boy who enjoyed all the things that most little boys enjoyed.

There was a particular picture of Cal at about twelve years old, bare-chested, leaping off a tire swing into a pond. He had a big smile on his face. It was a picture of pure joy. It intrigued Joe because he had a similar picture of himself at a similar pond. He had no idea where that pond was, but he started to wonder if maybe it was the same one.

"Was I here after that first time when I was a little boy?" Joe asked Robbie

"I don't think so. Why do you ask?"

Joe explained about the picture, but Robbie couldn't give him any insight as to where it came from. She did tell him about the pond and how much fun she and Cal had had there. She told about swimming naked together as little children and picnicking there as they got older. Joe did his best to try to erase the mental image of Robbie naked at any age.

They continued to go through the books, page after page. She had a comment for every picture of Cal. A different image of Cal was emerging for Joe. He wanted some of these pictures.

"Do you think you could let me borrow some of these pictures so I could make copies of them?" he asked.

Robbie agreed that she would spend the next day putting together a pile a pictures for Joe to take and reproduce.

As their conversation went on, Joe decided not to bring up the investigation. It was clear to him that Robbie truly loved his father and was only interested in talking about him.

Joe had been there for about six hours and was just getting ready to leave when Robbie said to him, "There is one more book I want to show you."

"I really need to get going," Joe said.

"This will only take a few minutes."

Joe sat back down, and Robbie set a much smaller book down in front of Joe.

He opened it up.

The first picture was of Cal holding a baby on a hospital bed. The woman in the bed was Robbie. It took Joe a few seconds to understand what he was looking at. He looked at Robbie, then back to the picture. Cal must have been around twenty-five years old, several years after he'd married Joe's mother.

"You and my father had a baby? I have a brother I don't know about?"

Joe looked at Robbie. She had a sad smile on her face

"I'd been contemplating contacting you to tell for the last five or six years and then, as if a prayer was answered, you showed up. Your coming here is God's way of telling me that he wants you to know. I'm an old woman. I don't know how much longer I'll be around. I don't want to take this secret to my grave. My son is fifty-one years old. He lives in California. He knows his father has another child, but he doesn't know your name. I didn't think it was fair to tell him who you were without giving you the same opportunity. I guess somewhere in the back of my mind I was hoping you two would meet."

Joe was shocked, and that was the only feeling he could get his mind around. He wasn't mad or bitter, at least not yet. His feelings toward Robbie hadn't changed. His feelings toward his father, well, he already knew his father had fooled around and that he wasn't a great husband.

"Did my father support the child?" Joe asked.

"He did what he could do, but we didn't need much. He would come and visit about once a year and call periodically."

"Did you ever marry?"

"No. There was no need. I had my boy and I had a little bit of Cal. That always seemed like enough, until he died and my son moved away."

Joe flipped through several more pictures. There seemed to be big gaps in time between pictures. He was silent until he got to the end of the book.

"Wow," he said.

"I hope I did the right thing by telling you. I thought about it for so very long," Robbie said with a look that showed she was happy to have unburdened herself.

"I'm glad you did. When I came up here as young child, did I ever meet him"?

"Yes. You two played as if you were natural brothers. Neither of you knew the truth."

"Do you have pictures of us playing together?"

"No. Your father thought it was a bad idea." She looked away as she answered, obviously regretting that she didn't.

"What was his relationship like with my father"?

"Oh, they were pretty much strangers. I don't know why, but I always hoped they would have been more than that. Cal tried to have a relationship, but that isn't very realistic with a young boy. As he grew, it got worse. In fact, I think that Cal came to resent him for that. I think he felt that, in some way, my son was not grateful for the money Cal sent and the trips he made to see us."

"My father kept track of every slight or perceived slight anybody ever gave him," Joe said. "He was incapable of forgiving and forgetting. I forgot his birthday when I was twelve and he never let me forget it."

Robbie went on for almost an hour telling Joe all about their relationship, loving every second of being able to recount her one and only relationship, as sparse as it was.

At one point Robbie put her hand on Joe's knee. "Cal and I were in love from the time we were young kids. Well, maybe I was in love with him," she said with an aching sadness.

Joe almost wanted to hug her.

"We spent all our time together. He almost never wanted to be home if his mother or his father were around. When he was happy, I was the one he wanted to tell about it. When he was sad or after a beating from his father, he would always come to me. I was the one who cleaned up his bloody nose or put ice on his welts and scratches. Never did his mother once raise a hand to stop the beatings. I hated that woman. I think she would have let him beat Cal to death."

Joe couldn't believe the irony of what Robbie was saying, but didn't have the heart to break hers and ruin her memories of the only man she ever loved.

Joe remembered times when he was getting a beating from Cal and his mother always got involved. Whether he deserved the beating or not, she would only let them go so far. If they were undeserved, she'd simply throw herself into the middle and draw his rage away from Joe. She suffered as a result, but she stood between him and Joe on several occasions, once with a butcher's knife in her hand. If Cal had gotten too far out of hand, Joe thought she would have used it

One day, Cal had come home from work in a particularly foul mood. Joe, his mom and his brother were walking around on egg shells, but there was no way they weren't going to incur his wrath that night. Joe was sitting at the dinner table, eating quietly and quickly, when Cal backhanded him off his chair onto the floor and then started screaming about something to do with school work and chores.

He got up and stood over the crying boy, undoing his belt to continue the beating. Joe's mother sprang up and ran up behind her husband and grabbed him in a bear hug and yelled for her boys to run. They both bolted for the door and ran down the street. They returned about an hour and half later and saw the family car was not in the driveway. They went inside and saw their mother sitting on the sofa in obvious pain. She'd changed into a long sleeved shirt and had sunglasses on. Both boys ran up to her and started crying.

She told her boys that he wasn't bad man. He just drank too much sometimes. Joe stopped crying and got very mad. He had gotten a huge welt on his face where Cal had hit him. He told his mother that he was going to tell everybody that his father had done this to him so they would know what a son of a bitch he was.

Joe's mother made him promise that he wouldn't, that he would tell everybody that he had gotten hit in the face with a football. Joe defiantly refused to protect him. He ran to his room and slammed the door. The next day at school, he didn't tell a soul the truth about what really happened. As far as anybody knew, he had gotten hit in the face with a football.

After an incident like that Cal would always return home the next day, acting as if nothing happened, being as nice as he could. And they would all forgive him. They loved their father.

Joe had now spent the whole day with Robbie, and the surprise and the emotion of the day was more than Joe had banked on. He got up to leave.

"So what do you think about all this?" Robbie asked him.

Joe knew she wanted to ask something else, but she was afraid of what his reaction would be. Finally she asked if Joe wanted to contact her son, his half brother.

"I have a lot to think about. I will call you again before I leave town, I promise."

Robbie wanted more, but she knew that for now she would have to be content. She walked him to the front door to say good-bye. She hugged him awkwardly, but very tightly, as if she could have some piece of Cal back by hugging Joe harder.

Joe walked back to his SUV. The little dog was lying down be-hind the rear wheel.

"Why don't you just stay there, you little crap machine," Joe said under his breath.

Robbie called the dog from the porch. She stood there smiling, hoping that she hadn't upset Joe too much. Joe smiled back at her, they waved good-bye, and Joe headed back to his motel.

# Chapter Ten

The door to Joe's motel room had been fixed with a padlock on the outside. There was a note from the super to stop into the main office.

"Shit," Joe thought. He walked into the office

"The police want to talk with you," the super said.

The words cut through Joe. "What about?" he asked defensively.

"About the break in, of course," the super said with a puzzled look on his face. "What'd you think they wanted to talk to you about?"

"Oh, okay. Yeah, of course."

Joe felt like a fool and again realized how unprepared he was for all this secret investigation stuff he was involved in. He was, by all measures, an amateur.

The super gave Joe the key to the padlock and a business card for the policeman and told him to call the guy before 7 p.m.

Joe had no intention of calling until 7:30 to make sure he wasn't there when he called.

Joe went back to his room. He fumbled with the key, stuck it in the lock and went inside. All the lights were off and all the shades were drawn. It was pitch black in the room. The only light was coming from the half open bathroom door.

Joe closed the door and swept his hand across the light switch to turn it on. It didn't go on.

"Shit. You must be kidding me," Joe laughed to himself.

He felt his way over to the lamp between the two beds. He reached for the switch and knocked over a bottle of water he had by the bed from the night before.

"Oh, great."

At that moment, a voice from behind him said, "What's your interest in the Wrin house murders?"

"Holy fuck!" Joe screamed and fell back onto the bed, his heart racing. "Who the fuck are you?"

"Don't worry about it. Just shut your mouth and sit down."

Joe looked in the direction the voice was coming from. Whoever it was, he was sitting in the corner closest to the door. Joe couldn't make out any of his features. He had purposely positioned himself in such a way as to obscure his features completely.

The intruder was calm, but there was a threat of violence in his voice and Joe assumed he had a gun, but couldn't tell. It occurred to Joe that this guy could be a cop, but that didn't seem logical. On the other hand, how did he get past a brand new padlock?

"What's your interest in the Wrin house?" the man repeated.

"How'd you get in here?" Joe asked. "What do you want?"

"I want you to answer the question."

Joe was terrified. He was actually crossing his legs because he was afraid he'd pee himself. He was trying to form an answer, but at the same time he was looking for an escape route. Then it occurred to him that the mysterious man in the corner might not be alone.

"I'm interested in the Wrin house because my father wrote a book about it years ago and I was thinking of doing a follow up on it."

The answer seemed to satisfy the man. He didn't say a word for long time.

"Where's the broach?" he finally asked.

Fucking Strong, Joe thought. "I don't have it. It's at the jeweler's."

Immediately Joe realized what a stupid lie that was. If Strong had told this man about the broach, he probably told him that they gave it back to him. Maybe he wasn't the buyer Strong had mentioned.

"You're not a very good liar."

A fleeting thought crossed Joe's mind. That's funny. I come from a long line of liars. I ought to be pretty good at it.

"Empty your pockets. Joe did as he was told.

"Is it in your car?" the man asked once he realized Joe didn't have it on him.

"No, but you're welcome to check," Joe said, stuttering all the way and holding the keys up as if he wanted the man to take them.

"Joe's eagerness to have the man check his car apparently didn't appeal to him. Joe realized the man knew there was no way he could keep Joe in the room and check the car. If he sent Joe to check, Joe might run.

The man seemed to be weighing his options.

"Forget it," he finally said. "But your investigation is over. Do you understand?"

"What? Who are you?"

"You'll find out if I hear you're still around tomorrow."

His threat was clear. Leave or die.

He told Joe to stand up and turn around. Joe wasn't sure if he was going to be shot or not. He did as he was told.

He shut his eyes as tightly as he could to be braced for a bullet between the shoulder blades. Instead, he heard the door open and close.

He was alone, but still afraid to move. After a few seconds he went back to turning on the lamp by the bed. He looked around. The room was empty. Nothing had been disturbed. It was if Joe had imagined the whole thing.

He took a step toward the door and realized that he had indeed peed his pants.

Adrenaline had been pumping through Joe's veins. He had never been scared like that before.

"The hell with this," Joe said out loud and grabbed his suitcase and started throwing all his clothes in the bag. "I'm getting the hell out of here now."

In about five minutes he had everything together and was in his SUV heading south out of town. He drove for about fifteen minutes until he calmed down.

He pulled off at a rest stop, got out and just started walking. He had to clear his head.

"I can't just leave," he said. What about Corra? What about Robbie?

What about Melissa?

What about everything he had learned? Was he just going to forget about it all? Let the world go on thinking that there was no connection between the murders of the two policemen and the country club robbery. Maybe the kids of the slain officers needed to know the truth about how and why their fathers died.

The fear Joe had been feeling subsided and he started to think rationally.

"The hell with this," he said again.

He turned his vehicle around and headed back to Gold's Lake. Two exits before Gold's Lake proper, he saw a Hilton hotel advertised on a road sign. He pulled off that exit. The hotel had an underground garage that gave Joe some comfort that he could operate in anonymity.

He got a room on the fourth floor. For the next day or so, Joe was going to work the phones rather then cruise around Gold's Lake for everyone to see.

His first call was to Melissa.

"Melissa, I need you to meet me at the Hilton at exit 32. I'll explain why when you get here."

If it wasn't for the fear in Joe's voice, Mellissa would have assumed she knew exactly why he wanted her to meet him in a hotel.

"Okay. What room?"

"I'll meet you in the lobby."

Joe had registered under a false name and he didn't want Melissa asking for him by name.

"I'll see you at 8:30," she said.

"Okay. But don't tell anybody who you are going to see."

Joe wanted to add, "Make sure you're not followed," but he didn't want to freak her out any more then he already had.

Next he called Corra.

"Hi, Corra. It's Joe."

"Who?"

"Joe!"

"Joe who?"

"Joe Mann, the guy that's been looking into the cop murders."

"I knew it was you. I was fooling with ya a bit. I've been waiting for you to stop by."

"I won't be stopping by any time soon."

"Why not?"

"I had an uninvited visitor today in my motel room and he threatened to kill me if I didn't get out of town."

Joe knew that was not exactly what was said, but that was certainly how he had interpreted it.

"Now you're messing with an old lady, aren't you?" Corra asked.

"No, I'm absolutely serious."

"Who was it?"

"The fuck if I know. Oh, sorry." Dropping the F-bomb to an old lady wasn't Joe's style.

"Did he want the broach? I told you to be careful."

"No, he didn't, but he asked about it."

Joe stopped for a second and thought to himself, he knew I had it, but he didn't take it, yet he probably knew what it was worth. Maybe he was forgoing the broach in order to get the full score.

Joe went on and told her everything that happened in the motel room, but what he really wanted to know was what she had found out about Ed Kutz.

"I found out a lot. Want me to give it to you over the phone?"

"Do you drive, Corra?"

"How old do you think I am? Yes, I drive. Where do you want me to meet you?"

Joe told her to meet him at the Hilton as soon as she could. It occurred to him that he had already given his hideout to two of the same people he at one point suspected could be the leak.

"Forget it. It just can't be them," he said aloud after Corra had gotten off the phone.

Corra got to the hotel in a remarkably short period of time. Joe assumed it would have taken at least that long for her to just get to her car. Again, he was underestimating her.

"You're the best," Joe said when he met her.

He led her over to an armchair in the corner of the lobby. Joe faced the door so he could see anybody coming in.

"What'd you find out?" Joe asked eagerly.

He was acting like a man who didn't have a lot of time. He'd been told to leave town by tomorrow and he wasn't sure if he would heed that warning or not.

"I found out a lot. I didn't have much in my files, but I do have a friend I bowl with who grew up near the Kutz family. She told me everything. Some of it could be rumors because the only thing she likes better then bowling is gossiping. Oh, my, she's got a mouth on her."

Joe wasn't too happy that she'd gotten someone else involved, but he hadn't given her any parameters, so he let it pass. He was glad to know that she found out where he lived.

Corra pulled out her notes. To Joe's surprise they were voluminous.

"They grew up on Old Barn Road and as far as I can tell, they never sold it. It's still owned by a Reginald Kutz. I found an obit on old Reginald. He died in an awful accident when Ed was ten. I'll tell you more about that in a minute. His wife Regina died about six years later."

"Reginald and Regina?" Joe asked.

"Yeah, kind of funny, ain't it? They had two children. Ed and an older daughter named Angela. Now, Angela was born with severe cerebral palsy. I don't have much info other than that on her."

"What kind of accident killed the father?"

"Patience," Corra said, obviously enjoying every bit of this.

"This part I got from my friend with the mouth." She said that Mr. Kutz and his son Ed were in their back yard cutting trees down to make room for a garage. They'd gotten their first new car and needed someplace to keep it. They were tackling a particularly big tree. It was too big to drop all at once, so Mr. Kutz climbed the tree about thirty feet up with little Ed watching from below. Mr. Kutz started sawing away at the top twenty feet. He thought the top half would fall away from him, but he was wrong. He didn't make it all the way through the tree with the saw when it folded in half right on top of Ed's father. It killed him immediately and his lifeless, mangled body fell right at little Ed's feet. The boy refused to leave his father. They found him later on that day when it started to get dark, his father's mangled head in the boy's lap. It was his mother who found them. Something short circuited in her head then and she was never the same. She crawled inside a bottle of Famous Grouse and never came out. She had a seriously handicapped daughter to care for, but she just couldn't do it. Folks who knew them say that Ed was the main caretaker of his older sister and his mother until the state came and took the girl away. His mom died a few years later. They say she died in her sleep, but everyone says she drank herself to death."

"God, that's awful," Joe said. "Doesn't sound like a cold blooded killer to me."

"People who knew him prior to that said he was a sweet boy."

Joe was shaking his head. "So he sees his father killed, his mother drink herself to death, and his sister taken away and probably put into some awful state hospital. Then he gets to spend forty years in prison before being crashed and burned in a car accident. He had nothing but the worst possible luck. By the way, where is Old Barn Road?"

"It's on the far side of town near the ball fields. It's easy to find. But if someone is keeping an eye on you and threatening your life, you'd better change cars."

Joe had already thought about that. There was a car rental place he had noticed as he pulled off the exit. He was going to rent a car from them.

Joe felt obliged to tell Corra about the break in and the man in his room. He didn't mention anything about having a stepbrother. It didn't pertain to the case and Joe didn't yet know how he felt about it.

Corra suggested he call the police, but Joe explained why he didn't think that was a great idea. Joe could tell Corra he was genuinely worried about his safety.

"Please be careful, Joe. I'd hate to lose you over this or see you get beaten up."

"I'll be careful. Just make sure you don't mention to anyone where I'm staying."

They said good-bye, but this time Corra couldn't help but give him a hug.

Joe made more notes about everything that had happened that day. He was amazed at how much he learned in such a short time and how events were speeding up, and he started to worry that his luck was going to run out soon. He planned to meet with Melissa around 8:30, but was not planning on leaving the hotel.

Who knows where that could lead, he thought to himself. Then tomorrow I'll rent a car and go see where Ed Kutz grew up.

Since he had to keep a low profile, Joe thought he'd drive by the homes of George Allen and Bill Hollar also. It looked more and more to him that, assuming he survived this adventure, he was going to have to write this book, and having more local flavor was going to be important.

He finished making his notes and then just stared off at nothing in particular, lost in thought about everything that happened that day and in the preceding week and a half. The lobby was fairly empty and quiet.

About forty-five minutes after Corra left, Melissa came in. It was just eight o'clock. She would have had to have left work early to make it there by eight.

Joe wondered if she was as excited about seeing him as he was about seeing her.

As she approached, Joe wasn't sure how to greet her. Should he stand up and give her a big hug in full view of everybody in the lobby? Should he shake her hand? That seemed a little impersonal after what they had shared two nights earlier.

He decided to let nature take its course. He stood as she approached and gave her a quick hug and then sat down again.

She had a big smile on her face, as did Joe.

"So what's the big mystery? I love this cloak and dagger stuff," she said.

He told her about the man in his room and his warning to get out of town. He told her about the break-in the day before. He told her about his meeting with Robbie and his new stepbrother. He told her all about the pawn shops and Strong's offer to sell his broach.

"That guy at Strongwaters' is an asshole," she said. "He doesn't know anything and he doesn't do shit at the store. I know several of his employees from the bar. They say he's a do-nothing with crappy ethics."

Joe was amazed at how universal the opinion of Walter Strong was. He wondered if Walter Strong knew what most people thought of him.

Joe was becoming uncomfortable sitting in the lobby in full view of everybody.

"I need to get out of sight," he said to Melissa.

"Do you want to go out, somewhere in the other direction from Gold's Lake?"

Joe knew his answer was going to sound like a not too subtle attempt to get her to his room, but he said, "Let's just go up to my room and talk awhile."

"Talk?" she said.

"Yeah. No expectations. I need to talk."

She had a doubting smile on her face, but she agreed and they went up.

As soon as they were in the room, they both stopped and stared at each other. Joe tried, but he couldn't resist. He grabbed her around the waist and kissed her as deeply as he'd ever kissed anybody before in his life. He wasn't sure if it was because he wanted Melissa that much or because he was still just so pumped up from the events of the day before.

Or was it because this was the perfect situation that he'd always wondered about? He was far from home and there was no chance of his wife finding out.

He didn't care. He just wanted her.

Melissa reacted in kind. She was as into him as he was into her. As they stood there kissing, hands were going in all directions and clothes were flying everywhere. The fact that Joe was a married man was far from his thoughts. He was lost in the moment.

If there was going to be any guilt about cheating, it would have to wait.

Two nights earlier in his SUV, they had fooled around, but something had stopped them from going all the way. Joe wondered if it had been guilt. His or hers? Was it that she didn't want to be seen as a home wrecker? Was she just trying to play hard to get? Joe thought she might even have been worried that he would think that she fooled around with all her bar patrons.

When she had finally pulled away in his SUV, Joe felt he could have easily persuaded her to go all the way, but he didn't. He had settled for some very heavy petting.

He remembered wondering, what's the difference? His wife would be as mad at a deep tongue kiss as she would be for full sexual intercourse. Wouldn't she consider both a betrayal? In some ways Joe believed that a passionate kiss was more serious than meaningless sex.

Joe had always thought that if a man or woman cheated, it was symptomatic of a deeper problem, like there was some deep irreparable issue and cheating was its manifestation. Now he didn't believe that anymore, and he was pretty sure his father hadn't believed that either.

If Barbara finds out about any of this, I'm dead. Why not go for it?

But in the car that night, Joe still hadn't resolved for himself if he was as bad as his father when it came to honoring his marriage vows. Now, this night in the hotel, all that was resolved.

The two bodies crashed onto the bed and wrestled around for the better part of an hour until they were both exhausted. For the first time in twenty years of marriage to a woman he loved very much, he had had sex with someone else.

He had always assumed that he would feel badly if he cheated on his wife, but now he didn't. He wondered if there was something wrong with him that he didn't feel badly, but he saw the two events, being married to Barbara and having sex with Melissa, as separate and distinct. One had nothing to do with the other. Love was not sex. Sex was not love.

He knew that no woman, let alone his wife, would buy that as an excuse, but that's how he felt and there was no getting around it.

He and Melissa lay on the bed staring at each other.

"How much longer do you think you will be hanging around?" Melissa asked.

"I don't know," Joe responded.

"Well, I'll miss you. I hope you'll look me up if you ever come back into to town."

The comment startled Joe. This woman was too good to be true. She saw their relationship much the same way he did, devoid of any moral or ethical components. They were two adults, attracted to each other, who wanted to have a good time while it lasted.

Her comment made Joe want her again and their wrestling started anew.

Afterward Joe ordered a bottle of wine from room service and they sat on a sofa in their room and talked. The conversation came easily. There was none of awkwardness that could come from two people who'd just had sex when they weren't supposed to.

Eventually Melissa said good bye. Joe promised to call her in the morning.

"If you do, you do. If you don't, you don't. Just don't leave town without saying good-bye."

Joe had no intention of not seeing her again.

Melissa left and Joe fell back on his messed up bed.

# Chapter Eleven

Joe overslept the next morning and awoke to the sound of his cell phone ringing

"Hello," he said, before checking to see who it was.

"Hi, hon. How are you?"

"Hey, Barb. Good. I'm glad you called. I overslept."

"Out late last night?" she asked.

Joe was completely frazzled. He was still half asleep and was in no position to start explaining anything to his wife. Normally they would talk at regular intervals when he was away, but now she was calling randomly. He was surprised she now seemed to need so much reassurance.

"Hon, I really have to pee. I'll call you back in a minute."

He hung up and swung his legs around onto the floor. He knew that he probably made her a little uncomfortable, hanging up on her like that, but it was better than fumbling through an account of what he'd been doing when another woman had been right here in his room seven hours earlier.

After getting his head together, he got back on the phone. He apologized for hanging up on her and she said it was fine. They talked a lot about what was going on. He told her about finding out he had a half brother, about the break-in, but not about the man in the motel. He was afraid she'd insist that he come home. She could try to insist, but she knew she couldn't compel him to anything he didn't want to do. He just didn't want her to worry.

They talked for awhile. Joe was surprised at how easy it came to make up an alternate account of how he'd spent his time when he'd really been with Mellissa. He didn't mind having sex with another woman, but he really hated lying to his wife.

He could imagine his father saying, "It comes with the territory, son."

He told her he was planning on winding down and coming home soon, although he wasn't sure if that was true of not. He knew she wanted him home badly and to his great surprise, he missed her, too.

One minute he wanted to leave, the next he wanted to stay. He had Melissa pulling at him to stay and Barbara pulling at him to come home. And there was a scary man urging him to get out of town.

All were compelling

He also had to finish his investigation. He couldn't leave until he had all the answers. With that in mind he headed to the rental car agency, rented the most nondescript car he could find, a white Camry, and headed toward the house were Ed Kutz was raised.

It didn't take long to find it. Joe thought about stopping to get a map, but he figured he'd try to find it himself rather then get out of his car in Gold's Lake where there might be people looking for him. Corra had given him good enough directions that he found the house quickly.

It was a nondescript small colonial with a big wooded area behind it. Joe tried to imagine which tree it was that killed Ed's father and dropped his body at little Ed's feet. There were still many trees there that all looked the same. The house itself was in desperate need of maintenance. The roof shingles were almost devoid of the granules that came with them. In many ways it was similar to the Wrin house except there were other houses around it. It was obviously a house that had not been cared for in years.

There was one difference. There was a relatively new handicapped ramp leading up to the front door.

Didn't Corra say something about a sister with cerebral palsy, Joe thought? She'd probably be in a wheelchair, wouldn't she, if she were still alive?

Joe wasn't an expert on cerebral palsy. He assumed that people could have it and not be bound to a wheelchair, but by the description that Corra gave him, he assumed that Angela's case was severe enough.

Joe drove past the house several times. He was worried about arousing suspicion. As he approached the house from the opposite end of the street, he pulled over to make some notes. While he was sitting there, a shiny new van pulled up to the house.

The driver got out on the opposite side from where Joe was parked. He went to the sliding door on the side of the van. From what Joe could see, the van was equipped with a lift to get a wheel chair in and out of a van.

Am I about to see the sister of Ed Kutz, Joe wondered?

Joe put down his pad and rolled down his window. After a few minutes the driver closed up the van and started to push the chair. As he emerged from the front of the van, Joe saw a tall, older man, about sixty-five, pushing the chair, with what could only be described as dead eyes.

He wasn't positive, but Joe was pretty sure he was looking into the face of Ed Kutz.

The cold wet weather had continued and Joe needed some place to think. He went to his favorite coffee shop. He walked in and sat at a table without ordering coffee or even taking off his jacket.

He'd seen something that defied logic. His father had described Ed Kutz so well that even as an older man, Joe imagined him just like the man he saw pushing the woman in the wheel chair. But Kutz was dead.

That fact had gotten him to Gold's Lake in the first place. Whoever he saw could not have been Ed Kutz.

"But that's exactly what I imagined him to look like before I even got here," Joe said aloud, causing some patrons of the coffee shop to turn and look at him.

Am I going crazy, Joe thought. Maybe it was a relative. Maybe it was a twin. Maybe Corra had gotten the story wrong and Ed actually had a twin. That would explain it. But Joe had underestimated Corra one too many times already. If she said he only had one sister, then that was good enough for Joe.

"What the hell do I do now? I could go to the police," he said, still almost audibly. "I could tell them that a killer is among them again. That the person who died in that car wasn't Ed Kutz. But what crime has he committed? All I saw was him caring for his elderly infirmed sister. Not exactly a patrol violation. Well, breaking into my motel room certainly was. But I'm not even sure that was him. But somebody had broken into the Wrin house. Oh, yeah. I did that too."

Joe internal dialogue was getting him nowhere.

"I need someone to talk to. I could call Melissa, but then we'd just end up back in bed, not exactly what I need at this moment. Corra? Yeah, she can keep a secret and she gets information for me. I'll drive to the library and meet her. No, I can't do that. I'm in hiding, remember, dick weed? In fact, what the hell am I doing in this coffee shop? I'd make a really bad criminal."

With that, his rambling dialogue ended and he heading back to the Hilton. When he got there, the first call he made was to Corra.

"Corra, I need you again."

"Glad to hear it. What's my assignment?"

"I think Ed Kutz is still alive."

"Hang on. Let me turn my hearing aid up. I thought you said Ed Kutz was still alive."

"I did. I'm not fooling around here. I think I saw him out in front of his house pushing his sister in a wheelchair."

She asked what made him think it was Kutz, and all Joe could offer was that he looked the way his father had described him as a nineteen year old. There was doubt in Corra's voice, but she asked what Joe wanted her to do.

"I want you to find out why they thought the driver of that car was Ed Kutz. Was an autopsy ever done? Was there enough left of whoever was driving the car to do an autopsy? For God sake, now I'm wondering if Ed was ever released from prison. I just assumed he was because the paper said that he had died."

Joe was more emotional then he had been in long time. Nothing was making sense. He hung up with Corra and squeezed the sides of his head with both hands. He wanted to leave so badly right now and forget he'd ever heard the name Ed Kutz.

After sitting for five minutes, he stood up abruptly. A decision had been made. He headed for his rented car, got in and started back in the direction of Ed Kutz's house.

He picked up his cell phone and called Corra, but there was no answer. He wanted to tell her that if he didn't return, he had probably been shot through the head and was buried under Ed Kutz's house.

Once Joe got there, he parked in relatively the same spot he had parked in before. He just stared at the house. The van was in the driveway and the house looked still and dark. Joe had no plan. He just wanted to see him again, to see if his eyes were playing tricks on him. He was pretty sure they weren't, but he wanted to remove all doubt.

He sat there for ten minutes when the front door opened again. The man Joe thought was Ed Kutz walked out and got into the van. The van pulled down the street and made a left hand turn around the first block.

Joe thought about following him, but the idea of following a convicted double murderer wasn't sitting that well with him. Maybe he was trying to lure him away from his house to kill him like he had killed Hollar and Allen. Maybe he had a taste for killing and was hungry again.

Joe's courage seemed to rise and fall with the moment, and right now it was at low ebb. Joe figured he'd just sit there for a few more minutes to see if Ed came back. Joe took his note pad out and started scribbling furiously. He steeled himself to get it all down and then he planned on leaving. He was wishing he was in Melissa's arms right then rather than sitting outside Ed Kutz's house.

The thought of seeing Melissa moved him to action. He put down his pad and pen and started searching for his keys. He looked to the passenger seat and as he did, he heard a knock on his window. The knock startled him, and he was so frozen in place he was momentarily unable to turn his head to see who was knocking.

When he was able to move, he looked up and all he could see were those dead eyes he'd heard so much about.

# Chapter Twelve

Joe fumbled with his window button and then realized he needed to turn on his ignition key to lower it. He had to open the window. There was no way out of it. Speeding away wasn't an option.

"What are you doing here?" the man asked.

It seemed like a logical question, but Joe was simply unable to answer it. Whatever he could come up with in that instant inside his head just sounded wrong. He started two or three sentences, and kept starting them over again.

The man with the dead eyes seemed to sense his discomfort. "We need to talk," he said.

Talking is good, Joe thought. Killing me is bad. He didn't like the sound of his own humor. He knew it was a knee jerk reaction of his nerves, but he couldn't help it.

"Okay," Joe was finally able to stutter in a cracking, scared voice. He cleared his throat and repeated it.

"Not here. I think I'm being watched," the man said.

He's being watched? What a coincidence. So am I, Joe thought.

"Where are you staying?" the man asked.

He asked it so matter-of-factly that Joe thought it would almost be impolite not to answer him truthfully.

"I'm staying at the Hilton off exit 42."

"Okay. I'll see you there in an hour. What room?"

"Room 412," Joe answered again.

Joe couldn't believe he was inviting back to his hotel room the man that had been his idea of a monster for his whole life.

At least he didn't offer to meet me in the basement of the Wrin house, Joe thought.

The man started to back away from Joe's window.

"Hold on," Joe said. "What's your name?"

"You know my name," the man said and walked away.

Joe couldn't decide whether he wanted to just start driving back to his wife and kids and his warm bed, where there were no impending meetings with multiple murderers, or if he should just pull over and puke.

Those are not mutually exclusive, Joe thought. I can do both.

He drove his car down the street and headed back to the Hilton. He thought that if he was going to have this convicted killer in his hotel room, he should let someone know. Just in case the dead eyed man added another person to his body count, someone would know where to find Joe's body.

"Corra, it's Joe."

"Who?"

"Joe Mann from the policemen murders."

"Oh, yeah. Are you looking for that information already? Didn't you just ask me for it? Are you forgetting how old I am?" Corra asked Joe sarcastically.

"Yes, I did just ask you for it and, yes, I want it as soon as you get it and, no, I didn't forget how old you are. An interesting situation has arisen. I think I have a meeting with Ed Kutz in an hour."

"Isn't he dead?"

"I thought so, but I'm not so sure."

"Well, I did find out some information that might help," Corra added. "No autopsy was ever done. There simply wasn't enough of him left after the car fire, I guess."

"What about dental records?"

"There weren't records to check them against. Remember, he'd been in jail for over forty years."

"What about dental records at the prison? He must have seen the prison dentist."

"I don't know about that. All I know is that no formal autopsy was ever done."

"Then what made them think it was Ed Kutz in that car?"

"They found his prison ID dog tags in the fire as well as his wallet."

"He was still wearing his prison dog tags months after getting out? You'd think he'd trash them as soon as he passed through the prison doors."

"Well, they aren't sure if he was wearing them or they just happened to be in the car.

They also found a wallet and some kind of ID."

"Everything was burnt to ashes. How'd the wallet survive?"

"It was partially burnt. They found it on the ground beside the car. Look, Joe, everything I'm getting is second hand. All I can tell you is what I heard."

Joe thanked Corra profusely and added that he didn't know what he'd do without her. Corra's mood changed as Joe was getting ready to hang up.

"You be careful. I don't want this story ending with you being dead and me having to explain it all."

"I'll do my best to stay alive," Joe said with a nervous laugh.

Joe drove in deep thought down highway 100. He passed his old motel. He noticed that the damaged door to his room hadn't been permanently fixed. He wondered if the policeman was still looking for him to come in and answer some questions. Joe idly wondered if he'd have to answer questions from Bull, Jr. He passed the coffee house and the Oval Bar. He didn't see Melissa's El Camino.

He arrived back at his hotel and headed to the elevators. There was a young family just checking in. Twin seven-year-old boys were devouring complimentary cookies at the check in counter. Their parents didn't seem to mind.

Joe would encourage the same with his kids so he wouldn't have to buy them dessert that night. Joe laughed to himself.

Maybe I am cheap, like my father and his father before him.

Joe was trying to forget, albeit temporarily, about what he was about to go up to his room to do.

"I'm going to meet with a murderer upstairs," he felt like saying as he passed a sloppily dressed businessman. "What are you doing today?"

Joe went into his room and sat on the bed. This room was much nicer than the one at the Dead Roach motel or whatever it was called. It was clean, recently refurbished, and it had mints on the pillows. There was a round table in the corner with a pitcher of fresh iced water and two glasses. The drapes were closed. Joe decided to open them, thinking that more light was better than less light in this situation.

Joe arranged the chairs and then rearranged them so he could sit nearer the door. If he had to run, he didn't want to be stuck in the corner.

The room was ready. It was clean and well organized. Joe put a yellow pad and pen on the table to give credence to the story that he was an investigator.

He went over to the window to watch for Ed, or whoever it was. He was there for one minute when a pickup truck pulled into the parking lot. It stood out because it was so old. Every other car there was fairly new. Joe had been expecting the handicapped van, but still he instinctively knew it was Ed when he saw the truck.

Sure enough, the man who spoke to him through his driver's side window was heading up to his room.

There was a sharp knock at the door. Joe's heart jumped. He was scared and excited at the same time. He knew that when this meeting ended, everything would look a whole lot different.

He waited a second so as to not look too anxious. He stood there and then felt foolish and opened the door.

"Come in," Joe said.

The man at the door didn't say a word. He had a hat and sunglasses on to hide his appearance. He walked in and sat at the chair Joe had reserved for himself. Joe took the other chair.

Since the man was still not talking, Joe starting the meeting.

"Are you Ed Kutz?"

"Yes."

"The papers said you were dead."

"They got it wrong and I'm not in a big hurry to correct them. Now who are you and why are you watching me? You don't seem like press and you sure aren't a cop."

Joe didn't now how much to tell him. He wasn't sure where to start nor when to stop. He sure wasn't going to tell him about the broach, but Joe had a feeling he already knew about it. Joe wasn't sure why, but he wasn't afraid. He was pretty sure that he was safe.

Ed seemed more afraid then he did.

"I'm the son of the man who wrote the book on the murders. I came back here to research it and to see the town where my father grew up. That's about it."

"You went into the Wrin house."

Ed said it like a statement and not like a question. He was so sure, it seemed silly for Joe to try to deny it.

"I stopped by," Joe said coyly.

"You did more than that," Ed said.

Joe, feeling emboldened, said, "I don't mind telling you what I'm doing, but you have some explaining to do also. First, how is it the papers think you are dead?"

Joe realized Ed probably wasn't going to be ready to start spilling his guts to him until he knew a lot more about him.

"Where's the broach?" Ed asked.

"How do you know about the broach?" Joe asked, although he thought he knew. Somehow the word had gotten back to Ed after Walter Strong had shopped the broach around, maybe through that scary local cop who always seemed to be snooping around.

Ed sat there silently, still sizing Joe up. Both man had answers they wanted and secrets they wanted to keep.

Joe was afraid that Ed would just up and leave and he might never get the answers to his questions. Joe made a daring decision and told Ed he was going to tell him everything and then in turn Ed would tell Joe everything.

Ed gave a barely perceptible head nod.

Joe explained everything. He told him what brought him to Gold's Lake, even the stuff about his relationship with his wife. He talked about the Harding Country Club and about the torched Porsche and about the broach, although he didn't tell him it was in his pocket. He picked up his yellow note pads and flipped through the pages, trying to tell Ed everything. He told him about the cop who pulled him over.

Ed broke his silence and asked, "What was his name?" He asked the question as if he already knew.

"Bull, Jr."

Ed's face went hard.

"Do you know him?" Joe asked.

"Yes. But please go on."

Joe continued. He told Ed everything. He kept looking at Ed's face for signs that what he was saying was right or wrong or if his assumptions had been on target or not. When he mentioned the Harding Country Club, there was no sign that he was accurate or not. Joe finished up.

"Your turn," Joe said with more courage than he thought he'd be able to muster before the meeting had started.

"What do you want to know?"

Joe had so many questions he didn't know where to start. He wanted to know about the Harding Country Club, the car accident. Why the authorities thought Ed was dead. Who had been his accomplice in the robbery? Did the accomplice have anything to do with the murders? Did Ed recover the items stolen from the club?

The questions came flooding into Joe's mind. He literally didn't know where to start.

Ed interrupted Joe's thoughts. "I'll start from the beginning."

"After my father died, I was the only caretaker for my sister. My mother started to die herself when that tree killed my dad. I was a young boy. I wasn't smart enough, strong enough and money was running out. Neighbors had been helpful for awhile, but people had their own troubles and soon we were left on our own. Once my mother drank herself to death, the state took my sister. She and I were very close. I was the only person who could understand her. We had our own language. It was as clear as you and I speaking right now."

Ed stopped a second and poured himself a glass of water. There was a sad twinge in his voice when he talked about his mom and dad, but that twinge turned to an aching sadness when he spoke of his sister.

"I was sixteen so the state didn't care about me. I was old enough to care for myself. I drifted around for a while. I tried to visit my sister when I could. She was in a horrible place, surrounded by full blown mental cases. My sister wasn't retarded. In fact, she was very smart, but since nobody but me could understand her, they simply lumped her in with everybody else. The stench of the place was appalling. Everybody was dirty. They stayed in wheelchairs for twenty-three hours a day. It was a holding pen and nothing more. Each time I visited my sister, I could see her slipping further and further away. I was afraid she'd die if she stayed there much longer. I complained to the staff, but no one listened. After a while, when I stopped by, she wouldn't even talk to me. My ability to understand her was disappearing. I was lost, depressed, angry and feeling completely useless. That's when Hoot Gibbons came into my life."

# Chapter Thirteen

J ust the mention of Hoot's name made Ed stop, stand up, turn toward the window and stare. The regret in Ed's eyes made Joe want to look away, and the silence was so awkward Joe felt Ed might not continue with the story, as if it was just too painful for him to relive. Finally, Ed sat back down and started talking.

"Every town has one: a small time, small minded criminal that everybody knows. If a store is broken into or if graffiti is sprayed on the train trestle, everybody has a pretty good idea who did it. In Gold's Lake in the early fifties, it was Hoot Gibbons. He grew up in a lower middle class family with three brothers. Their father flew the coop early on. No one really remembers him at all. That's probably where the problems started. Their mother made ends meet as a crossing guard in town. Nobody in the family ever seemed all that clean and they all got in trouble in school. To some degree, each was a troublemaker and had run-ins with the law, but Hoot was a special case. He wasn't just a mischievous kid, he was mean."

"The entire family was built the same. They weren't that tall but they were all naturally stocky and very strong. Even at a young age, older boys wouldn't mess with them because they had the physical maturity of much older boys. Being that their last name was Gibbons and they looked like gorillas seemed like more than a coincidence to the town's people. While his brothers seemed content with shop lifting and stealing lunch money, Hoot preferred fighting."

Joe was listening intently and scribbling furiously, all the while wondering how Ed knew so much about Hoot. He considered stopping him and asking him, but thought better of it. He'd ask that later. Ed continued.

One late fall day when Hoot was a teenager in the midst of a sophomore year -- he rarely went to school so to call him a sophomore is not all that accurate -- he was shoplifting from Ward's 5 and 10 shop. He wasn't being particularly sneaky about it. The manager was a recent graduate of the local high school and approached Hoot, his pockets full of merchandise. Hoot didn't run or make excuses. He just stood there while the manager insisted that he open his coat and empty his pockets. Instead, he walked up to the manager casually and smashed him in the side of the head, sending him sprawling into the aisle. Hoot slowly turned around and walked out."

"He got arrested for the assault, but was never convicted. Townspeople were pretty sure that the manager was intimidated by the rest of the family so he withdrew the charges, but the cops knew that Hoot was no good and they kept their eyes on him."

"Hoot had gotten a taste for the power that his physicality provided and he liked it. He would go out at night and look for fights. He would hit on bigger men's girlfriends just to get them to fight and then he would annihilate them. Older boys routinely underestimated his strengthen and his brutality."

Joe marveled at how Ed was able to retell the story of Hoot's life as if he had been his biographer. The two of them must have spent a lot of time together at some point, Joe realized, for Ed to have known so much about him, besides what he knew from just living in Gold's Lake.

"As he grew into a man, his reputation preceded him everywhere he went. People didn't want to hire him or associate with him and that even extended to his family. The police were constantly watching him. Gold's Lake became intolerable for him. Even his family wanted him gone. He would leave for months at a time, be chased out of another town and then end up back in Gold's Lake. He could be seen at bars until all hours of the night. When the cops found out he was back in town, they kept an eye on him. They'd occasionally stop him, just to roust him and remind him that they hadn't forgotten him. It was on one of those late night binges that I met up with Hoot Gibbons."

Joe noticed an almost imperceptible smile fleetingly cross Ed's face. It wasn't a happy smile, he thought, but one filled with regret, one that said, how could I have been so foolish?

Ed stood up and walked back toward the window. When he started talking again, Joe felt like he was talking about someone else.

"I had turned bitter. My father was dead. My mother was dead and the only other thing in my life that I cared about was locked in a living hell. I was grief stricken when they first took her away and then I became despondent and then bitter."

"Our house was modest, but it was paid for and the insurance or inheritance paid the taxes, although I wasn't really sure which, and to tell you the truth, I didn't give it much thought. I couldn't stand to spend time in that lonely, sad place, so hanging out at a bar after work was where you could find me most nights."

"My drink of choice back then was a double gin and tonic. I was already a little tipsy when Hoot first approached me. I knew of him from living in the same town and he was aware of me, as were most people in town because of the tragedies I'd endured. To say we'd struck up a friendship wasn't exactly accurate. Hoot was a few years older and much more confrontational. If he wanted to start up a conversation, no one, including me, was going to say no. At first he seemed to have real affection for me. I was lonely so I wasn't about to push back. After a while we would meet a few times a week. We'd only known each other as 'friends' a few weeks when Hoot suggested the robbery. At first I just laughed and when I realized Hoot wasn't smiling, I felt my stomach sink."

Ed's face turned white and Joe thought his stomach might be sinking at that very moment simply from retelling that part of the story. The color came slowly back into Ed's face and he continued.

"Hoot always relied on tacit threats whenever he had to get a point across. He directed me away from the bar over to a table in the corner to give the conversation added seriousness. It became clear to me right away that Hoot wasn't kidding, that he already made up his mind to rob the Harding Country Club and that if I wasn't with him, then I was a liability. With Hoot's reputation for brutality, I was trapped and I knew it.

Hoot continued to press. He always used a two pronged attack. He would stand over me, his massive forearms leaning on the table more for effect than support. Then he went at me, explaining how life had dealt me a shitty blow and how the town had done nothing when they took my sister away. He made up stories about how the town thought my mother was an embarrassing drunk and thought she may have even sold sex for alcohol. Prior to going to jail I was never a fighter, but I wanted to kill Hoot at that point. But I was scared and knew I couldn't, so I directed my anger and hate right where Hoot wanted me to, right back at the town."

Retelling the story about what Hoot had said about Ed's mother was almost too much for him. He excused himself to use the bathroom, but Joe was pretty sure he had to regain his composure. While Ed was in the bathroom, Joe realized that he been listening so intently to the story that he'd stopped taking notes. He quickly tried to remember what he was told. He couldn't ask Ed to repeat this story.

Ed came back, visibly refreshed, Joe thought, and started where he had left off.

"The alcohol kept flowing and Hoot kept the pressure up. If I had had one ethical, reliable adult in my life that I could have turned to at that moment, I probably could have resisted Hoot, but I had nobody. I reluctantly agreed to his plan and even in my drunken stupor, I knew two things. First, I would regret this for the rest of my life and two, I was completely locked in and Hoot would probably kill me if I tried to back out."

"The plan had already been hatched when Hoot first approached me. He knew about the jewelry show from a friend of his who had worked it as a waiter the previous year and told Hoot of the unbelievable display of wealth and riches. Hoot had acted unimpressed, but was intent on robbing it from the first moment he heard about it."

"It wouldn't be Hoot's first robbery. When he needed money, he robbed. He robbed liquor stores or general stores. He would usually punctuate his robberies with a punch to the face to emphasize his brutality and to dissuade anyone from coming after him."

As Ed told this part of the story, Joe could sense the growing disdain for his partner.

"He robbed several bars after spending the night drinking at them. He had gotten very good at laying in wait for a bar manager to leave the store with the day's take and then sneak up on him from behind and turn him around and punch him in the jaw. He had been told by a boxer once that if you punch someone in the side of the jaw, it was "lights out" because it was completely disorienting, more so than a punch directly to the face."

"Word had gotten out about these late night robberies and bar managers had stopped leaving with their bank roll. Some installed floor safes while others hired private security people to come and get the money. Hoot had tired of these penny ante robberies anyway. He wanted a big score so he could leave the town he had so much contempt for -- and it for him -- and go settle somewhere where no one knew him. The country club was going to be his retirement plan."

"Hoot had a big mouth. He loved to talk about his past exploits. The more he'd drink, the more he'd talk. For the few weeks that he and I had been hanging out, Hoot told me of several robberies and fights he'd been in. He told of one robbery in which he had turned on his partner in the end and hadn't split the money with him. Instead he kicked the shit out of him for a perceived slight. Hoot thought the story was a riot. It scared me to death. I saw it as my future."

"As the day approached, Hoot laid out in detail how everything would work. He could see how uncomfortable I was. He kept assuring me that nobody would get hurt and that I wouldn't have to do anything but stand by the door and help him collect the loot. Hoot had scoped out the club. He actually had gone in to use the bathroom to get the lay of the place. He planned on nailing the doors shut from the outside so nobody could escape. He even planned on creating a diversion for the police by claiming that he'd seen a boy fall into a local lake, thus keeping the cops busy while the robbery took place."

"Hoot would have been a natural salesman. He kept reinforcing the reasons for my helping him and how good it would be for my sister. He said I could take my sister out of that place. He kept up his attacks on Gold's Lake and how badly they'd treated my family and me. It didn't seem to matter that the country club we were about to rob was fifteen miles outside of Gold's Lake."

"That night we headed to the country club on foot because neither of us owned a car. I was shaking, but Hoot didn't seem to have a care in the world. He really seemed to be enjoying it. I would have liked for the cops to show up and arrest us both. At least I'd be safe from Hoot. Hoot had omitted whatever the slight was with the partner that he almost beat to death rather than split the take. I wondered how I couldn't avoid the same slight."

Ed kept shaking his head and as he told Joe this part of the story, Joe felt as if he was trying to go back in time to try to stop himself from going along with Hoot.

"When we were about two hundred yards outside the club on the edge of the woods, Hoot pulled out a gun and handed it to me. Until that moment, I'd never held a gun. I knew a gun was part of the plan, but I never considered holding it, much less using it. But there I was with a gun in my hand. I felt as if I wasn't even inhabiting my own body."

"The robbery took 10 minutes, but it seemed like ten hours to me. I was told nobody would get hurt, but the first thing Hoot did was viciously smash the maître d' in the mouth. The sight of him on the ground with his head resting in the lap of a waitress and blood coming out of his mouth, his nose, and the cut on his head reminded me of the day, many years earlier, when my father's lifeless body was on the ground and his damaged head was resting in my lap until the neighbors found him. I had a powerful urge to run, but I would have been signing my own death warrant if I did that to Hoot. The casualness with which Hoot moved around the room was infuriating to me. All I wanted to do was flee, while Hoot just wanted to enjoy the party."

"When we left the country club, I was carrying the bag and both of us were walking fast. When our paths diverged due to an oncoming police car, Hoot became enraged that I had gone the other way into the woods. Would this be the slight that I was worried about? Not only did I have stolen merchandise and the gun and the police after us, I now had Hoot chasing me and that scared me most of all. I never really had thought Hoot would split the proceeds evenly. I felt like I was more likely to get ten percent. If I was lucky. I also felt that Hoot believed that I would crack under police pressure. Eventually Hoot would see me as a loose end he couldn't afford to have."

"It occurred to me that Hoot had chosen me because I was in the world pretty much alone. There was no family to come looking for me. The shadows in my mind were already working overtime to scare me as I ran through the woods from the police car, and that was before I ever even got to the Wrin house."

Joe had given up writing again and was now just listening. Ed didn't seem to care. Joe felt the tone of the story change when Ed mentioned the Wrin house.

"As I finally slowed to a walk in the woods, I felt the weight of the bag in my hand. I was terrified. I'd have loved to dump it, but my life would have been in grave danger if Hoot didn't get his share. I'd been walking another hour and twenty minutes when I emerged from the woods at a cross road, but I still didn't feel safe so I reentered them and walked about thirty minutes further. When I emerged again, I was in the back yard of the Wrin house."

# Chapter Fourteen

Ed and Joe had been talking in the apartment for well over an hour. Joe felt they were starting to trust each other more. They seemed to be developing a mutual interest in each other, perhaps because they both had something to hide. Joe knew he had to ask about the murders. He wanted to know if maybe Hoot had done it, and Ed took the wrap. But Ed put that idea to rest fast.

"I entered the Wrin house as a hideout. It wasn't preplanned. It was available and I was desperate. Relieved to find it empty, I stayed there. It gave me time to think, but it also cut me off from the rest of the world. It cut me off to the reaction to this brazen robbery from the community. It cut me off from the erupting fury that was Hoot Gibbons and who by that time must have been thinking that I had ripped him off."

"The water had been shut off when the Wrins left on vacation. The only things to eat in the house were dusty canned goods. The refrigerator had been cleaned out and left open. The freezer had been defrosted and was equally as bare. I was afraid to go upstairs. I didn't want to be seen from the outside. I was afraid someone would be checking on the house. I preferred to stay in the basement until I could figure things out."

"After two days in the basement, I ventured upstairs for a can opener and to see if there was anything to drink. I was becoming lightheaded and fatigued from lack of water. The liquid from the canned goods sustained me for a short time, but I was afraid I would have to go outside to find something to drink. I had attempted to catch water from a leaky rain gutter that was dripping in front of the basement window. I gathered a little, but decided the risk wasn't worth it."

"I decided to go out and find something to drink. Otherwise my dried out body would be found on the basement floor when the Wrins returned, I thought. I decided that I better alter my appearance lest someone recognize me from the robbery. I went into the Wrin's master bedroom and found a razor and some scissors. I cut my own hair with the dull shears. The scissors pulled the hair out more than it cut it. It was a terrible job. The hat I was wearing was the one from the robbery so I couldn't wear that. The house was dark even during the day so I couldn't tell what an awful job I had done cutting my own hair. Later, when I finally saw it in a mirror, it looked like I had cut it with an eggbeater."

"When I went to shave, the lack of water wreaked havoc on my face, too. I shaved with a straight edge razor I'd found and cut my face with every stroke. Although I couldn't really see myself then, I knew I couldn't go out until my face cleared up a little bit. It rained a bit that night and I was able to gather some more water from the leaky rain gutter, but I was quite literally dying of thirst."

The level of detail Ed was giving was more then Joe could have anticipated. Joe was sure that Ed had rehearsed this or that he had at least thought of it in great detail and desperately wanted to tell someone who could relate the story to others.

"I woke up later that night after sleeping on the basement floor. The cold slab chilled me to the bone. I decided that I would venture out at first light, buy some milk or soda and return as soon as I could. I crawled out through the basement window even though I could have easily walked through the front door, but my paranoia was only increasing with my dehydration. I stayed close to the tree line as I went. I wasn't exactly sure where I was, but I knew that if I went in a southwesterly direction, I would arrive at a small cluster of stores. It was still early so there was really no one around on the streets or in the shopping area. When I arrived at the store, it wasn't open yet. I laid back in the trees that surrounded the store, hidden from view. My panic and paranoia made me want to sprint back to the Wrin house, but I was so weak I didn't think I could sprint anywhere and I was afraid that I wasn't thinking straight."

"You must have been a sight," Joe said, if only to give Ed a break.

Ed ignored Joe's comment and went on. "The owner of the store pulled up and parked his car in the back. The lights to the store went on. I didn't want to be the first in the store. I wanted to mix in with some townsfolk, get what I needed and head out. A few patrons showed up, and I quickly fell in behind them. My appearance made me hard to ignore, even to these sleepy eyed people. I avoided eye contact, got what I needed and went up to the counter. I was desperate for some news about the robbery, but heard nothing. A newspaper with a heading that mentioned the Harding Country Club was obscured by an older man's grocery bag. I had to know what was going on with the crime so when I got up to the store clerk, I grabbed the paper and put it face down on the counter. The clerk picked it up and turned it over to see the price, but I was sure he was turning it over to compare the picture on the front of the paper with mine. I was ready to run. There were no pictures of me or Hoot, but my terror was about to boil over. I felt that everybody in the store was staring at me and every single person knew exactly what I'd done. I assumed the police were already on their way. I quickly paid and walked out of the store without the paper and without ever making eye contact with anyone. I headed back to the woods, pretty sure every eye from the store was still on me."

"Once safely back in the cover of the woods, I stopped to get a drink. I didn't think I would make it back to the Wrin's house if I didn't. The milk calmed me a little. I was walking slower now, but was still sure to stay out of sight. As I was making my way to the Wrin's house, I realized that Hoot and I had never discussed what to do after the robbery, much less what to do if we got separated and I had all the money. Was Hoot going to stay in town? Everybody knew him. It wouldn't take long for them to arrest him. His plan must have been to skip town. What were his plans for me, I wondered.

"Do you think his plans were to eliminate you soon after the robbery?" Joe asked, feeling a bit like a professional interviewer.

"I don't know, but the thought sure crossed my mind," Ed said with a half laugh. "I crawled back in through the basement window and settled down to sleep for awhile. When I awoke, finding a hiding place in the basement for the stolen jewelry and cash became a priority. I decided that if I was going to leave once in awhile, the loot better be out of sight."

"I spent the better part of the morning trying to find a perfect place, but the basement had very few items in it. I thought about hiding the stuff on top on the foundation wall between the floor joists. I climbed up on the old asbestos covered furnace to get a better look. It was almost pitch black so I couldn't see anything even though my eyes had been adjusting to the darkness for hours. But I could reach and feel around. I stuck my hand through the cobwebs. The little void simply wasn't big enough to fit everything. I was disappointed because I didn't want to split up the stuff for fear I'd forget where I put it all. I started to climb down. I found a foothold on a rock towards the base of the river stone wall. The rock held for a second and then gave way and sent me sprawling to the rough concrete floor. The jewelry went all over. I was annoyed, but not hurt. I started to collect the stuff when I noticed that the rock that had given way had split in half when it hit the floor. I got up and investigated the hole left by the rock. It was of a perfect size and the rock proved the perfect false front."

"With the stuff hidden, I had to decide what my next move would be. I was concerned that my appearance at the general store had tipped off the police and quite possibly Hoot Gibbons. The police scared me because spending my life in jail wasn't very appealing. Hoot scared me because he was extremely motivated to find me and I was now more convinced then ever that Hoot's plan was to kill me rather than to split the take. In fact, I was convinced that even if I did have the stolen merchandise, chances were I would not make it through another meeting with Hoot."

"The days wore on. I had been in the basement over a week. I wasn't sleeping because of the cold basement and the possibility of Hoot Gibbons showing up with a meat cleaver. My paranoia was increasing with each passing hour. Venturing out again was not going to happen. My dehydration had returned. I was starting to worry about my own mental stability. This is the state I was in when I heard the footsteps upstairs."

# Chapter Fifteen

Ed and Joe had been sitting in the hotel room for several hours when the moment arrived for Ed to tell what actually had happened that day in the basement. It was something that Ed really didn't want to talk about, Joe thought. He had done it. He had killed them and he had to live with it. Why go into it any further? Joe wanted to respect Ed's wishes to continue their newfound friendship, but he just had to know if he did it alone. Joe had still been secretly hoping that he was going to find out that Ed hadn't shot the policemen at all. That it was Hoot.

"But why did you do it?" Joe asked.

Joe could see that Ed was terribly uncomfortable with the topic. He was in his sixties, but the topic made him squirm like a high school boy trying to get out of telling his parents he'd failed a subject.

"I was tired, hungry, scared, thirsty. Take your pick. Until the day we robbed the country club, I'd never held a gun. I've fired three shots in my life and each tore into a police officer. I wasn't thinking right. I had been asleep and awoke in a fog and just started shooting. I thought Hoot was coming to kill me."

"Where'd you go after that?"

"I was horrified when I realized what I'd done. Both men were clearly dead, but to this day, I wonder if one of them had only been wounded, would I have stayed and tried to help? I'd like to think I would have, but in the state of mind I was in, I doubt it. I grew up without a father. I knew the pain of losing a parent. I couldn't believe that I had taken a father away from someone else's kids. I ran until I found another house to hide in. It wasn't long before they came for me. I gave up without a fight."

"And the stuff from the country club?"

"I left it where it was, inside that wall."

"Did they ask you about it?"

"Never. Not a word. I would have told them everything, but they never asked. I didn't actually forget about it during the trial, but it seemed unimportant. I never even entertained the thought that maybe one day, I would get it back. That seemed ludicrous considering my situation. I'd just killed two police officers. I was assuming I'd be executed for what I did, and that didn't sound too bad. I deserved it."

"And what about Hoot? Did you ever see him again?"

"Oh, yeah, unfortunately, but not for a while. He made himself scarce after the robbery and the murder. He had to be sure I wasn't going to rat him out for the robbery to get some leniency, but none was ever offered or requested. I'd been in jail for two years when I was told I had a visitor. He used a false name. When I sat down at a glass window and saw him, I wanted to kill him. He had come into my life and destroyed it. Don't get me wrong, I did what I did and take responsibility for that, but if I hadn't met him, I wouldn't have robbed the club and I wouldn't have been in that basement."

Joe watched silently as Ed looked down and stopped talking for a few moments. Then Ed just stared off into space, as if he were wondering what his life might have been like if he had not run into Hoot that first night at the bar.

"I guess I know why he came to see you. He wanted the stuff."

"You guessed right. He pretended he was concerned with my well being. The guy who was going to kill me instead of splitting the loot was there to see how I was doing. It didn't take him long to get to the point, but he couldn't ask directly because all the conversations are monitored."

"Hoot told me we had some 'unfinished business,'" Ed said.

"It sounded more like a threat than a question, but I wasn't the same scared kid I'd been when he first showed up at the bar. That's not to say I still wasn't scared of Hoot. I was. Hoot had no conscience and he liked violence. I'd become hard because I had to, not because I liked it. Our conversation was spoken in hushed tones and in an impromptu code."

"Hoot asked me where 'it' was."

"'The cops got 'it,' I assume,' I said, although I was pretty sure they hadn't, since they hadn't discussed it with me. Hoot didn't believe me and he told me so. He finally asked me where I'd stashed it. This was a no win question for me. If I said where it was, I'd lose it all. If I didn't, I ran the risk of incurring Hoot's wrath. Being in jail didn't offer me much comfort for two reasons. One was that Hoot most likely had friends in prison who could easily knife me in the back for fifty bucks and a pack of cigarettes. The other was that I thought it more than likely that Hoot might end up in prison himself some day with the way he was going."

"'You'll get it when and if I get it,' I told him. I got up and started back to my cell."

"I was surprised at my nerve to do that to Hoot. I had taken a calculated gamble. I intentionally left the possibility open that Hoot would some day get his share and I hoped that would ensure that he wouldn't have me shanked while I slept. Hoot's eyes had almost burned their way through the three-inch safety glass that separated me from him when I spoke those words to him. I looked back at him as I was walking back to my cell. Hoot's face was contorted with confusion and hatred. He was dying to start screaming at me, but was in no mood to be noticed by the guards."

"That was ballsy," Joe said, getting up from the table and stretching his hands out. They had started cramping up after he began writing down again all that Ed was telling him.

"Was that the last time you saw him?"

"Oh, no, far from it. He was smart enough not to come around too often. He sent messages through friends in prison. He sent me threatening letters disguised as letters from friends or family. He once sent me a picture of the home my sister was at, nothing more. He implied that if I didn't tell him, something would happen to her."

"Luckily, Hoot was in a bad position. He couldn't show his face in Gold's Lake, Harding or anywhere around the area. He had robbed the club without any kind of disguise. He was easily identified from his picture in the paper the day after the theft. Coming back to Gold's Lake required a lot of planning by him and a little luck. If one person recognized him, he'd be arrested. While he was long on brute strength, he was short on smarts. He had to make sure he made the most of each of his visits to the prison, but there wasn't much else he could do. He tried to make offers to me for splitting the cash, but I would have none of it. In some ways I felt that the hidden treasure was keeping me alive."

"But I don't think the bag of jewelry was ever very far from

Hoot's mind, even after he came to terms with the fact that if he was to ever get the cash, he would have to wait until I'll got out of prison."

In Joe's mind, Hoot was guilty of the robbery and of ruining Ed's life. Joe had now come to regard Ed as nothing more than an unwilling accomplice and another victim of Hoot's. Hoot, on the other hand, had become despicable to Joe. He wondered how his father had investigated so thoroughly and yet had missed this main character.

I guess he didn't know what he didn't know, Joe surmised. His father did suspect another person was involved, so Joe had to give him some credit.

Joe sat back down at the table. He got the feeling that Ed was relieved to finally be telling someone who understood everything that had happened in his life and to his life. There was still a chance that Joe could turn Ed in, but Ed didn't think so.

"So when was the last time you saw Hoot? Does he know you're out?" Joe asked him.

"Oh, yeah, he knows. I hadn't heard from him for almost twenty years and then he came to visit me a week before I got out. I hardly recognized him. I had thought, had hoped anyway, that he was dead or in jail himself. At the least, I thought he'd forgotten about me. When I heard I had a visitor, my skin started to crawl. The only person who ever came to visit me was Bull and his son and my attorney, and I'd seen my attorney that morning. Hoot was old and skinny, not the hulk he used to be, but he still had that menacing swagger. I remember thinking, what could make a man wait thirty-seven years for a payout? Or, I thought, maybe he was simply waiting for his revenge."

"Wait a minute," Joe said, "Bull and his son?"

"We'll get to that," Ed said. "We'll definitely get to that."

"Okay," Joe said, "back to Hoot. Have you seen him since your release?" Joe was now pushing hard for answers and was anxious to find out where this story would go.

"Yes, he was waiting for me as I left the prison. You would have thought we were best friends. He picked me up at my house shortly after Bull dropped me off. We actually went back to the bar we met at, although it had changed names and owners and was almost un-recognizable. We chatted like old buddies. I didn't drink, much to his disappointment. He wanted me drunk so I'd let my guard down and tell him where everything was. He got drunk before he finally brought up the loot."

"He asked me where the money was. I said I didn't know if it was still where I had left it. I told him he would get his half, but it had to be on my terms because I didn't trust him at all. I would not have spoken to him that way thirty-seven years earlier, but while I'd maintained my strength and had stayed in shape in prison, Hoot looked terrible. His teeth were stained yellow from smoking and if you got in the way of one of his exhalations, his breath would make you make you vomit. His skin had that leathery tone to it that most longtime smokers get. His God-given strength was gone. He was hunched over and while he was skinny overall, he had a pot belly."

"His attitude, though, contradicted his physical form. He still had his swagger and his evil eye, but he could no longer back them up with an overpowering physique. I thought there would be a lot of people in the world who would like to take a crack at him then, such as the guys whose girlfriends' butts had been grabbed by Hoot just to start a fight."

"I laid out my terms to him regarding the loot. We would meet here in a week and if the stuff was where I left it, I'd be back with it. 'Either way,' I said, 'I'll be back.' But Hoot wasn't even close to being satisfied by that, and his vicious streak came out. He told me that as he saw it, if it wasn't there, I still owed it to him. The threat was clear. Then, without another word, Hoot walked out. I knew that I'd have to worry for the rest of my life if the stuff wasn't there. Worse yet, I didn't feel I could skip town. I had to get my sister first."

Ed got up from the table and Joe did too.

"I think that's enough for tonight," Ed said.

"You mean there's more?" Joe asked.

"Yes. There is much more."

"I got all night," Joe responded. "Let's just stay and finish it." But Joe knew the conversation was over because Ed had said it was. One doesn't survive all those years in prison being wishy-washy, Joe realized.

"Tell me why you broke into my apartment before you leave," Joe said, thinking quickly in case he never saw Ed again.

"I didn't."

"Who did?"

"Good question."

"Can you at least tell me who was driving the Porsche when it crashed?"

Joe heard Ed start to laugh at the question as he was walking out of the hotel room. Afterward, even through the closed motel room door, Joe heard Ed's laughter echo more and more loudly as he walked down the motel hallway.

# *Chapter Sixteen*

Joe was exhausted, but exhilarated at the same time.

So much had happened that day. His meeting with Ed Kutz had taken up an entire pad of yellow paper. He had started the day just hoping to see the house were Ed lived and he had ended up spending the rest of the day with him. He wanted to talk to someone about what had happened, most of all to his father, but of course that wasn't possible.

He wondered if Melissa was around. He called her phone, but there was no answer. It was probably a busy night at the bar. He really wanted to see her. He knew his time in Gold's Lake was limited and was destined to end altogether in the next few days. He felt like he was living in a parallel universe. Anything that existed back in New Jersey didn't matter. When he returned to that universe, it would matter again, but all that mattered was right here, right now.

Joe threw an old baseball cap on and a pair of sunglasses. He got into his rental car and headed for the Oval bar. The bar was as crowded as could be. A local Jaycee group had their Thursday night gathering there. It was an excuse for those thirty and forty year olds to go get drunk in the middle of the week. They were mostly the local up and coming businessmen and women. They were loud and obnoxious, but they tipped well. And they were all well connected. This concerned Joe because now that he knew it wasn't Ed who broke into his motel room, he thought it could even have been one of these people.

Despite the crowd in the bar, Melissa noticed Joe as soon as he walked in. She looked up quickly and smiled. He kept a low profile and headed toward the corner. Melissa came around the bar and headed to the storeroom where they kept all the liquor stock. Joe followed in behind her. They immediately hugged and kissed and Joe would have kept going, but Melissa had to get back to the crowd.

"You'll never believe my day. I'm dying to tell you about it," Joe said.

"I'll be here 'til at least three if you want to come back and see me."

He definitely wanted to see her, but he couldn't sit out in the open. He went back out into the bar, finished his Gimlet and left.

Joe went back to his motel room, but despite his best efforts, he couldn't stay awake long enough to make it back to the Oval bar. He fell asleep fully dressed and only managed to kick his shoes off in the middle of the night.

The shades in the hotel room were like black out shades. When there was a knock on the door, Joe still thought it was the middle of the night. He was already disoriented from being in a strange town and in a new hotel room and now by being woken up in the pitch dark.

He jumped out of bed and ran directly into a wall.

"Damn," he screamed.

He got his bearings and felt around for a light switch and turned on the light. He paused a second before heading to the door.

"Who is it?" he yelled.

"Open the door. It's Ed."

What in the world is he doing here at this hour, Joe thought. Had he had second thoughts about telling me everything and was now back to shut me up for good?

Slowly Joe was getting his balance and waking up a little.

"Why are you here so late?" he yelled through the door.

"Its six a.m. I'd call that early."

Joe opened the door and let Ed in.

Ed explained to Joe that after thirty-seven years in prison, getting up at 5 a.m. was a hard habit to break. Joe looked at his clock and opened the blinds. It was a bright day despite the early hour. It was the first nice day since Joe had been in Gold's Lake.

"What are you doing here?" Joe said, still trying to get his eyes to adjust to the light.

"I'm here to finish telling you the story."

"Why didn't you finish last night"?

"Trusting people is not something I come by easily these days. Every time I did that in the past, I paid for it."

"You checked me out?"

"No, I just thought about everything. For some reason I feel like I can trust you."

Joe went to the bathroom, brushed his teeth and called for room service. He ordered eggs and bacon, juice and a bagel and then told them to double the order for his recently arrived room guest.

"I haven't showered. I smell like crap," Joe said

"In prison everything smells bad all the time. It either smells like shit or disinfectant. After a while you can't tell the difference."

Ed went on about a lot of the small details of prison life. At first Joe thought he just wanted somebody to talk to, but after awhile it occurred to him that Ed was providing those details knowing that Joe might write a sequel to his father's book. Ed wanted it right this time. When Ed finished talking about life on the "inside" as he called it, Joe changed gears on him.

"What did you think of my father's book?"

"What makes you think I read it? I'm an ex-con. What makes you think I can read?"

"Oh, you can read. You seem pretty smart to me."

"Yeah, I read your father's book. It pissed me off at first. He had me all wrong. He should have worked harder to get an interview with me, to hear my side of the story. He should have learned about my past and my family life. He made me seem like an amoral monster. I remember thinking that my parents would have been so insulted after all the hard work they did raising me. I was glad they were dead and didn't have to read it."

"Would you have shared everything you shared with me with him?"

"Probably not back then. I was angry, bitter and full of guilt. I was a twenty year old facing the rest of my life in prison."

"So what'd you think of it?"

"Since it was only based on a true story, but was really a work of fiction, I got over it. And he killed me off at the end. I just wished he'd have gotten to know me."

A wave of a responsibility washed over Joe. He now felt he had a duty to get Ed's story down properly. He grabbed a yellow pad and a pencil, put the date at the top of the paper, and started writing.

"Where do you want to start?" Joe asked. He could see by Ed's expression that he had a topic in mind.

"I want to tell you about Bull, Senior," Ed said.

"Senior? Don't you mean Junior?"

"I see you've met his evil little offspring."

"Yes, he stopped me, seemingly for no reason, soon after I got here. He seems like a menacing little prick."

"The only person I hate in this world more then Hoot Gibbons is Bull Senior, and I'm on my way to hating Junior as much."

"Why do you think he stopped me?"

"He knows you're a stranger and were asking around about a broach. In this town you are either with him or against him, and you don't want to be against him. Everybody reports back to him, whether they're on the police force or not. In that way you stay on his good side. Townspeople have to build up chits to keep in reserve if Bull ever comes after them. He learned everything from his father, but the kid isn't smart enough to tie his own shoes. His father amassed a tremendous amount of power during his reign of terror that lasted for thirty-five years. He was able to pass it to his son. The town hoped the son would be better, but he's as bad, just without the brains."

"Tell me about senior first."

The way Ed settled into his chair made Joe feel he was getting ready to tell a long story.

"Bull Senior was my first jailer. I stayed under his care -- or lack thereof -- for a year and a half before being sent upstate to Plattsburg to serve my forty year sentence. In that year and half, Bull did nothing but abuse me anyway he could. He had known me to be a pretty nice kid while growing up in Gold's Lake. He even showed up at my father's funeral. He was kind to me on that day, but once my mom starting drinking heavily, she ran afoul of the law a few times. She'd crashed her car into the side of the senior center. The car ran straight through the wall. Nobody was hurt, but it made for a great picture the next day on the front of the Gold's Lake Gazette. Eighty percent of the car was in the building. My mom's name was mentioned and a few days later the story ran again, this time mentioning that alcohol was involved

"When I was brought into the police station after the murders, I was put in a cell that was usually home to drunks and domestic abusers. They were all simply released when I showed up. I was a young kid who had just done a monstrous thing, gunning down two of Gold's Lake's finest. There was absolutely no sympathy anywhere in the entire state for me, and my jailer was the all-powerful Bill Timothy, aka Bull."

"Like his son, Bull Senior was short and fat. He liked to pretend that his barrel chest was all muscle when in truth it was all fat."

As Joe sat listening to Ed's description of Bull Senior, he sounded identical to Bull Junior.

"He had naturally massive forearms and would always wear short sleeves to show them off. They were the only positive physical attribute he had, so he let the world enjoy them. His mentor on the force had been a nice old gentleman who was fair and friendly to everyone, even the guilty. Despite his best efforts, he couldn't instill Bull with the same qualities. As time went on, Bull started to challenge him on a lot of issues. No one knows for sure, but everyone in city politics says that it was Bull who started the senility rumors that lead to his mentor being forcibly retired and Bull taking over. Bull's willingness to go after even his friends had won him the respect of the "fry-'em-all-and let-God-figure-it-out" crowd in town"

"You seem to known as much about the two Bull's as you know about Hoot. Did you major in all three?" Joe asked Ed, but his attempt at a joke got no reaction from Ed.

"You couldn't live in this town without being informed about Senior and Junior. They are an institution around here. Kinda like a cancer you just can't cure."

Joe had gotten Ed off track and resolved not to do it again. He didn't want to make Ed forget any part of his story.

"Bull took over and then immediately started to consolidate power by getting rid of anybody who was a challenge or a threat to him. He didn't care what it took or the damage he would do to those people. He would slander, intimidate, lie, start rumors, whatever it took, and he could justify it all as a means to his lofty goals, which were quite simply to have all the power, to keep all the power and to not have to answer to anybody.

George Allan and Bill Hollar were holdouts. They stayed clear of Bull and did what they were told. Bull didn't like them because they weren't the hard-ass, goose-stepping sycophants he wanted. Had they not been killed, he would have eventually turned his attention to them and converted them to his way or run them off the force."

Joe was impressed by Ed use of the word "sycophants," and Ed had meant him to be. He wanted to show Joe that he had done a lot of reading in prison. That's probably about all he did, Joe realized. No more cracks about majors or reading, Joe resolved. Maybe Ed should be writing his own book.

"I had just killed two of his policemen and now I was in Bull's custody. Media was swarming around the police station. In public Bull put on a very professional face, explaining the process when a microphone was in his face. He feigned sorrow and almost forced out a tear. He was the picture of law and order. But once inside, an evil sneer appeared on his face as he leered at me."

"'You're mine now,' he told me."

"I had been lying face down on my cot the first time Bull entered the cell. I didn't turn to face Bull and that either infuriated him or simply gave him the justification for what he was about to do. He walked right over to me and pressed his massive forearm on to the back of my neck, backed by his enormous weight. The pressure on my neck forced my face into the pillow so I couldn't breathe or scream. Bull then took the opportunity to explain to me the rules of his jail. I was to stand at attention whenever Bull was anywhere in sight and remain that way until Bull said I could relax, but that was never going to happen so I would just stand ramrod straight, sometimes for hours. Bull told me, all the while smothering me and crushing my spine, that he would feed me if and when he felt like it. Bull seemed to be enjoying himself and was in no hurry to finish. He'd let me up every so often just so I wouldn't pass out."

Joe averted his eyes from Ed's. To him, it seemed the memory of the physical abuse mixed with the humiliation of being treated like an animal was almost too much to take. Joe wasn't sure, but he thought he saw a tear well up in Ed's eye.

"This part gets to you, huh?" Joe said sympathetically.

"Yeah, it does. I guess I'm sad for that young man that made such a horrendous mistake. Sometimes it feels like it happened to someone else, and to this day it still amazes me that that young man was me."

Ed rubbed his faced with both hands as if trying to wipe the memory out of his head. Joe was surprised at how much all this was still tormenting Ed.

"Yeah, poor me, right?" Ed said to Joe with a forced smile, embarrassed that he had gotten so emotional.

Joe felt like crying for him.

"That was not to be the last physical punishment I received

from Bull, but it was the most severe. I was not sure if I would survive it. The rest of the abuse was verbal assault or food and sleep deprivation. Bright lights would be left on all night long. And when I could manage to fall asleep, I never knew when I would be woken by a slap in the face, a kick to the ribs, or a cold bucket of water thrown through the bars. The abuse was not always at the hands of Bull, but it was always with his tacit approval."

"The lack of food was the worst. Morning time rarely meant breakfast. And noon and dusk had no relationship to meals. All the smells of food wafting in from the policemen's meals were torture, and the cops paraded past me gleefully eating over-stuffed éclairs or egg sandwiches. The food odors would get my stomach juices flowing with the promise of food soon to come, but more often than not, it didn't come. At one stretch, I was given nothing for three straight days, at which time I stood up and promptly fainted, falling forward and smashing my face into the bars and getting a deep gash in my forehead."

Ed pulled back his hair so Joe could see the scar.

"This incident happened a day before my preliminary court appearance. Bull must have been worried about how it would look, so a doctor was brought in to stitch me up. Afterward Bull came into my cell and sat down on my cot. I was sure a beating was coming, but Bull just sat there and explained in a calm voice that I'd better tell anybody that asked that I'd slipped, and that was the end of the story. The message was clear. If Bull got any bad press out of this scar, there would be hell to pay. I'd already decided not to complain and to my not too great surprise, neither my lawyer nor the judge asked me anything about it. It was at that point that I realized how little empathy there was for my plight. I could have been beaten to death and no one would have really cared. In fact, a lot of townspeople would have preferred that to a long trial. As Bull got off my cot and left the cell, he pointed to the dried blood on the cell floor from my fall and ordered me to clean it up."

"Bull became unhappy with only physical abuse and food and sleep deprivation. Humiliation became a constant for the year and half I spent with him. In my cell, there was only a cot and a toilet. Of the four holding cells, mine was the most central and the most visible. Any visitor that came into the police station could see me. I had no privacy whatsoever. There was no privacy screen for me to put up so I could pee and shit in private. When I put a makeshift screen up using the sheet from my cot, the sheets were removed from my cell. I was allowed one shower a week. The bathing area of the prison was on the opposite end of the building. I would be made to strip naked in my cell, turn away from the door, and than the guard would come in, put the cuffs on me and parade me through the corridors bare naked."

Joe was embarrassed for Ed, but Ed went on talking as if he was talking about someone else.

"On one occasion, one of the more sadistic of Bull's minions was removing me from my cell to the shower when a phone call came in for him. He sat me, stark naked, in a chair in the office and proceeded to spend forty-five minutes on what seemed to be a very unimportant chit-chatty phone call."

"It got to the point where I would look forward to my court appearances and meetings with my lawyer just to get out from under Bull's boot heel. I had no money to speak of so the court appointed me a lawyer. He was a fleshy, pot bellied attorney approaching retirement age, although he couldn't afford to retire. He hadn't been very hard working during his career and he never cared very much for his clients, and that wasn't about to change for my sake. He had hair all over his face. One might refer to it as a beard and a mustache, but it was really just a tortured web of matted hair, let grown wild, because he was too lazy to shave. He didn't like me and didn't care to make any kind of small talk or inquire as to how I was being treated. He also didn't give me any updates on the goings on concerning my trial."

"After the trial ended with a bizarre scene of the prosecutor being pummeled by a massive farmer, I was taken back to Bull's cell to wait for sentencing. The day before I was to be sent upstate for the rest of my life, Bull came into my cell as if he was saying good-bye to a good friend, as if he hadn't been abusing me for the last year and half. I jumped to attention, but Bull told me to relax. He made some mention of how he had treated me, but it was less of an apology and more of an "I was just doing my job" speech. Bull explained that he had a lot of friends up at Plattsburgh prison and he could help make my stay there more comfortable. Bull got up to leave and actually put out his hand for me to shake. For a second I thought Bull was going to grab my hand and pull me in viciously for one last knee in the gut. But he didn't. He said good-bye and then headed for the door. Just before he left, he turned to me and said, 'So what do you know about the County Club Robbery in Harding last year?'"

Joe sat straight up at the mention of the country club

"The question hit me like a two by four to the side of my head. Questions started streaming into my brain. What had Bull heard? Had Hoot said something? Had Hoot been arrested? The robbery seemed like ancient history and something that happened to someone else in some other life. I had hardly even thought about it after the killings. After a year of not trusting Bull Senior, it was easy for me to act totally ignorant of the entire subject, as if I had never even heard about it at all. I said I really had no idea where Harding was, but that I may have heard the town's name once before. I knew I was risking a severe beating if Bull had even the slightest inkling that I was lying, but I took the chance anyway."

"Bull was obviously fishing, but I was not about to bite down on that hook. He had his suspicions, and if I could help it, I would keep them that way, just suspicions. Bull smiled and said 'okay' and left. Over the next several years, Bull Senior would stop in to the prison and visit me and each meeting ended with a mention of the Harding Robbery. And each time he asked, he would let a little more information out. On one visit he asked if I knew Hoot Gibbons. On another one, he mentioned that one of the robbers was about my size. The last time I ever saw Bull Senior, he mentioned that the cash and jewelry from the heist had never been recovered and asked if I knew anything about it."

"Bull Senior died a few weeks after that visit. By then I had been in prison for seventeen years. I heard that Bull had been eating hard candy in the office when a piece had gotten lodged in his throat. He was there with a few of his loyal policemen, including his son. They tried to dislodge it, but Bull had gotten even fatter as he had gotten older and doing anything for him was difficult. Rumor had it that Bull Junior had tried to stick his fingers into his dad's mouth to get the candy out, but that just set the candy in deeper."

Joe smiled because he could see Ed trying hard not smile.

"Frankly," Ed Said, "I couldn't keep the smile from my face then either when I heard that Bull Senior's last act on this earth was to shit and piss himself in front of his men."

Ed excused himself to use the bathroom. Joe thought it was probably more to regroup than to use the facilities. Ed returned with a towel in his hands that he had been using to dry off his face. He threw the towel in the corner with disdain.

Joe noticed an ugly sneer come to Ed's face as he started talking about Bull's son.

"It was no more than two weeks after his dad's death that Bull Junior made what would be the first of many visits to Plattsburgh prison to see me. When he first arrived, I thought I was looking at the ghost, albeit the much younger ghost, of Bull Senior. They looked identical. They dressed the same, and they carried themselves the same. The same feeling of dread shuttered though my body. I had already heard rumors of Bull Junior and his cruelty. Everybody had said that he was either as mean or even meaner than his father, just not nearly as smart."

"The position of police chief was bestowed upon him after his dad's death. The same council members who had supported his father and his brutal tactics had made sure his son had the position. It finally turned out to be an ill conceived move, one that the whole town would live to regret. On two occasions Bull Junior had wrongly imprisoned people who had the wherewithal to defend themselves, and they then sued over the abuse they suffered at Bull Junior's hand. He had punched one young man in the face and broken his jaw, permanently disfiguring him. For that the guy received a lump payment from the town's rainy day fund of two million dollars.

"Bull Junior was twenty-nine when he was given the job. He had been a way below average student at Southern Valley High School and everybody figured his dad had helped him pass the policeman's exam. He had gotten into a lot of fights in high school, but had always been bailed out by his dad. The other kids were afraid of Bull Junior, not because he was a good fighter or particularly strong, but because they didn't want to incur the wrath of his father. Bull Junior was a bully with the protection of his father, and most of the students hated him for that. The principal had stopped by Bull Senior's house once to discuss the problem of Bull Junior beating on the weaker kids. He was laughed out of the house. The principal then made the mistake of taking the issue to the town council and the school board. He was out of a job within a year. Nothing ever happened to Bull Junior."

"Bull's first meeting with me was to let me know he hadn't forgotten me. He was there for only about three or four minutes when the Harding country club was mentioned. His tone was calm, friendly, and yet he seemed extremely menacing."

"I didn't know what he could do to me from outside, but I wasn't excited to find out. After about four years on the force, Bull Junior had learned to work the system to his advantage. His father had shown him the ropes, but Bull Junior was indiscriminate with how he used his power. He had a lust for women, booze and money, and while his father had been around, I had heard he had been able to get away with things."

"On one occasion, late in the summer, Bull Junior had staked out a favorite teenage make out spot. On the north end of a multi-field ballpark in town there was a small access road where the local DPW could park their truck and tractors to work on the field. There was an even smaller road off it, which led into the woods. It was a completely private spot that only a few people even knew about. That night a young couple had stealthily approached the access road, shutting off their headlights as they pulled in. This couple had more on their minds than just some light petting, but they would end up regretting their impulses for years to come."

"In fifteen minutes the boy and girl had gotten completely naked, and the windows of the car were becoming more fogged up by the moment. Bull Junior had been waiting about a hundred yards away, sitting in his squad car with the lights out. He had disconnected his interior light so it wouldn't go on when he opened his door. He wanted his arrival to be a total surprise. He approached the car from behind, careful not to cast a shadow across the back window. He stood back and watched for as long as he could until his view became totally obscured by the foggy windows. He had his billy club in his left hand and an eighteen inch flashlight in the other. He walked up to the car and knocked hard on the window."

"The naked couple jumped apart in horror and started searching for their clothes. Bull tore the driver's side door open and ordered the couple not to move, but they both continued to grope for their clothing. Bull withdrew his gun and ordered them to stop moving. They did as they were told. The girl had not been able to locate any of her clothing and she sat there completely naked, trying to cover herself with her hands. The boy was able to locate his undershorts and had them sitting on his lap. Bull ordered them both to put their hands on the dashboard. The boy protested, begging Bull to let them dress and to get the flashlight off them, and especially off her."

"Bull had had enough. He ordered the boy out of the car. The boy continued to protest, but with each word Bull seemed to get angrier. He finally grabbed the boy by the hair and yanked him out of the car. Bull forced him up against the car and handcuffed him to the back door handle. By this time the girl was sobbing, her hands up on the dash and her breasts completely exposed. Bull calmly walked over to her side and told her to get out. She refused and begged him just to let her get dressed."

"'Now listen, honey,' Bull said to her, 'you get your pretty little ass out of that car or I'm going to call the boys at the station to come and get you out and then I'm going to charge you with indecent exposure and prostitution as well as with resisting arrest.'"

"'Prostitution?' she sobbed incredulously. 'He's my boyfriend!'"

"Bull was enjoying himself tremendously. He let the flashlight slowly track over every inch of her body. Her weeping had no effect on him whatsoever and her boyfriend's protests fell on deaf ears also. At one point the naked boy screamed that Bull was a pervert and that he was going to sue him. Bull casually left the naked girl, slamming her door shut so she couldn't get back inside to get dressed, and walked around the back of the car to where the boy was."

"'Now, son, you are the one out here molesting that girl on public property and endangering the morals of any innocent passersby. What if some young kids happened by and saw what you were doing to that girl? You should be ashamed of yourself. And you better be real careful with your tone toward me, seeing how I haven't even decided yet what I'm going to charge you with.'"

"The boy understood the implied threat. 'Just let her put her clothes back on,' he pleaded."

"'Now, son, I've got to check through the car and those clothes to make sure there isn't any contraband or weapons back there.'" Bull had an annoying habit of calling everyone 'son' even though they were his age or in some cases older. The naked boy who was cuffed to the car couldn't have been but two or three years younger than Bull himself."

"Bull thought he remembered the girl from high school, and he turned his attention back to the crying girl who was now standing outside the car with her hands trying to cover her private areas."

"'Hands down at your sides,' Bull said to her."

"The naked girl shook her head."

"'Put your hands at your sides or I'm going to be forced to cuff you and do a thorough cavity search. And I might need some help from some of my other officers to do it safely.'"

"The girl, sobbing uncontrollably, lowered her hands. Bull instructed her to turn around. All the while he danced his flashlight over her naked body."

"After he had gotten his fill, he decided to let them off with just a warning, but he reserved the right to charge them later if he changed his mind. The message was clear. If they caused any kind of fuss about the way he had treated them, he would charge them with several different crimes."

A look of doubt replaced the fascination that had been on Joe's face. Ed noticed it immediately.

"How could you know all this?" Joe asked. He didn't want to insult Ed, but he felt he just had to know.

Joe's doubt didn't bother Ed at all.

"I'd have a hard time believing it too if I hadn't heard it directly from the guy it happened to. Jim Switzer was an ex-private detective with extensive knowledge of recording and wiretapping. He had trouble holding a job, probably because of the abuse and humiliation he endured, thanks to Bull. He ended up in jail because he wiretapped his wife's lawyer during their divorce. When the lawyer started to suspect he was being recorded, Jim broke back into the office to retrieve the recorder and came across the lawyer working late. Since he was in trouble anyway, he punched the lawyer in the face and broke his jaw. He had gotten a ten year sentence for assault. He was in a cell not far from mine for a while. He saw Bull and me talking on one of Bull's visits to me. At first he thought we were friends, but once I told him I was no fan of Bull Junior or Senior, he told me what had happened to him."

"I believe Jim Switzer hates Bull even more than I do," Ed said as an afterthought.

Joe was trusting Ed more and more.

"Oh, and another thing," Ed said to Joe. "Bull obviously knew Jim Switzer was in prison and that he and I had spoken. One day he told me to say 'hi' to Jim for him and to ask him how his girlfriend was."

"Why didn't someone do something?" Joe asked incredulously.

"While Bull's conduct was reprehensible, he really hadn't committed a crime. They were publicly indecent. He was under no obligation to allow them to put their clothes back on since they had taken them off willingly. And while the girl was not engaging in prostitution, she would have had to defend herself of that charge and could have been found guilty. The potential humiliation alone was probably enough of a threat to prevent her from speaking out. Bull could say he saw money on the seat of the car and assumed it was a sex-for-money transaction. Shades of gray were Bull's guarantee that he would never have to pay for his perversion."

"Bull Junior had become surer than his father that I was involved in the Harding Country Club. It wasn't that Junior had any better information than Senior, but Junior was more willing to make wild accusations. Being wrong didn't concern him. If there were even half a chance that I might know something about the robberies, it was worth that chance. Junior was well acquainted with Hoot's past and had apparently heard some talk that there was a connection between Hoot and me."

"On Bull's second visit to see me in prison, he asked me again about the robbery. I, of course, said that I knew nothing about it. That cat and mouse game went on for years. Bull talked about it as if it was a hard fact and paid no mind to my denials."

"'Where'd you and that scum bag Hoot hide that stuff?' Bull

asked me once with a smile. "I'll go get it and I'll split it with you.'"

"'I don't have the slightest idea what you are talking about,' I said again and again."

"'Sure you do. Did you give it to someone to hold it for you? Maybe I should go try to find out from your retarded sister.'"

Joe watched as Ed's mood turned dark when he recalled Bull calling his sister retarded.

"I knew better than anybody else that she wasn't even close to be retarded. She was smarter than most people, but couldn't convey it because she couldn't speak in a way that people could understand. Her hand gestures were so herky jerky that she never learned to write, and no one ever took the inordinate amount of time it would take to teach her to read. Several years after my confinement started, she started to write to me via a computer with very large letters and voice recognition software. To write a two line letter to me would take her all day, but getting it really meant the world to me."

Joe looked away as Ed's eyes welled up when he spoke of his sister

"Bull's visits were always short and they always ended with an angry Bull Junior saying that it wasn't over and that someday I was going to tell him where the stuff was. Months would go by without a visit, and I would think that I had finally convinced him that I didn't have the stuff, but eventually Bull would return."

"After I'd been in prison for thirty-seven years, Bull Junior actually weighed in on my behalf to the parole board members and just like that, my prison sentence was up. Many of the people who remembered the killings had died and the ones who were still around got a visit from Bull telling them to stop contesting it. I had gone into prison at twenty years old and now, as a fifty-seven year old man, I was being released. The day I walked out the gate, Bull Junior was sitting in his squad car across the street from the prison, waiting for me. And about two hundred yards further down the road, with a pair of binoculars to his eyes, was Hoot Gibbons."

# Chapter Seventeen

Ed and Joe had been in the room for three straight hours as Joe devoured every word Ed said.

"And that brings us up to the present," Ed said with a sly grin on his face.

"Oh, no, it doesn't," Joe, said.

"Well, maybe that's all I want to tell you."

"You can't do this to me. I need to know."

"Know what?" Ed asked.

Joe got up and walked over to his nightstand, opened the top drawer, and pulled out a small item wrapped in tissue appear. He placed it on the table in front of Ed. Ed didn't need to open it to know what it was.

Joe pulled the broach out and handed it to Ed. Ed took it, looked at it, and at first seemed to be studying it, but Joe felt Ed was looking right through it at the same time to a place long gone where he could have made a different decision and lived a much better life. In many ways, when he decided to take part in the robbery, he sealed the fate of those two policemen and altered the lives of so many others. The broach was a bad luck charm to him and he let it fall to the table

"I remember the woman's face who we took this from. I got

the feeling then that it wasn't just about money to her, but we took it anyway. There were three or four pieces nicer than this one. Did you find out how much this one was worth?" Ed asked Joe.

"Yes, I did, but I'm not telling you until you finish the story." Of course, Joe knew that Ed couldn't really finish the story because the story itself was not finished yet.

Ed sighed once and started talking again. "Both Bull Junior and Hoot were very interested in my release from prison. Both of them wanted to get their hands on the money. Bull was now free to harass me in plain sight, day or night, while Hoot's past kept him on the police wanted list. The statute of limitations for the Harding robbery had expired long ago, but lesser crimes still dogged him. And Hoot was certainly on Bull's radar screen as he was the only other potential competition for the loot."

"Bull drove me from the prison to my childhood home. The tenants, who had been in the house for over thirty years, had decided to move out a few months before. I had the feeling that Bull facilitated that move so I could move back in, and Bull could keep his eye on me. His conversation in the car was simply to tell me that I didn't have the protection of the prison walls anymore. I was either going to get the loot for Bull or my life would be hell."

"That ride home was strange. He treated it as if we were old friends. He mentioned some people he thought I might know and told me if they were alive or dead. He pointed out the sites of a few buildings that had been demolished. I remember thinking that nothing seemed familiar to me. I didn't recognize anything until we drove through the center of town and even then only a few things seemed familiar. Our ride was almost over when he turned to me with a smile on his face and said, 'You're gonna wish you were back in that Club Med prison when I get through with you if you don't give me what I want.'"

"Shortly after I was back home, Bull and his entire department got embroiled in a scandal that wouldn't go away. Federal authorities had bugged the police department because of rumored financial improprieties. Money from the evidence locker had been disappearing at an alarming rate. Nobody in Gold's Lake had the nerve to accuse Bull Junior, so someone went to the FBI. After they set up their wiretapping, they heard talk about Bull's cops and possibly Bull himself arresting prostitutes and then letting them go in exchange sexual favors. Bull and his cronies had become so brazen that they'd pick up known prostitutes, even if they weren't currently plying their trade, and arrest them. They wouldn't even take them to the police station. They'd take them to the spot where those young lovers had been abused by Bull, have sex with them, and then bring them back home. In Gold's Lake policemen having sex with prostitutes was huge news in and of itself, and on one of the tapes a prostitute mentioned that she was still in high school. The FBI men could not abide what was happening."

"Bull's reputation had been taking hits for years, but his ability to intimidate everyone had still offered him protection. The current scandal now had the potential not only to have him removed as police chief, but threatened to have him put in jail. His time, for the next few weeks, would be spent on self-preservation. He hadn't forgotten about the money and me, but we had gone down on his list of priorities. Of course, I didn't know I wasn't being watched, but I definitely felt the pressure ease up and that seemed to coincide with the stories in the newspaper about Bull and his department's extra curricular activities."

Ed looked at Joe and shook his head as if he was still in disbelief.

SINS OF THE SON

"No sooner had the pressure from Bull eased up, than Hoot made his appearance again. One day he just knocked on my door. I wasn't surprised at all, even though I'd told him at the bar to wait a week or so. I had found myself hoping he might have died since then.

In the daylight I could now see Hoot more clearly than in the dim light of the bar. He was old before his time and he cut a rather pathetic picture. The physicality he had always depended on had left him, but he wasn't smart enough to realize it. He looked withered and weak. By contrast I had worked out in prison and had kept in top physical condition and looked to be twenty years younger than he did and in far better shape."

With half a smile Ed looked at Joe, hoping he would confirm the he still looked good.

"Well, I've never seen Hoot, so I have nothing to compare you to," Joe said, pretending to be serious.

Ed smiled at Joe's remark and continued

"But Hoot still had the willingness to be extremely cruel and one didn't need big muscles to shoot a gun or stab someone. Hoot was still the brutal human being he had always been, just without the strength he once had."

"'We got some unfinished business,' Hoot said to me in a raspy voice, damaged from his years of hard living. Maybe he suffered from blackouts, I thought, and had been so drunk in the bar he'd forgotten our whole conversation there.

His clothes were tattered. He was unshaven for many days and he smelled like he needed a bath badly. My first thought was that he must be homeless. If he had been anybody else, I would have invited him in for a meal and a bath."

"'Where's the stuff?' he asked me."

"I hadn't yet checked to see if it was still there. I wasn't even sure if the house was still there. And if I told Hoot where I thought it might be, Hoot would go there straight away and take it, never to be seen again."

"'I'm not sure if it's still there,' I told him."

"'It better be. For your sake,' Hoot hissed at me."

"I acted as if I hadn't heard a word of Hoot's threat. 'Like I told you, when the time is right,' I said, 'I plan on going to see if I can reclaim it. If its still there, I'll split it with you.'"

"Hoot smiled, exposing two rows of decaying yellow and brown teeth, and laughed, but then he started coughing uncontrollably."

"Once he had regained his composure, Hoot said, 'No way. I'm going with you.'"

"'No way to you,' I shot back. 'I don't trust you for a second. As I see it, you don't have a choice but to trust me.'"

"'I've been waiting for what's mine for almost forty years. I have a lot of choices. I could blow your fucking head off for you right now. How's that for a choice I could make?'"

"I wasn't the least bit intimidated. Years of prison life had taught me the folly of showing fear."

"'Hoot, you cost me forty years of my life. I should kill you right now.'"

"'I didn't tell you to kill those policemen. You did that all on your own.'"

"'You know, I thought it was you coming to kill me,' I snarled at Hoot."

Joe could see Ed getting angrier with each word as he continued.

"'If I had had one half a thought that you might honor our deal, none of that would have happened. My plan is to go after the money and the stuff when the time is right. I'm not risking going back to jail.'"

"Hoot knew he was defeated. He could bark all he wanted at me, but that wasn't going to get him any closer to his money. He was too old to be taken seriously, and he didn't have any other options, if he ever wanted his money, but to trust me."

"'Just remember this,' he suddenly said to me, 'if you take off with my money, I will spend the rest of my life hunting you down, my hand to God.'"

"Like God cares about your hand, I thought, but didn't say it. From the looks of him, the end of his life was already pretty close at hand."

"Hoot turned to leave. I knew he wanted to storm out, but his weakened body made that impossible. He was able to slam the door, however, hard enough to smash one of the side lights."

"Surprisingly, meeting Hoot again hadn't given me the dread I had thought it would. I now knew my nemesis was a hollowed out man living a pathetic existence."

"Then why even consider splitting with him?" Joe asked Ed.

"I had been given such a staunch sense of fair play from my parents that even thirty-seven years in prison hadn't taken that rightness from me. I planned on giving Ed his half if and when I ever got mine."

Ed and Joe sat quietly for a few seconds. Ed because he had just recapped the mess he made of his life from one bad decision, and Joe because all the answers he had been seeking for years were finally at hand.

Joe saw Ed starting to act restless, as if he were getting ready to leave.

"Oh, no, you don't," Joe said. "Let's finish this thing."

"I'm not going anywhere."

It appeared to Joe that Ed knew he had to continue the story, but that he really didn't want to. There was one major question, among several minor ones, that still had to be answered. They both knew what it was.

"Whose body did they pull out of that car?" Joe asked him. "I'm not sure of much these days, but I'm pretty sure the dead body they pulled out of that car wasn't you."

Ed gave Joe a sad smile and said, "Yeah, it wasn't me."

"So who was it?"

"There's more to tell before I get to that."

"Yeah?" Joe said. "Like when and how you recovered the money?"

"Both of my tormentors had backed off, at least temporarily. Bull was dealing with his scandal, but no doubt keeping at least one eye on me. Hoot had been convinced to wait, although I also thought he would be watching me when he could. I had been out of prison for over a month when I finally decided to make my move and return to the Wrin house. Getting back there wouldn't be easy. Neither Hoot nor Bull could have any inkling that I had any interest in the Wrin house. I had to get there, get the stuff and get home without being seen. I had purchased an old truck with the money that I had earned from renting my house for all those years. The money had been in a conservatorship for me which had done nicely. I wasn't loaded, but it afforded me enough money to get started. But driving there was risky. What if Bull had instructed his people to pass by the house a few times a day to report on my movements? The truck would have to stay in my driveway."

"Thirty-seven years ago I had walked through the woods to find the Wrin house. I would have to do that again, only this time under the darkness of night."

"The air was cool and dry on the night I started to walk back toward the house that had played such a pivotal role in fucking up my life. Going into that house was a mistake that lead to the deaths of two policemen and my being incarcerated for most of my life. Kids grew up fatherless and wives lived without their husbands because I had gone into that house. Years of guilt shadowed me because of that house. I wasn't able to care for my sister because of that house. The thought of going back in there turned my stomach upside down."

Joe watched as Ed struggled to tell the story. He seemed to be going back and forth from an emotional retelling of the story to a total detachment from it.

"The moon was bright and lit the way for me to walk. Without a map, I thought I might have some trouble navigating the wooded areas between my house and the Wrin house some five and a half miles away. But it was as if I was being pulled toward the house. My feet knew just where to go. The landscape had changed considerably since my earlier trip. A strip mall had been constructed half way in between. I hadn't anticipated going through a mall parking lot so I altered my plan and went around the back of a new Stop and Shop. I walked a little further and came upon a neighborhood that no longer looked new, but it wasn't there the last time I made that trek. When I saw that development, it made me sad feeling how much time had passed. Maybe it was built shortly after I went to jail, I thought."

"I carried three things with me. I had a flashlight I was reluctant to use, as it might be seen, a leather bag that used to be my father's, which he used to carry hand tools, and a pry bar to get into the house."

"What if the house was gone, I thought. That hadn't occurred to me before. I guessed I would have heard if it had been torn down, but then I started to doubt that. Who would have told me? I started to panic a little, but then decided just not to let myself even consider that it might be gone."

Joe had known that the house was still there before he left for Gold's Lake because he had heard it had been broken back into.

"Maybe you heard it had been broken into again," Joe said.

Ed shook his head and said, "I don't think so. As I walked on, the day we had robbed the Harding Country club came flooding back to me. I remembered the fear I had of Hoot finding me. I had visions of the maitre d' that Hoot smashed in the face. I remembered perfectly the feeling then that I had made a huge mistake, but couldn't take it back. I remembered being so scared then, and I had to acknowledge that I was scared now. If I got caught, I would definitely go back to jail. I would never be able to care for my sister. She would die in that awful hell hole. The rest of my life was riding on whether or not I could get in and out of the Wrin house safely."

"I had always taken responsibility for what I had done in that basement. I had never tried to make excuses or blame it on someone else. I could have tried to lessen my sentence by selling Hoot out, but I didn't. But some part of me felt like life hadn't been fair to me. My father had been killed and hadn't been around to redirect me when I went off course. My mother's drinking left me with a mother to take care of at a time when I was still reeling from my father's death. Was it just bad luck that Hoot approached me or had I held myself out as someone who could be approached by the likes of someone like Hoot? I didn't have a parent to say 'stay away from that guy because he's bad news.' My safety net had been torn to shreds and I was cast out a window. There was no one to catch me when I fell. I fell hard. Some part of me still thought that the Wrin house owed me something. And that something was a bag of old wallets, purses, cash and jewelry. My luck just had to change."

Joe was fascinated by the moment of self-reflection that Ed was going through. At times he made no excuse and at others he seemed to feel so sorry for the little boy who lost his parents. Joe knew what it was like to be without a father, even when that father was alive.

Ed continued. "My heightened sense of right and wrong had already dealt with the question, was it right to take the cash? I felt that if I could use that cash to help my sister and get away from Gold's Lake to start a new life, then it would be well used. I couldn't speak for Hoot's portion. Hoot would have to make peace with his maker by himself. I wasn't so naïve to think that Hoot would have any ethical quandary at all over this stuff. It was probably not right for him to get it because he would waste it in short order on frivolous, illegal, immoral things. I was sure he didn't deserve it, but I had made a deal and wasn't going to go back on it."

"I was pretty sure I was close to the Wrin house, but the brush around it had gotten thick and almost impenetrable. I circled around it to see if there was an opening. I didn't want to enter from the driveway side. Most of the yard had grown in with weeds and saplings that had grown into sizeable trees since I was last there. It was hard for me to get my bearings because the open yard simply didn't exist any more. The detached garage in the back left corner was almost entirely reclaimed by the earth. I couldn't tell the vegetation from the structure. In a while I had re-acclimated myself to where everything was. I started to head to where I remembered the basement window being. The brush was so thick I had to stamp on it to get it to stay down so I could approach the house. Much of the brush was taller than I was. Thirty-seven years earlier it had all been grass. The window I had climbed through was still boarded up, but the board was so rotted that I didn't need my pry bar to remove it. I simply pulled and I was suddenly looking into the space that had changed my life. The glass in the window had been replaced, but then it had been broken again. I couldn't slip through because of the shards and I hated to admit it, but my own stomach had grown in the last three and half decades. I wasn't sure if I could squeeze through even if I wanted to. I stood up and headed for the front door. The wooden boards on the porch creaked under my weight. Although the noise was barely audible, I was afraid some-one would hear. I got to the old wooden door that George Allen and Bill Hollar had opened on the way to their deaths. The door was twisted now and couldn't be locked anymore. I leaned on it and it opened enough for me to get through."

"It hadn't changed much, I remember thinking. It was messier, but everything looked pretty much as I remembered it. But I was in no mood for a walk down memory lane. I was anxious to get in and get out. I had been subconsciously dreading having to walk down the basement stairs and step over the spot where the two policemen had lain dying all those years ago. The constant guilty pang that I had always had, but never verbalized, was going to have to be faced. In the dark recesses of my mind, there was always the question of whether or not either or both of those policemen could have been saved if I had stayed and called for help. Sure, I didn't know they were policemen when I fired, but I knew it before I ran out. Did I not only shoot them, but then leave them to bleed to death? The coroner's reports had been pretty clear. They died almost instantly and nothing I could have done would have saved them, but it still weighed on my mind."

"I made my way to the stairs and started to head down. It was surreal for me to see the basement from this vantage point. For a second the thought occurred to me that someone might be down there lying in wait for me. How poetic would that be if I was shot dead in the same way those policemen had been killed? What a story that would make."

"I reached the bottom of the stairs and stepped on the spot where the men had died. I was afraid I'd see discoloration on the basement floor where the blood had leaked out or maybe the chalk outlines would still be there, if they were ever there. But there was nothing. The years of moonlight and sunlight combined with time and dust had washed the evidence away. It looked like any other basement floor in the world. Nothing was left to testify to the tragedy that I had caused."

"I just stood there for a minute. I had killed two men I'd never met, family men who by all accounts were good people. I'd left children fatherless and wives without their husbands. I felt I owed them more than just to rush by them in search of the valuables that led to their death. A deep sense of sadness came over me like a blast of frigid air. Bumps erupted on my skin from head to toe. I wondered if the men knew how sorry I was for what I'd done, and even though I'd served thirty-seven years of my life for my crimes -- yet still didn't think that was enough -- did they know that I had had no ill feelings toward them? I wondered if they could have forgiven me."

Joe was sitting there listening, but he felt that Ed was talking more to himself or to those two policemen than he was to him. This was not the man that his father had written about in the book, Joe realized. His dad had gotten that part dead wrong. Ed was smart, well spoken, and a seemingly well read guy with a sensitive, introspective side.

How could my father have gotten it so wrong, Joe wondered.

What about the story had blinded him so badly? Joe stared hard at Ed, trying to figure it out, but Ed had started talking again.

"I moved on from that spot at the bottom of the stairs and went over to the furnace. The furnace was the same one, and little else in the basement had changed. I felt the place was smaller than I remembered, as if the walls had moved in and the ceiling had been lowered. I'd spent almost two weeks in that basement. It was seared into my memory."

"I approached the stones in the wall. They all looked to be tight. I began to get nervous when I couldn't pick out the stone that I'd removed to stash the take from the robbery. 'Oh, God, please tell me nobody found it,' I yelled out, forgetting my need to be silent. Just one time in my life, I thought, let things work out for me. I'd made mistakes and I've been punished. Give me the ability make some good out of an awful tragedy. Let me care for my sister in the last stages of her life. I had never been a praying man, but I was suddenly deep inside my own head talking to someone. Was it God? I don't know, but what I was saying sounded an awful lot like talking to him."

"I ran my hand over the stones in the wall. 'Which one was it?' I mumbled. I reached for one that resembled the right size stone, but it was lodged securely and the mortar hadn't been compromised. I pulled my flashlight out and started to focus on the mortar instead of the size of the rock because they all looked similar to me. I reached for two or three more stones, but they wouldn't budge. Sweat started to run down my back. Had someone found it and then re-mortared the stones? Why would anyone do that?"

"I expanded the area of my search. I could have sworn I'd hid the stuff directly behind the furnace, but maybe my memory was off or had been altered over the years. I definitely remembered it being low to the ground because I discovered it trying to find a place to step on to reach up high to hide the stuff. I bent down and felt the lower stones. The first one I touched moved slightly. My heart skipped a beat. This was it. It had to be."

"I hesitated. At this point there was still hope. If I pulled it away and found nothing, that hope would be gone. I took a deep breath and started to wiggle the stone out of its hole. The stone fit in so perfectly that no one would have noticed the missing mortar. I rocked the stone back and forth. There was barely enough room to fit my fingers around the rock to move it. It started to come out, millimeter by millimeter. I didn't remember it being this difficult thirty-seven years earlier, but I was glad for the difficulty in getting it out. If I found the loot still in there, the tight fit would be the reason."

"There actually was no pleasure in any of this for me. I hated every second of being in that basement. I'd rather have been almost anywhere else in the world. I felt my chest tightening. Just as the rock was about to break free, a shadow came across the window. I froze and ducked to the far side of the furnace. I could see a pair of legs in the window. I was sure they were woman's legs. Old woman's legs. The legs stopped there for a second and then a little dog poked its head into the basement and barked twice. I fully expected the person outside the window to bend down and peer inside, but she didn't. She moved on."

"I think know who that was," Joe interjected. "It was a woman my father used to know as a child. She walks by the house every day."

Ed listened carefully to what Joe was saying. Joe figured this was one of the few areas of the story that Ed still hadn't filled in. Everything and everybody else seemed to have been thoroughly studied and researched by Ed, at least in his mind.

Ed nodded and seemed to make a mental note of what Joe had told him.

"What's her name?" he asked Joe.

"Robbie," Joe said.

Ed nodded and went back to his story

"I was sweating now. Was she going to come inside to check it out? Would she call the police? I didn't know and didn't want to know. I wanted to get out. The rock fell free. I got down on my knees and reached into the hole. It was deeper and further back than I remembered. But my hand knew where the bag would be if, in fact, it was still there. I turned my hand downward and clutched. To my great relief, the bag was there and it felt as if the stuff was still in it. As I pulled the bag from the hole, I realized it had almost completely disintegrated. Everything that was in the bag fell into the dirt as I tried to retrieve it. Damn, I thought, this was going take much longer than I wanted it to."

"I removed the bag I had brought with me and opened it up. I pulled the old bag out of the hole and threw it on the basement floor. I stuck my hand back in and started grabbing handfuls of cash, jewelry and dried dirt. I had no time to be careful. Handful after handful came out. I was sure I was getting some run-of-the mill rocks, too, but I could sort through everything later. I didn't take time to look at what I was removing. My heart was beating furiously with a sense of relief that the stuff was still there, but also with a sense of dread that I wouldn't be able to enjoy it because the cops might be on their way. Or worse, Hoot might be waiting upstairs to blow my brains out."

"I felt around the entire hole. I was pretty sure I'd gotten everything. I grabbed the old burlap bag and threw it back into the hole in the wall. I scooped up handfuls of dirt that had fallen on the floor and replaced the rock. It didn't fit as well as it had, but no one would see it unless they were looking for it. I picked up the leather bag and headed for the stairs. It was heavier than I remembered, mostly from the dirt, but still there was a lot of stuff in the bag. I turned to look to make sure everything was in order. Although I was in a panic, I realized I was again standing right on top of the spot where the two men had died and where I may have left them breathing, but bleeding to death. I stepped to the side, looked down, said, 'I'm really sorry,' and headed up the stairs."

# Chapter Eighteen

"I had no intention of going out the way I'd come in. No way was I going to be shot down by Hoot or arrested by Bull Junior. I'd come too far. I walked to a bedroom in the back of the house and tried to pull up on the window, but it wouldn't budge. I looked out the back and saw no one."

"'The hell with it,' I said."

"I swung the bag full of the jewelry, rocks and cash into the window and smashed it in. If there had been people out front, they most certainly would have heard. I shot through the window, cutting the underside of my thigh badly. Despite the blood running down my leg and into my shoe, I ran for the cover of the woods as fast as I could."

Joe felt as if he hadn't even been breathing while listening to Ed's story. The noise of the breath from his own lungs might have caused him to miss a word. He had so many questions, but Ed was such a methodical story teller, he was answering the questions before Joe posed them. It still surprised Joe that Ed was telling him all this without knowing all that much about him.

Sure, Joe thought, I said I was there to investigate the car accident and how it related to a forty year old murder, but that was just the story I had told. That might not have been true. Hadn't

Ed's years in jail taught him to be more suspicious?

Joe was becoming more and more convinced that Ed wanted a truer accounting of his life than Joe's father had given him and of the events before and after the murders. Ed was nearly sixty. Maybe he was afraid he wouldn't live that much longer and he didn't want his family to be remembered only for what he did. Even though that would probably be exactly what would happen, at least one person would know that Ed was a human being with parents, with a sister and with a conscience. Maybe dying and thinking he would only be remembered for eternity as a heinous murderer didn't sit well with Ed.

Joe was adamant about getting it right this time.

"Do you want to take a break?" Joe asked Ed, hoping he would say no.

"You are the one writing so furiously. Maybe you need a break," Ed replied back.

"No, I'm fine. Let's keep going."

The men had been in the room for the better part of five hours.

"So you jumped out the bedroom window and had cut your leg," Joe said. "Since you're not back in jail or dead, I assume nobody was there?"

"That's right. I ran once I made it into the woods. I wanted as much distance between the Wrin house and myself as I could get. I wasn't a big believer in karma, but I thought that house had really bad karma."

"I made the decision that I would not take the bag back to my house. There was just too much of a chance of Hoot or Bull showing up and tossing my home in search of the stuff. A neighbor on the street parallel to my house was old and in a nursing home. His detached garage was not locked and hadn't been since I returned from prison, and it was easy for me to step through a large hedge that shielded his garage from the road. The back door to the shed was open so I made use of it. After that, I never walked through the back of this man's property to get back to my house in case someone would wonder what I was doing there."

"No sooner had I returned home and cleaned up my leg than Bull showed up at my house. It was after nine at night. Bull must have been home when he learned that someone had been to the Wrin house."

"'Looks like someone was at the house you killed those cops in this evening,' he said to me after I let him in."

"'Really?' I said, as if I couldn't care less."

"'Wasn't you, I'll bet?'"

"'That's right,' I said."

"Bull didn't believe me, but not because there was a defect in my story. It's just that Bull had no other explanations, suspects or motives. He wasn't a deep thinker. His mind wasn't cluttered with other possible reasons. He didn't look at alternate scenarios. Sometimes that lack of reasoning got him into trouble. In this case his weak intellect and his lazy way of being a policeman served him well because he happened to be right."

Joe wasn't sure if he completely followed Ed's logic, but he let him go on.

"Bull was in no hurry and seemed to be taking his time. But something had changed. Bull seemed like he was less interested in the money and jewels for himself and more interested in solving the robbery and putting me back in jail to make people forget about the scandals that gripped his department and threatened the job he loved so much. He kept walking around my living room, peeking into the adjacent rooms as if he thought the bag would be sitting in the open."

"'I could have a warrant in two minutes and have this entire place tossed tonight. Would I find anything interesting?' he asked me. I said nothing."

"'I don't guess I would. You're too smart to bring it back here.'"

"Denying it was pointless. Saying nothing made more sense and might cause Bull to leave sooner. The crude bandage on the back of my leg was soaked with blood and in danger of falling off. Blood was already pooling in my shoes and threatened to seep through my new white sneakers. I guessed that the window I cut myself on might have some blood on it. Even someone as dim as Bull could put that together."

"Bull kept wandering around my house with a fake smile on his face to mask his anger and frustration. I knew he would have loved to try torturing it out of me. That's likely what he would have done if he hadn't had so much pressure on him and his department."

"'I'll be seeing you real soon,' Bull finally said to me and tipped his hat with mock sincerity as he walked out the door."

"I had certainly not anticipated someone coming by the Wrin house while I was there. I thought if I got there and got the stuff, no one would know. But now everybody knew that someone had been in there and I was sure that Hoot would find out very soon. I hadn't had a chance to even look through the bag to see what I had or to clean out the dirt and worthless rocks. It took all my restraint, but I decided to wait. After all, I'd waited for thirty-seven years. I could wait another two weeks if I needed to make sure I wasn't caught."

Joe stood up and grabbed the water pitcher off the table and headed for the bathroom to fill it up. He felt like he wanted a break before Ed revealed what he found in the bag.

Why was Ed telling me this in such intricate detail, Joe wondered again. Was he planning to bring his story to a publisher himself if I hadn't stopped by? Was he waiting for me? But then, Joe went on with his internal conversation, that couldn't be. I only decided to come here a few weeks ago myself. Joe stood in front of the mirror, gathered himself and then walked back out into the room. Ed had just been sitting there, completely quiet and still, while Joe was in the bathroom. What if he was going to get a publisher himself and was just using Joe for practice telling his story?

"Are you ready?" Ed asked.

"All set," Joe said, putting his worries aside. "So, what was in the bag?"

"Patience," Ed said. "Sure enough, Hoot had found out too, and he was at my house the next day. I knew if I denied it, Hoot wouldn't believe me and he might think I was ripping him off. That could be dangerous. Hoot would kill me out of spite if he didn't get his stuff. But if I'd told him I got it, he'd want to know where his share was or where I had stashed it. I definitely couldn't do that."

"I opened the front door for him, but wouldn't let him in."

"'So?' Hoot said, not bothering with any niceties. 'Where is it?'"

"'All I will tell you is that something was there, but I didn't have a chance to look through it. I will get you your share next week.'"

"'My share? Of what? What was there, goddamn it?' he yelled."

"'That's all I'm going to tell you,' I said."

"Hoot looked as if he could kill me right there. A big lumpy vein bulged out of his forehead like there was a bloodsucker worm under his skin. He was furious, but now he was yelling at me under his breath, in hushed tones, so as not to rile the neighborhood. He was trying to keep his composure, but was failing miserably."

"'I want my shit now,' he said."

"'In a few weeks,' I responded."

"The hatred in Hoot's eyes was enough to scare me, which is saying something since I'd had just spent that many years in prison with some of the worst criminals in the country. But I was no good to Hoot dead. If he killed me, he knew he'd never get his stuff. He started to threaten me, but I brazenly cut him off in mid sentence."

"'Save the threats. I'm not nineteen anymore.' With that I slammed the door in his face."

"I laid low for the next three days. I felt like a prisoner again because I was afraid to leave my house and I felt like I was being watched. The police cruisers driving up and down the street increased ten fold. Neighbors commented on how nice it was for the police to be so attentive. Only I knew the real reason they were there."

"I had a routine that I followed almost every night. Most of the lights in my house would go on at six p.m. Around eight all but the living room light and the glow of the TV could be seen from outside. Around ten the living room went dark and the bedroom light went on for a few minutes. Then, shortly after, the last light would be put out, signaling that I had gone to bed for the night. The night I would go to retrieve the stuff I would follow that exact routine, only I wouldn't get into bed. Instead I planned to walk in darkness down to the basement and go out the back door. Then I planned to walk through several back yards to get to the end of the street, where I would make a left and another left until I arrived at the shed."

"I knew that it was too soon and that I was taking a big risk, but

I had to get the stuff. I sensed the noose tightening. Hoot was getting ready to blow a gasket and Bull's public relations issues were getting more severe. Either's issues could be resolved if one of them got the stuff from me."

"My plan worked well until I made my first left and woke up a ferociously loud dog. The dog barked so aggressively, I almost ran, but decided against it when I saw a man in his boxer shorts standing on his back porch. I calmly backed into a hedge and let it close around me. The dog knew exactly where I was and if the man had let him off the leash, he would have found me instantly. The dog continued to bark. I watched the dog and the road intently. I was afraid the dog might raise the suspicions of the police who were monitoring the area. One call from a neighbor about a noisy dog in that area would have the place swarming with cops at Bull's insistence. The man went back inside with his dog, who continued to bark loudly. I darted across the yard, and four houses down the road, the dog was still at it."

"I made it to the shed, but on the way there I saw people looking out their windows. I saw a few lights go on and front doors open. The dog was still barking. While I may have been being paranoid, I was also really scared. Finally, I crawled to the shed, opened the door and went in. I was too terrified to use my flashlight. I felt around on the floor under the old workbench. I retrieved the bag and started to back out on my hands and knees when a pitchfork that had fallen off its perch on the pegboard wall stabbed me in the exact spot where I'd cut my thigh leaving the Wrin house. It hurt so much that I had to bite down on my arm to keep from screaming. Then it started to bleed. I remember saying whispering, 'Oh, God, give me a break, will ya?'"

"My leg was killing me and bleeding again, but I had the stuff.

I stood up and peered out the door to see if anything was stirring. The dog had stopped barking and things had gone back to normal, so I walked back to my house, keeping to the shadows as much as I could. I brought the bag to my basement where I could finally look through it, but that would require turning on a basement light and that would be a dead giveaway. I waited til morning."

"Early the next day, a hard rap on the door woke me. I went downstairs and Bull was standing there with his billy club out and that same smile on his face. He asked me if I had been roaming around the neighborhood the previous night."

"'No,' I said. I didn't know if he was fishing or if someone did call the cops after that dog made such a ruckus."

"'Here's what I'm gonna do,' Bull told me. 'I'm gonna find a way to bust you back to prison and then I'm gonna to make sure you stay there forever if you don't come clean to me. You got one week.'"

"I was nervous and I was in pain. I'd worn red sweat pants to bed. If I'd worn any other color, Bull would have seen the dried blood on my leg."

Joe interrupted. "Maybe by amping up the pressure, Bull thought he could force your hand."

Ed nodded and said, "Maybe. But as soon as Bull left, I went down into the basement and opened the bag. My memory had diminished the take. There was much more in the bag then I had thought. There wasn't much cash, but I counted forty-five pieces of jewelry that looked to be very valuable. One piece in particular stood out. It was a diamond necklace that draped down like lace. I guessed there had to be sixty diamonds on that one piece. I remember thinking, 'Oh, God, I hope this is real.'"

Among the necklaces, and bracelets, diamond laden watches, wallets and purses were smaller items like rings and broaches with inscriptions on them, deeply personal stuff, the real value of which was what was written on them. One silver heart shaped broach had two dates on it, April 13, 1938 – December 22, 1940, and the words "Baby Emily" etched on the back.

Joe noticed Ed's voice grew quieter as he talked about these items, as if he were trying to remember whom he had taken them from.

"I separated out the dirt and the worthless rocks from the stuff we had stolen. At first I was elated and then a second later I felt ashamed because of what these jewels had led to. So much pain and suffering were so directly linked to them that it was hard to be happy, but I was happy. I put everything back in the bag. My paranoia was growing and I felt the pressure increasing by the minute. I couldn't wait any longer."

"I got the roll of medical tape I bought for my injured thigh, but I had other ideas for it now. I taped several pieces of the jewelry to my uninjured leg. Hiding things on or in my body was another skill I'd perfected while in prison."

"You know, you haven't spoken much more about your prison years," Joe interjected.

"Yeah, and I don't plan to. Prison is boredom and humiliation followed by more boredom. I did, however, learn to be a criminal. I learned to fight and steal. I learned to be brutal when I had to be. Oddly enough, being a cop killer gave me a certain amount of prestige with the other inmates. If they'd known that I was scared, delirious and incredibly ashamed of what I done, they might not have accorded me the same respect."

"So what did you do all that time?"

"I kept to myself as much as I could and I read everything I could get my hands. I was determined not to let my life be a waste after all my parents had done for me."

Joe noticed that whenever Ed spoke of his parents, his voice got very low and almost too quiet to hear.

Ed shook his head back and forth as if to change the subject. "Where was I?" he asked.

"You had just taped the stuff to your leg."

"Right. I went outside and got in my truck and headed out. I reasoned that since Bull had just been there, I had a few minutes before another cruiser came by. By that time I'd be gone. Before leaving I taped the remaining pieces to the underside of an old table saw in my basement just in case anybody stopped by while I was out. I had made a list of pawn shops to visit, the closest being an hour outside Gold's Lake."

Joe smiled because he'd done exactly the same thing, but he decided against mentioning it to Ed right then.

"The first three I went to were not right. They each seemed to be too low end to move the kinds of goods I was interested in selling. I was starting to think that this wasn't the way to go about this, but since I had no other idea, I pushed on. The owner of the fourth pawn shop was hugely fat and in his mid fifties. He wasn't going to make it to sixty if he didn't so something, I remember thinking. Just moving his massive head seemed to take a tremendous effort. The store was strangely cold and yet this large man was sweating. He barely noticed me as I walked in and then he pretended to be uninterested in the earrings I showed him and only made a low end bid for them. He was so uninterested that it actually gave me hope."

Joe gave a quizzical look to Ed.

"I also learned the art of negotiation in prison," Ed said. "I looked at him with eyes that said, I'm not the kind of guy you want to screw with. It was a look I'd perfected over those thirty-seven years. I have a prison tattoo on my left wrist and I pulled my shirt up far enough so the shop owner could see it."

"'Is this it or is there more?' he asked me sheepishly."

"'There could be,' I said."

"'Well, I'm not the right buyer for these, but I know who might be.'"

"'You got a name, I asked him coldly."

"'I'll try to get him on the phone.'" The man got off his stool with great difficulty and went into the back room and made a phone call."

"The area behind the counter was completely hidden by black drapes. I could only imagine it was a stock room filled with all kinds of stolen merchandise. I looked around the store and saw glass case after glass case filled with jewelry, none of which was close to as nice as the stuff I bought in. It looked like old estate items, probably stolen, I surmised, just like the stuff I brought in."

As Joe listened, he couldn't help but wonder if they had both been to the same pawnshops.

"I could hear the man explaining the earrings to another man on the phone. I heard words like 'clear,' 'antique cut' and 'huge.' I was getting excited, but was doing my best not to show it."

"The man waddled back and said, 'I'm authorized to offer you ten grand for these.'"

"I was shocked, but did a masterful job of not looking surprised. I made no counter bid. I just stared at the man as if I was unimpressed. It was another skill my years in prison had honed. The first offer was never the best."

"'Okay, twelve grand,' the man said."

"I let him squirm for a few more seconds and then I finally spoke. 'Let's go with the ten grand, but I want it in cash and I may have other pieces. Is your friend a buyer for more of this kind of stuff?'"

"The fat man seemed to brighten up a bit. 'If you are going to continue to be so reasonable, absolutely,' he said."

"I was pretty sure I could shop these pieces around to several different pawnshops and haggle to get the best price, but I was motivated to get the deal done quickly and quietly. I would have loved to find a single buyer who understood discretion to sell all the pieces to at once. I was also aware that I could be being set up, but I was out of time and out of options. The man may have just pretended to call some deep-pocketed buyer and had actually called the police and was trying to get me to bring all the jewelry in there at once so they could arrest me and recover the stolen merchandise. Maybe he figured he'd get a handsome reward. I realized there was no way that he could legally pay me cash now. How did he know I wasn't a cop working under cover on a sting operation? I was surprised at how trusting the pawnshop owner was of me. Then I realized my tattoo might have made him think I was one of them."

"I asked how quickly he could make this deal happen. The man went back to the phone and told me to come back in an hour. Everything was going too well. I was getting the feeling that everything could come crashing down on me."

"When I returned, I hadn't un-taped any more jewelry in case I was the victim of a sting or worse, a robbery. A thin man in a dark, wrinkled suit with a jewelry loop attached to his eyeglasses greeted me coolly from behind the counter. He had a beard that looked to never have been groomed. Personal hygiene was real high on his list, I thought. They made an interesting sight together, the fat man and this thin sloppy one."

"The pawnshop owner now had a self-satisfied look on his face.

He stood to make some good cash for facilitating the deal, I figured. The pencil neck geek with the loop extended his hand, not to shake, but to get the diamond earrings. I handed them to him. He looked at them and then looked at the shopkeeper and nodded. The shopkeeper handed me an envelope containing ten thousand dollars cash."

"'What else have you got?' the geek asked me."

"I was still not convinced that I was in the clear, so I kept going outside, getting in my truck, driving away for five minutes and then driving back to make them think that I had the stuff stashed nearby and not on my person. Each time I went in, we went through the same routine of the thin man viewing each piece through his loop and then making me an offer that I quickly accepted, the fat man going in the back room and coming out with another envelope full of money."

"No sooner had I gotten rid of most of the jewelry than I started to worry that I might get mugged with all this money in my truck. I kept up the charade of driving away and then coming back so that they might think I had someone else with me watching my back. Each time I brought a piece of jewelry in they had no problem giving me large amounts of cash. I wondered if I brought double the amount of jewelry in, would they have been able to keep paying me? It occurred to me that the thin guy was representing someone else, someone with very deep pockets and probably also well connected and well protected. I was fairly sure I was dealing with some version of organized crime. By the time I left the pawnshop, I had sold eight pieces and had a bag full of cash totaling $105,000."

"I left the pawnshop and went straight to a bank forty-five minutes outside of Gold's Lake. I opened up a checking account with $500 and also opened four safety deposit boxes. I neatly placed all the money in the boxes, save one thousand dollars. I left the bank feeling as if every eye was on me. I needed cash and contemplated asking the bank teller to break up the hundred dollar bills, but was afraid that might clue her in to what had been in my bag. I was now weighing every move I made. People were going to find out what I was up to. It was just a matter of when. I got back in my truck and looked at that money in my hand. I was fifty-seven years old and as far as I could remember, I'd never held a hundred dollar bill."

Joe smiled. "That must have felt pretty good."

Ed went into one of his reflective stares and looked out the motel window for a minute.

"Yeah, well, I guess if you could say that if any of this awful story was good, that was about it. It felt good to have pulled it off. Now I had to figure out how I was going to get Hoot his money and or his jewelry. I had just successfully converted a small portion of it to cash without raising any suspicions. I didn't think Hoot would do as well and might bring the whole thing down. I decided that I would convert it for Hoot and give him the cash. This would be a decision that almost cost me life."

"For the next few days, I returned to the pawnshop and each time the fat man and the thin man were there to meet me. Each time I left with a bag full of money and returned to the bank."

"I did my level best to divide the jewelry up evenly. I put the jewelry for Hoot into a canvas bag. I hid his share under the table saw. I was afraid to put too much high-end jewelry on the market at once. It was likely to raise suspicions. I wanted to fly as far under the radar as I could. I wasn't a jeweler and had no way of assessing the stuff. And I wasn't even sure whose share was worth more. I did keep the big necklace for myself. If one of us was going to get more then the other, it should not be Hoot. He hadn't spent thirty-seven years in prison. His sister hadn't been confined to a hellhole. I was the one who kept the secret for so long and the thought of doing something good with money was a thought that would never cross Hoot's mind."

"I sold Hoot's share and put the cash in safety deposit boxes at a different bank. My plan would be to put the money in the boxes and then give Hoot the box numbers and the keys to them. That way I wouldn't be there when Hoot got his money, and the chance of Hoot shooting me would be greatly reduced. I stuffed five safety deposit boxes for Hoot with $338,000. He didn't deserve it. He'd waste it on booze and girls, but a deal is a deal."

"That's a lot of money," Joe said incredulously

"Half the loot from the robbery had been converted and half was still in my basement. I was halfway home. The scandal surrounding Bull was still raging. The newspaper reported the same day that I converted Hoot's jewelry that one of Bull's cops was on video having sex with a prostitute and snorting cocaine. He had taken the video himself and had kept it at his own house. A jilted girlfriend dropped it off at the newspaper. There had been a steady stream of bad news surrounding the department for three straight weeks, but Bull hadn't been implicated directly. Somebody was protecting him. The question was how long could that last. I believed that if it hadn't been for that scandal, Bull would have been harassing me day and night. Maybe my luck was finally changing."

"Getting Hoot his money and out of my life was the next challenge. I really didn't know where to find him although I was pretty sure he was watching my house. I really didn't want to wait around for Hoot to find me again. The walls were closing in and I had to move. I decided to make myself visible around my home and see if Hoot approached. It didn't take long."

"As I made my way back home after visiting the banks and the pawnshops, I noticed an old man fast asleep in a beat up car with the side panels rusting out. When I first saw him, I thought he might be dead, but the sound of my car startled him awake. Hoot must have been sleeping for a while because it took him several seconds to get his bearings and I saw he'd been drooling down the front of his filthy shirt. I pulled up to his car so both drivers' side windows were facing each other."

"Both of us rolled our windows down. I just stared. Was I really going to make this wreck of a man who ruined my life rich? This man who had so willingly and happily ruined so many lives? Who had beaten up so many, humiliated so many, violated so many."

Joe heard the combination of rage and disgust rising up in Ed's voice.

"He was a bad dude. There was no getting away from that. I could have easily rationalized not giving him the money or not giving him a fair share. As I was about to speak, another thought came to me. Since Hoot couldn't validate if what he was about to receive was actually half or not, or even somewhere south of half, would he take my word for it? Would he just automatically assume he'd been ripped off? Hoot only dealt with scummy people. Most everybody he'd known his whole life would have eagerly ripped him off. The concept of my being fair because I had given my word was completely foreign to him."

"The transaction was never supposed to have been done in public. I had an idea that I would meet Hoot at some restaurant way outside of town to make the exchange. But we were both there and I wanted Hoot out of my life forever. I decided on the spot that now was the time."

"'I recovered the stuff,' I said without any type of greeting. 'I converted it to cash and divided it up equally. I've put yours in safety deposit boxes.'"

"Hoot stared, skeptical, but hoping what I was saying was true."

"'How much is it?' he asked."

"'A lot. More than you deserve.'"

"Hoot didn't appreciate the insult, but the good news allowed him to look past it."

"'How do I get it?'"

"'First, I want to make sure that you are out of my life forever.' I knew it was a pointless statement," Ed said, looking directly at Joe. "Hoot was a skilled liar. Of course, he would agree, but that didn't mean much. He'd see how much I put in the boxes for him so he'd know that I had gotten at least as much. That made me a robbery target for Hoot. Imagine that, stealing the same stuff twice, forty years apart."

"Naturally Hoot swore up and down that I would never see him again. He'd have sworn he was the Pope if it got him closer to his money. He looked like he probably didn't have a penny left to his name. I removed an envelope from my shirt pocket and tossed it dismissively at Hoot. It contained the bank address, five keys and a list of box numbers."

"'The boxes are good for six months,' I told him. 'You better get it out of there before then.'"

"With that, I rolled up my window and drove away. I hoped I would never see Hoot again, but my gut told me differently."

"With Hoot placated and Bull's scandal still raging, I felt I could afford to lay low before cashing in the rest of the stuff. Whoever was buying it would certainly be reselling it for a profit. Somehow news of all this expensive jewelry on the market would raise questions. I'd been away for most of the day to convert Hoot's take.

Bull's guys may have noticed my absence and would be ready if I disappeared again. I could have made a strong case for moving quickly, but moving slow won the day."

Ed's mood became somber as he began telling Joe the next part of the story.

"Just as it seemed that Bull's world was collapsing, the clouds parted and the sun came out. The cop who had been caught on the video had fallen on his sword for the whole department, but mostly for Bull. He admitted to being the only one involved and that no one else in the department had any knowledge of it. It reeked of a cover up, but it seemed to calm the populace and the offending cop was placed on leave and probably would eventually be fired. Rumors that a deal had been cut ran rampant and most of the community felt that Bull's supporters had orchestrated it."

"No sooner had the scandal lifted than Bull was back in my life. He could be seen sitting out in front my house. He'd sit there until he was sure I had seen him and then drive on. He made it clear that he wasn't going to let up until he got what he wanted."

"It was probably a mistake on Bull's part. I had been starting to relax a little, but the sight of him sitting outside my house got me on my toes again."

"I had been able to convert the rest of the jewelry to cash, with the exception of the big diamond necklace. Despite my best effort to divide the stuff up equally, I had taken a bigger share by twenty thousand dollars plus the diamond necklace. I felt it was the luck of the draw and had no intention of looking up Hoot to tell him of the error."

"I put the money in a safe deposit box. I felt a great relief to have gotten the jewelry out of the Wrin house and converted it to cash successfully. When I first started, I gave myself a fifty-fifty chance of pulling it off. The key had been finding a willing buyer so easily. Several things had worked out well for me in the last few weeks, but the skeptical side of me didn't expect it to last. I was afraid an anvil would fall on my head. The anvil did fall, and it came in the form of a cherry red Porsche a little over a week later."

# Chapter Nineteen

"I had noticed the car as I was pulling onto my street. The car seemed out of place because it was such an expensive car in my modest neighborhood. I drove past it and didn't think much of it. I pulled my truck into my driveway, got out and headed to my front door. As I walked around my truck, the Porsche pulled in behind me. It was Hoot, with a big smile on his face. My first instinct was to be completely pissed to see him again. Then I thought he just wanted to show me his new toy, as if I was someone he would want to share an exciting event with in his life."

"He couldn't possibly think we were friends, I remember thinking."

"Hoot motioned to me. Maybe he just wanted to thank me for my honesty, I laughed to myself. It wasn't hard to figure what Hoot had done with some of the money. The Porsche looked good, but not new. I figured it was hot."

"I walked over to the passenger side door. I walked very slowly as if part of me was saying don't go. Hoot leaned over and pushed the door open rather than just rolling down the window. I contemplated making some small talk but was not in the mood, so I just stared at him."

"'You like it?' he asked me.

"'What do you want?' I said.

"'Let's go for a ride.'"

"'No thanks.'"

An awful feeling came over me as I looked into that beaten up face. I could tell he had something on his mind other than showing me his car.

"'We had an agreement,' I said to him and reminded him he'd agreed to stay out of my life."

"'Get in so we can talk about it,' he said."

I told him to leave me alone and get out of my driveway. Hoot pulled out a small handgun and pointed it at me. His big smile had disappeared, replaced by a sneer.

"'Get in the fucking car or I'll drop you right here.'"

"I had actually smiled when he first pulled out the gun. It struck me as funny. Maybe only because I had been stupid enough to think he might honor any kind of agreement."

"I realized it wasn't a joke, though, and a feeling of resignation came over me. Life was just not going to let me win or give me another chance. I wasn't scared when I got into the car with a gun pointed at me. His hands were so wrinkled and shaky that I was pretty sure I would have been able to run before he could have gotten a shot off. I wondered if he even had enough strength to pull the trigger while holding the gun up. I'm still not sure why I got in the car. I remember thinking this is where it started, so this is where it should end. We were not going to be able to coexist."

"Once inside his car, I thought maybe I could overpower him, but I suddenly felt annoyed with myself for wasting my life. Would I live through the day? Suddenly I wasn't sure. Probably not. I regretted that I'd made such a mess of the life my parents had tried to give me. I regretted that my sister might have to live out her days as she'd lived them for the last forty years. I'd never loved a woman. I'd never had kids. I'd never done anything to help anybody. It was likely that I'd end up dead soon with a bullet in my head. It would make the papers and then I'd be gone forever."

"Now, in retrospect, the thoughts I was having with that gun pointed at me made sense. There was no getting around what I'd done or what I'd become. If I was going to die, those were the things I regretted. I just sat there as Hoot backed out. Once we were moving down the street, he stuck the gun in his pocket. That seemed strange."

"Now there was no question that I could overpower him if I wanted to. I remember thinking how pathetic he was, almost senile. Did he still see himself as the powerful hulk of a man he used to be? He was almost laughable. I asked him where we were going."

"'For a ride.' he said, although I got the feeling he had no real idea of where he was going or what his plans were for me. Then I wondered what Hoot had found out. I wondered if somehow he learned that I had gotten a bigger share of the loot or if he remembered something from the robbery that I hadn't told him. I couldn't imagine what it was, but I was about to find out."

"'I want the rest of the money,' Hoot snarled in his raspy voice and with his stinking breath."

"'And you think I'm just going to give it to you? Why in the world would I do that?' I asked with a disgusted laugh. 'I already gave you a lot more than you deserve.'"

"It was obvious to me that Hoot hadn't thought anything out, but then that started to worry me. I thought he might just shoot me out of frustration."

"'I want the money,' he repeated, as if he was a spoiled child and by repeatedly saying the same thing, he could get me to give in."

"'Do you really think I would give it to you?' I asked him, shaking my head as if in disbelief."

"'That's right. Or you're done.'"

"'I'd rather be dead than give you the rest of the money,' I said bravely, but the truth was I didn't think Hoot would want my blood on the inside of his car. As long as I was in the car, I thought I was pretty safe. Although I was a little concerned about Hoot's weakened state of mind, his kidnapping me wasn't working out the way Hoot had hoped. Beyond demanding the money, he had no plan. He must have known that I would never trust him to keep his word.

"'Oh, you're going to give it to me,' Hoot kept saying. 'You're going to be begging me to take it before I'm done with you.'"

"Hoot's attempts at scaring me were pathetic. I'm sure I even had a thin smile on my face. He lacked the physical strength that had been his hallmark for so long. His wit, which hadn't been that keen to begin with, seemed to be slipping fast as well. I figured that I could incapacitate him with a quick chop to the throat, but a part of me wanted to see where this little trip was going to take us."

"Hoot turned the car onto route 100 and started to speed up. The speed limit was 40 miles per hour and Hoot reached that quickly and had it up to 60 a few seconds after. Was he trying to scare me by driving fast? It wasn't going to work. Up ahead was a stop sign at the highway crossing in front of us. We were cruising along at 70 miles an hour and Hoot didn't seem to be slowing down. At first I thought maybe he was just showing me how fast the car could go and how well it handled."

"Hoot started glancing over at me to see if I was scared, I guess. As the stop sign approached, I was getting a little nervous because Hoot was in such poor physical condition that he wouldn't be able to stop quickly enough if a car was coming across the intersection. I was afraid that Hoot had overestimated his own physical abilities. The oncoming cars must have seen the cherry red Porsche from a distance screaming at them because they all had stopped to let us pass."

"'Hoot looked over at me as if to say, you see how crazy I am. Now give me the money. He slowed after the intersection and repeated that he wanted the rest of the money."

"I calmly said, 'No way.'"

"Infuriated, Hoot stood on the gas pedal. We got to 90 miles an hour when the rear of an eighteen wheel oil tanker came into sight in the distance. We were on a two lane highway that was about to converge down into one lane. A few widely spaced, modest homes were set back from the road, but beyond them were only acres of fields. Telephone poles lined the highway on the right side. I looked around us to see if any other cars were there, but there were none. Just us and the oil truck, getting closer by the second. I hadn't put my seat belt on when I got into the car and I wasn't going to do it now. That would have been an admission that I was scared."

"Hoot shouted over at me, 'You want to play chicken with me? We'll see who has the balls.'"

"Hoot approached the back of the oil truck and attempted to pass on the right. Passing on the left would have been logical and safe because there was no oncoming traffic. He would have to push the car well over 100 miles an hour if we were going to make it around the truck on the right hand side. I was scared now. Hoot was out of control and I think he was just starting to realize it, too."

"The truck wasn't slowing and the lane was ending way too quickly. The Porsche came even with the rear end of the truck as the truck pulled to the right. The trucker never even saw the Porsche. Hoot's maniacal laugh suddenly stopped. He knew that he was getting ready for a sharp, sudden, and violent crash. He must have realized that not only was he not going to get any more money, he wasn't going to be around to spend any more of his own."

"The Porsche hit the telephone pole squarely on Hoot's side. Six inches more toward the center of the car and we both would have been dead. The stop was abrupt and complete. The front end collapsed like an accordion and forced the firewall and the dashboard into the driver's seat. The steering wheel speared Hoot in the chest, crushing all his ribs and breaking his neck and several vertebrae.

"The front windshield, instead of shattering, simply flew off and away from the impact in one piece. There was no glass. Smoke started spewing from the rear engine compartment and a thick stream of oil was oozing out from under the car."

"The force of the crash had exploded the passenger side door open and sent me flying out. So many aspects of the crash could have and should have ended my life. As the metal tore and ripped around me, all my limbs were imperiled. My head could have smashed into the metal frame of the car, decapitating me instantly. The jarring impact could have caused all my organs to rupture. My leg, ankles, femurs and pelvis all should have been shattered. Instead I was thrown clear. I rolled a few feet and then I turned to see the wreckage just as the top of the telephone pole broke off with a whiplash effect and fell straight down. Hoot's head was pinned between the dashboard and his seat and his face was turned toward where I was lying on the grass. His eyes opened in a kind of startled look. Our eyes met in that split second before the telephone pole came down. I'd like to say I saw in that look regret for what he had done to me, but I didn't. I also don't think he noticed the pity in my eyes for such a pathetic man."

"I watched the telephone pole coming down as if it were happening in slow motion. Hoot wasn't going to survive and I just watched the events unfold. There wasn't anything I could or would have done anyway. The full force and weight of the pole came crashing straight down through the top of the car and ripped through the roof as if it wasn't there. It came down squarely on Hoot's head, crushing it."

Joe was mesmerized. "Are you telling me the dead body was Hoot's and they thought it was you? He's short and you are tall," Joe said incredulously.

"Let me finish," Ed said to Joe. "Hoot was very dead. The semi never stopped. To this day he doesn't know what happened. Maybe he had his radio up too loud or was talking on his cell phone and didn't see the horrific crash in his rearview mirror. Maybe he was only looking on his left side where the passing cars should have been."

"No one was around. A small fire had started under the car. I think the gas line had ruptured. When I get nervous, I play with my ID necklace, and I had gotten so nervous that I had ripped it off before the crash and left it in the car. I considered trying to get it, afraid that the police would know I was in the car with a known criminal and that I'd be sent back to prison. I got up off the ground, still stunned, but uninjured. I approached the car, but the fire was spreading rapidly. The carnage that was Hoot hardly resembled a body anymore. His head was gone, literally driven into his abdomen. That's when the idea of my being thought dead came to me. I knew it was a long shot. I took out my wallet and put it on the ground near the driver's side door. I looked around again. No one was watching or coming down the highway in either direction. I couldn't get my ID chain so I started to back away, getting ready to run, when I saw a bag in the back seat. It was a canvas bag like the ones I'd seen at the bank. I reached in through the flames and grabbed it and headed for the woods."

Joe was rapidly running his fingers through his hair while contemplating the accident.

"How did you survive a crash like that? And you weren't even hurt? I saw that burned out car. You should be dead. For God's sake, you were in the death seat. Why weren't you sent through the windshield?" Joe was almost screaming.

Ed stopped a minute. "I have a theory, if you want to hear it."

"Oh, please," Joe said sarcastically. He had gotten up and had started pacing around the room as if he weren't sure he should believe this story.

"As I told you before, I'm not a religious man, but on that day I think God had had enough of Hoot Gibbons. The man had been a menace all his life. He ruined lives wherever he went. He was bad, through and through. Maybe the money was the last chance God was going to give him, and when he screwed that chance up, God said 'enough.' If the crash didn't get him, God sent the telephone pole, and if He missed with that, He knew the fire wouldn't miss. He was right."

Ed stopped and stared at Joe to measure his reaction, but Joe said nothing.

"And for the same reasons, I think He spared me. I wasn't a bad person. I had done something awful and not a day had gone by when I didn't still feel badly for what I had done. But I was a kid who had had a lot of bad luck. Even in prison I stayed out of trouble. I tried to be as good as I could be. God knows I wouldn't be a bad person if given another chance. I think He thinks I deserve it."

With that Ed went silent. Joe had just seen a part of Ed that no one had ever seen. He was a guy who had been denied a life because of a mistake. He accepted his crime and now wanted a life to atone for his sins. Was that too much to ask?

"How much of Hoot's money was left?" Joe asked.

"About $75,000. That means he blew through 263 grand in less than two weeks. He mentioned to me before the accident that he got the Porsche for $55,000 and it was in fact hot. He got it from a chop shop over in Glens Falls from a prison buddy of his. He was also a gambler and a womanizer, although by the looks of him any woman who would go near him would have to be paid well. I also noticed he was wearing a Rolex watch when he picked me up in the Porsche."

"I guess you could run through a couple hundred grand pretty quickly if you weren't careful," Joe said.

"I could hear the sirens in the distance from the emergency vehicles headed to the crash. I remembered thinking, 'Don't hurry, guys. There's nothing anyone can do.' I kept feeling my own body, taking a physical inventory of what could possibly be broken. Maybe I was in bad shape, but the adrenaline was keeping me going. But no, I was fine, unscathed, un-bloodied, and very much alive."

"So there I was again, trying to make my way through to the woods to get back to safety. So much of my life had been lived out of view of the pubic, in the shadows. I wondered would I ever be able to walk down Main Street with my face turned toward the sun? Was that too much to ask?"

"I arrived home about an hour later. I hid Hoot's money in the shed across the street while mine was still tucked safely away in the bank. I was too afraid to put his in the basement. It also occurred to me, as I made my way toward the basement door, that since Hoot was dead now, I couldn't stay at my own house very much longer. The police would surely come to investigate. But investigate what? I lived alone and now I was thought to be dead. One thing I knew for sure. When Bull Junior found out I was dead, he was going to do a thorough sweep of my house to see if he could find what he'd been trying to get from me for so long. I wished I hadn't left my wallet under the car. The ID necklace would have been enough for them to identify the body, but it would have taken them a few days. Once they found that wallet, they'd be at my house soon after. I hoped the wallet was lost in the fire."

"I went inside and took the remaining items from the robbery including the necklace as well as a few items that I didn't want to lose and headed back to the shed. I thought I'd stay there for a day and watch my home. To my surprise no one stopped, and there was a precipitous drop off in the number of police cars cruising the neighborhood."

"The accident made the early edition of the paper the very next day, but with no mention of my name. A picture of the car graced the entire first page above the fold. One would have to look very carefully to identify the mangled mess as a Porsche. The fire had burned all the paint off the car and left it looking as if it was rusted. Everything that could burn was reduced to ashes. I wondered if the fire hadn't consumed the wallet too. Maybe it would take them longer to identify the body, I thought. The article did mention that the VIN number had been removed and that it was most likely a stolen car. But no mention of the dead man. That made sense to me. They wouldn't have had time to do an autopsy. I wondered if it wouldn't take a few days."

"After a full day of sitting in that small dank shed, I decided to move to a motel for a while. I needed a place that wouldn't ask for

ID and where I could pay cash. I knew of just the place. It had a bad reputation when I was a kid and time hadn't improved it. It was a worn out Scottish Inn off the exit ramp from the highway. It was clean, but badly in need of remodeling. I couldn't have a cared less. It was many steps up from the prison I had lived in most of my life."

"My first morning there, I walked to the main rental office in hopes of finding a newspaper. There was a pile of them sitting on the front counter. I reached for one and the young lady behind the counter said with a smile, 'It's free to our renters.'"

Joe smiled. It was such a small point and really not relevant to Ed's story, but Joe thought that Ed now really wanted to give him the flavor of what that motel was like. Joe realized Ed had been teaching him a thing or two, even if inadvertently, about telling a story.

"I thanked her and sat down on a chair in the lobby to look it over. The story had come off the front page by then, but I found the article easily enough buried among all of the small stories that required follow up. As I looked at it, I didn't try to read it, I just scanned it for any mention of my name. There was no mention of Hoot, the actual dead man, and they said little about me besides giving my name."

Joe realized that, 340 miles away in New Jersey, he had read the same story.

"I left the hotel only once and that was to pawn the rest of the jewelry. I was getting more and more uncomfortable with using the same pawnshop even though everything had been working out well. I was afraid, though, that if this was organized crime, they might tire of spending all this cash and just rob me, put a bullet in my head and bury me in a shallow grave. But it was a chance I just had to take. I called my contact there to arrange another visit. He couldn't hide the glee in his voice that I was coming back and I knew he was salivating at another payday for himself. He asked me how many items I was bringing, but what he really wanted to know was how much money would his partner have to bring."

"'I've got about a dozen items and one extraordinary item,' I told him. I would be there in an hour. He hesitated, but I jumped in and told him it was in one hour or I was going somewhere else. Of course, I had nowhere else to go, but he didn't know that. He started to panic and then agreed. Maybe he had more juice than I anticipated or maybe he was making a commitment he couldn't keep. Either way I was on my way to his shop."

"In the past, I kept leaving the pawn shop to go get the rest of the stuff from some imaginary hiding place so he wouldn't think I had it all with me or that I was working with someone else. It was a hedge against getting robbed. But this time I stopped about a mile and half from his shop, wrapped the necklace in a dirty rag and hid it carefully beneath a large rock on a stone wall surrounding a farm by the side of the road. The area was well hidden and I made sure I wasn't seen."

Joe chimed in. "So you hid the necklace beneath a rock again. Interesting."

Ed smiled and resumed his story.

"The fat pawnshop dealer and the thin geek were there again in the same spots. The thin one didn't say hello. He just stood there with his jeweler's loop in and his hand out. He seemed annoyed that I couldn't be more accommodating to his schedule. Every time I had been in the store in the past, I was always the only customer. This time there were two large men paying no attention to me, but were seemingly interested in some antique china dolls. Here we go,

I thought. I contemplated running but if they were there to rob me or worse, they probably had someone outside in case I ran."

"The fat pawnshop owner picked up on my uneasiness. He told me they were just bodyguards for the jeweler who often carried around large sums of money."

"'Hey! You two. Scram,' he said."

"With that they walked outside. They both had looked me over as they headed for the door. I was pretty sure I recognized one of them from prison. I felt a little better now that they were outside, but not much. They could always grab me as I left."

"I started handing the jeweler my pieces and he kept offering me cash, most of which I accepted on his first offer. At one point he went too low and I rejected his bid. I told him I didn't appreciate him low balling me. He reconsidered and we agreed quickly. I was setting the stage for the necklace. Once we finished, I had an enormous bag of cash in my hand."

"'I understand you have another piece,' the thin man said. 'Let me see it.'"

"I didn't tell him if I had it or not, but I did tell him I had had it appraised at $225,000 and if he agreed that it was that valuable, he would be able to buy it today."

"You had it appraised?" Joe asked.

"No. But I had to fake it."

"He asked if I'd be willing to offer him a discount. I told him yes, I would give it to him for $165,000 today only. He told me to come back in an hour, which was perfect for me because it would give me time to get to a bank and stash the rest of the money. The two goons were sitting on their car hood when I emerged from the pawnshop. I wondered if I had the necklace with me, would they have jumped me. Before I left, I told the two guys behind the counter that I'd be happier if the two guys were gone when I returned."

"Why'd you give him such a huge discount?" Joe asked.

"I was thinking on my feet. I figured if I gave them such a good deal, they wouldn't need to rob me. It was like I was already getting robbed by giving them such a great deal."

"But you didn't even know what it was worth," Joe said incredulously.

Ed smiled. "Thirty-seven years in prison teaches a man how to be convincing."

"I returned to the wall, uncovered the necklace, careful that I hadn't been followed and headed back to the store. The goons were gone and so was the car they were sitting on. Maybe the jeweler told them to take a ride for a few hours or maybe they told them to remain out of sight until the deal was made. If I could pull this last transaction off without getting killed, I would be amazed."

"I walked in. Both men were sitting, obviously waiting for me. The thin man seemed especially eager to see what I had. I pulled the necklace out of the rag and showed it to him. His face lit up. By his expression I got the feeling that I had undersold it. He counted the diamonds. There were 32, 16 large ones and 16 smaller ones. He nodded his head and the fat man went into the back behind the black curtain. He made a phone call and in two minutes the goons were back. Maybe they will just take the necklace and not kill me, I thought. Neither of the men behind the counter tried to make me any more comfortable. They could see how uneasy I was. The goons walked up to me, and put two large sacks on the counter in front of me and then walked out. For the fist time since I'd been dealing with the jeweler, I saw him smile."

"Who deals in that much cash?" Joe asked.

"I guess people who deal in hot diamonds," Ed responded.

Joe put his pad down and rubbed his eyes, more to calm his amazement than to wipe the tiredness from his eyes.

"So you were rid of Hoot and you had a ton of cash. Things were going pretty good for you."

"Yep," Ed said. He got up and started to roam around the room.

"Am I the only person who knows you're not dead?" Joe asked.

"You were until you started pedaling that broach around a week and a half ago. Now the only person in the world I didn't want to have know that I was still alive will have figured it out."

"Bull Junior?"

"You got it."

"How would he have put it together?"

"The best I can figure is that when you gave the broach to the damn jeweler, someone recognized it as a piece stolen from the country club. It doesn't make any sense to me how they would have done that, but that's the best I can figure."

"It makes sense to me," Joe said. "As a piece of bad luck, I brought the piece to the very jewelry store that designed and created the piece. It was their signature piece. I probably would have been arrested except that the dumb ass son of the original owner was too dim to indentify the piece before returning it to me. I found it easily enough in a catalogue in the library, though. The jewelers must have reported it to the police. Since Bull Senior and Bull Junior both thought there was a connection between the two crimes, and Junior knew the house had been broken into shortly after I got out of jail, that confirmed it."

Joe thought Ed seemed unconvinced.

"Think about it," Joe continued. "You come back to town after thirty-seven years. Shortly thereafter the Wrin place is broken into and a piece from the robbery turns up."

Joe realized that in a way, it was his fault that Bull could have put it together, even if he put it together wrong and thought that Ed had been there, not Ed and Joe.

"I'm sorry, Ed. I found that broach and really wanted to know what I had."

Ed seemed to harbor no anger at Joe for mucking up the plan. Joe thought it was almost as if he still expected something to go wrong.

"So why aren't you back in jail?" Joe suddenly asked.

"For what? Impersonating a dead person? And if I go back to jail, Bull would never get his reward for all his years of shitty service to the town of Gold's Lake."

"How did he find you if you were living in that motel?"

"I would return home periodically to see if anything was happening at my house. There was no activity there and it looked like there hadn't been any, so I came back to get some pictures of my family. I'd been going in and out without a problem. I would come back and stay for a few hours and still no one interrupted me. On my fourth trip down, I walked in the house and Bull Junior was sitting in my living room, wearing his street clothes, drinking one of my Black Label beers. He had a grin on his face that he couldn't contain."

"'So you're not so dead,' Bull said to me, still grinning at me before breaking off into his rough laugh."

"Bull told me about how much he admired what I had tried to do and how I had almost gotten away with it, but he said his 'keen intellect' had been up to the challenge. I had to laugh. Then he told me he would almost feel badly about having to send me back to prison."

"As soon as Bull heard that they had found my ID bracelet in the car, he took over the investigation. He realized pretty quickly once they got the body to the morgue that it wasn't me. He'd seen me many times in prison so he knew I wasn't as short and squat as Hoot. Even though the body was all charred up and had no face, he was pretty sure it wasn't me. It wasn't hard for him to cancel the autopsy. Having people think I was dead might work well for him, he probably assumed."

"'It was that worthless son-of-a-pig Hoot, wasn't it?' Bull said with a huge smile. 'Some of my guys reported that they'd seen him around a few times lately and guess what? No one can seem to find him now. I wonder why,' he asked me with all the sarcasm he could muster."

"I thought about running, but I wouldn't have gotten too far. I wasn't sure if Bull was there to arrest me or to make an offer that would exchange my freedom for the jewelry."

"'Where's the stuff? And don't lie to me. People already think you're dead so if you were to meet with an unfortunate accident, you'd be buried without a name. No one would be looking for you. I'm pretty sure I'd get away it.'"

Ed looked away from Joe before he changed gears a little.

"I had always hoped to be reunited with my parents in death," Ed said, "so Bull's comment about being buried anonymously really bothered me."

"I asked him why he couldn't just leave me alone, and then wished I hadn't. I knew why. Because Bull was a greedy, crappy human being, just like his father, who felt he deserved more than he was getting out of this town."

"'I will leave you alone,' Bull said, 'just as soon as you give me what you stole from those nice people all those years ago.'"

"I realized that Bull was not yet aware that I'd converted all the jewelry except the necklace to cash."

"'You see,' Bull said, 'I win either way. If you don't give me the money, I arrest you and I become a hero for solving a forty year old robbery. Remember there ain't no statute of limitations since you've gone and done something in continuance of the original crime. It's like you did it yesterday. And I can easily prove you were in that house again because of the blood on the window.'"

"The grin returned to Bull's face and he started laughing as if he was just so extremely impressed with himself. His big belly was bouncing up and down like Jello."

"Then he stopped laughing and looked me straight in the face and said, 'You can go back to prison for the rest of your sorry life or you can remain free. Either way you're never gonna see that stuff again.'"

"I felt beaten."

Joe looked away so as not to witness Ed's embarrassment.

"Finally I said to Bull, 'I'll get it for you, but it will take some time and I need your word that you will leave me alone for the rest of my life.'"

"'Of course,' he agreed in a very friendly way. 'Once I got all the money, I won't have no more use for you,' he said and he started laughing again. 'You got one week.' A snarl appeared on Bull's face as he got up, with some difficulty, and left."

"I realized something at that point. No matter what I did, if I stayed around here, he was never going to leave me alone."

# Chapter Twenty

J oe didn't know much about writing or journalism, but he had heard that it was wrong of a journalist to become part of his own story. Well, Joe realized, he was certainly part of this one. Should he stand back and see where the story led or should he see if he could help Ed. He was, after all, partially responsible for Ed getting caught.

Both men were tired of being in the hotel room, but it seemed risky to go out. They ordered food from room service again.

"So what are you going to do?" Joe asked after they'd eaten.

"I don't know."

"Maybe you can offer him what was left of Hoot's money."

"I thought about that, but if Bull thinks I haven't been fair with him, he'll never let me be."

"Would he really leave you penniless? He'd let you keep something, wouldn't he?"

"You don't know Bull. To show any kind of mercy would be considered weak in his mind. For God's sake, his father thought just feeding a prisoner was a sign of weakness."

Both man sat on opposite beds silently thinking. Joe would have loved to come up with a plan that would let Ed keep some of the money and get back together with his sister. He'd developed a genuine affection for Ed. He wasn't the man his father had described at all. Instead of being a monster, he was a moral man, a man of character. Maybe Joe's father had something to do with the way Ed had been characterized over the years and that was why the police felt he was just an easy mark. Maybe Joe could help right the mistake his father had made.

After a protracted, but comfortable silence, Joe spoke.

"What would Bull do if he got a pile of expensive jewelry that had been stolen forty years ago and that no one cared about anymore," Joe asked, even though he knew the answer to the question. He wanted to make sure Ed agreed.

"He would keep it for himself and no one would know anything about it."

"So basically, he's going to steal it."

"No doubt at all. He's said as much several times."

"Then I got a plan," Joe said.

Joe's hand shook as he dialed the pay phone in the lobby of the Hilton.

"Dispatch," a voice on the line said.

"William Timothy, please," Joe said.

"Who's calling?"

"Just tell him it's about the Harding Country Club."

The voice on the other end didn't bother to ask if Joe minded being put on hold.

"Bull, Timothy," Bull answered in the deep voice that he had practiced as a way of intimidating callers when he answered the phone.

Joe felt the effects of Bull's tone and for a second contemplated just hanging up and forgetting the whole thing.

"This is Joe Mann."

The name instantly registered with Bull.

"I thought you'd be out of town by now."

The comment rattled Joe because he thought back to the man who had broken into his hotel room and told him to leave town. He hadn't thought it was Bull, but now he was sure Bull had known who he was.

"How do you know I'm not already out of town?" Joe realized that with that comment they both knew that Joe wasn't out of town and that Joe had just admitted that he knew Bull had been watching him.

"What can I do for you, Mr. Mann?" Bull asked, ignoring Joe's previous comment.

"You can meet me at the Oval Bar in an hour."

"You mean your girlfriend's bar? Sure, I can do that. Do you have something for me? And where is Mr. Kutz? I assume you are calling on his behalf."

Joe was doubly amazed. Bull knew that he and Ed were connected, and he knew that Joe had been seeing Melissa. He was also impressed at how easily Bull would say the most cutting things, as if he was just making polite conversation. This was a man well versed in verbal combat. I may be way out of my league, Joe thought to himself.

Joe started to wonder if Melissa would be impacted by any of this and he wished he had chosen a different bar to meet at. If Bull knew about Joe and Melissa, meeting there had the potential to really complicate things

"It needs to be discussed," Joe said responding to Bull's inquiry about the jewelry.

"Alrighty, then. I'll see you in an hour."

Stunned, Joe just kept the phone to his ear after Bull had abruptly hung up. Joe went over in his mind the points he wanted to make and the demands he was going to throw out, but he began to think Bull was simply not going to allow him to dictate the terms of their conversation, or of anything else for that matter.

After Joe realized he hadn't been able to maintain control of a simple phone call, he began to wonder how was he going to control a face-to-face meeting.

Joe started to scramble. He wanted to be at the bar before Bull arrived so he could settle himself and get prepared for anything Bull came up with. He wanted to have at least a little control of the situation. He collected his stuff, changed his shirt and jumped in his car for the twenty-minute drive to the Oval.

As he drove and had a few seconds to think, he wished he'd spoken to Melissa to let her know what was going on and to tell her that if Bull or his men asked her if they were seeing each other, it would probably be best if she didn't deny it. They obviously knew something was going on.

"Hell, they might even have pictures," Joe said out loud in his rental car.

He also wanted to tell her that if they mentioned the Wrin house or the jewelry, she had to adamantly deny that Joe had ever mentioned anything to her about them. He couldn't remember if she was working today or not. Hadn't she said something about not being there? Joe really hoped so, but he also realized it might just be wishful thinking. So far Bull had been one step ahead of him in every situation. He or one of his henchmen might be grilling Melissa right now.

Joe needed the time to sit and think and get his nerve up for what he was about to do. The last thing he wanted was to show up late and see Bull sitting there.

Bull wasn't accustomed to doing what other people told him to do. Joe assumed that he would be forty-five minutes late out of disrespect. But Joe was wrong. He pulled into the parking lot of the Oval bar and his heart dropped as he saw Bull's car there a full twenty-five minutes early. Joe had only suggested they meet a half hour ago and there Bull was already.

Maybe he had been here before I even called, thought Joe, and the dispatcher had just patched the call through to him.

Joe had been nervous before he saw Bull's car, but now he felt as if his heart was beating so loudly that everybody would be able to hear it. Turning around and leaving the parking lot was an appealing idea at that moment. Joe's inner wimpy voice was screaming at him to leave.

"You've never served me well in the past so I'm not listening to you now," Joe said out loud to the voice.

The front door of the bar was open in order to take advantage of the nice weather. The sun had now been shining for three straight days, starting with the day Ed and Joe first met at the hotel. Joe walked in slowly and as his eyes adjusted to the dark interior of the bar, the first thing he saw was Bull sitting at a table facing the door. Joe didn't remember a table and chair even being there. He realized Bull had them move it for him so he could see everybody coming and going.

These were the moves of a man with serious distrust issues.

As soon as Bull saw Joe, he got up from the table and walked straight over to him and reached his big meaty paw out to shake Joe's hand. When Joe extended his hand, Bull pulled him in close to him as if they were old friends. He was greeting Joe as if he was thrilled to see him and holding him uncomfortably close.

Joe tried to pull away, but Bull pulled him closer. Joe understood instantly what Bull was doing. He was feeling his body to see if he had a weapon, a tape recorder or even the jewels on him. The embrace was excruciatingly uncomfortable and seemed to be interminable. When Bull finally released him, Joe couldn't tell if he saw relief or disappointment on Bull's face.

The restaurant was practically empty, as if Bull had it emptied for his meeting with Joe. Joe looked around to see if Melissa was there, but he couldn't find her. He couldn't remember if he'd seen her El Camino in the parking lot or not. The shock of seeing Bull's car there so early had really thrown him.

The stench of Bull's sweat mixed with what could only be described as "old man's" cologne hung in Joe's nostrils. Joe noticed enormous sweat stains under Bull's arms, accentuated by the light blue police shirt Bull had on.

"You got something for me in your car?" Bull asked, as if talking to a child in a friendly, but threatening manner

"No," replied Joe, a little afraid that Bull might reach out and slap him on the side of his head for disappointing him.

Bull's smile disappeared and the snarl returned.

"Why don't we go outside and check?"

Joe's comfort level had become non-existent. Everything he had planned was being disrupted. He wanted to control the situation and yet Bull had yanked control instantly. Joe had planned to do all the talking and to lay out his offer at a table in the restaurant. Now he found himself being led outside.

As they left the bar, the bright sun caused both men to squint. Joe turned right to head to his car, but Bull grabbed his arm and pulled him to the left towards his squad car.

"What are we doing?" Joe asked.

Bull didn't say a word. He just kept walking with Joe by the arm as a teacher might do leading an unruly child to the principal's office. As they approached the squad car, Bull told him to get in. Outside the bar several people were watching the event unfold, but Bull seemed not to care at all.

Joe was very nervous, but relieved that Bull didn't cuff him and sit him in the back. Joe got in the front and Bull got in on the driver's side.

"Where's your cop murdering boyfriend?"

"I'm here on his behalf."

"Look, boy, the only thing I'm interested in is the stolen stuff. You either have it or you're in a deep pile of shit. Don't forget. I know you were Kutz's accomplice breaking into that house."

Joe realized what Bull was saying. Whether Joe did or didn't help Ed, Bull was going to say he did and arrest him also.

There was no sense denying that the jewels existed now. Ed had already admitted to it.

Bull was becoming furious. The veins on his forehead and neck were pulsating almost audibly. Joe thought how Bull would love to get Joe inside his jail just so he could kick the shit out him.

Joe took a deep breath and began, "He wants to give part of it to you. He's willing to give you seventy-five percent. He's been in prison his whole life. He has nothing. He's an old man and he wants to do right by his sister. He's not asking for much. You can let him keep that much, can't you?"

Joe stopped talking, expecting Bull to jump right in with a response.

Bull listened quietly and let the question hang in the air for what seemed like two minutes, and then he smiled.

Bull was being careful now. He had his own agenda

"Tell me again why you're here and he's not, other than the fact that everybody but me thinks he's dead."

"There's a lot of bad blood between you, your father and Ed. He doesn't like you very much."

Bull smiled a contemplative smile, as if he'd love to have shared a laugh over that with his father.

Then the smile left his face and his sneer reappeared.

"Do me a favor, son. Don't you ever mention my dad in the same breath as that scumbag friend of yours or you and me are going to have a real problem."

Joe thought, if we don't have a real problem right now, I'd hate to see what a real problem looks like.

Smiling again, Bull said, "So old Ed doesn't like me much? Well, I'm really hurt. I'm a nice guy. Here's what I'm gonna do for Ed. Nothing. Not a goddamn thing. That bastard murdered two of my dad's finest men in cold blood and left them to die on a dirty basement floor. He should have been executed or at least died in prison. My dad was the only person in the whole state who knew he had that money and jewelry and that he robbed that country club."

Joe couldn't help but feel that Bull had suddenly taken on the persona of a twelve year old arguing with a friend about whose dad was better.

"I want every piece of jewelry and anything else he stole as payment for what me and my dad went through for all these years."

Bull continued his rollercoaster ride of emotion between smiling and sneering, yelling and whispering, moving closer to Joe and then sitting back. His unpredictability had Joe backed up against the driver's side door as tightly as he could be.

"But I am a nice guy," Bull continued. "I won't run you both in, him for violating his parole and you for not minding your goddamn business. And, by God, I got the power and the influence to throw you two in jail and keep you there as long as I feel like it."

Bull paused to measure the effect he was having on Joe.

"Oh, I get it," Bull went on in a quiet voice. "You think all that stuff in the papers lately weakened me. Don't make me laugh. Everybody who went against me is going to be out on their ass in the next election or fired from their jobs. All's that little episode did was to consolidate my power and let me know who my enemies are. Most of the people who went against me are already scurrying like rats on a sinking ship. One of them already put his house on the market."

Bull was full of himself. Safely inside his squad car he felt in control, out of the way from prying ears, listening devices or tape recorders. He wanted Joe to know who he was messing with.

Joe took a deep breath and went on. "If you agree to work with him on this, he's willing to make the exchange today."

The prospect of Bull getting his hands on his long sought prize seemed to appeal to him. It would be a final validation in his father's eyes for Bull. It was almost as if Bull was doing this for his father. He'd agree to anything because he had no intention of honoring any agreements. Both Ed and Joe were pretty sure that Bull would take the deal and then come back for the rest. They were prepared for him to reject Bull's offer, but planned to stand their ground that Ed should get something.

"He just won't agree if I have to go back and say he can't keep anything. Please just give him something so he can save face. He wants this to be over," Joe said, trying desperately to appeal to Bull's better nature, hoping he had one, and not really knowing what his next move would be if Bull didn't take the offer. He was pretty sure, though, that Bull had a next move.

Bull's demeanor had calmed significantly. He adjusted himself in his seat. They had been in the car for a few minutes now without the air conditioning on. It seemed intentional to Joe, but Bull was the only one sweating.

"Tell me again what your involvement is here," Bull said.

"I'm just a friend."

Joe had a sense that Bull knew a lot more about him than he was letting on. He had probably done a full background check on Joe as soon as he had first pulled him over the week before.

"What's your wife back in New Jersey think about you messing around with that waitress? Of course, she knows, right?" Bull said sarcastically. "Maybe I'll just give her a call and invite her up here and the four of us can have a nice little supper together."

Joe was amazed how easily Bull went from kindness to cruelty and back to kindness again. It was probably a secret of his success.

Joe didn't react. He couldn't let Bull know how much his threat had staggered him. He also didn't know if Bull really knew something or if it was just conjecture. Were there photos or video tape of them together? Could Bull have that much control? The thought horrified Joe. He didn't think it was possible, but underestimating Bull's power and willingness to use it was not serving him well. Without hard proof, if Barbara ever heard the rumors of an affair, Joe could deny it forever, which he already had decided he would do if he ever got caught. He was pretty sure Melissa would never tell either.

Joe was surprised at how fast his ideal situation for having an affair became so much less then ideal. The idea of having an affair in his mind had to carry with it the absolute impossibility of his wife ever finding out. Hurting her was something he never wanted to do. Maybe that was where his "plan" fell apart, he thought. There was never any such thing as an absolute certainty. What if there were photos or video tapes?

"We are here to talk about Ed," Joe said.

Bull laughed, knowing that he had scored a direct hit.

"We'll, I'd really like to meet her someday," Bull said as a poorly veiled threat. "There's always something a man doesn't want his wife to find out. My dad told me that a million times. Okay. Let your friend keep one piece, but I want the rest tonight."

Joe was relieved to get that one concession. Now their plan could move forward.

"Okay, I'll drop it by your house," Joe said, already knowing that wouldn't sit well with Bull, but wondering now if he might be risking a slap to the face for his insolence.

"The hell you will," Bull said, his veins bulging again. "You'll drop it off behind the equipment box on the Babe Ruth Field at Hollar and Allen Park no later than midnight tonight."

Joe wondered if Bull saw the irony in his dropping off the loot from a heist that led to the deaths of the two men at the field who it was named for. Probably not, he thought.

"If I find out that anything is missing from the robbery, all deals are off and you will both end up in jail with my foot up your asses."

Joe knew that there was really no way for Bull to know how many items there should be. They both knew that, but decided against factoring it into their discussion. Joe also knew that everything had been converted to cash. There were no "items" left to choose from.

Joe got out of Bull's car. Before going, he automatically reached his hand out to shake Bull's as if they had just concluded a mutually beneficial business transaction.

Bull shook his hand and smiled.

"I knew I liked you as soon as I saw you," Bull said, obviously elated to know he'd be getting his money that day.

# Chapter Twenty-one

After getting out of Bull's squad car, Joe walked back to his car. He noticed Bull stop his car before pulling on to the access road so that he could write down Joe's license plate number as well as the make and model of the rental car, Joe presumed.

When Bull pulled away, Joe sat there for a few minutes to contemplate what had just occurred. Happy to have gotten out of the car in one piece and without being arrested, Joe felt pretty good about himself. He wanted to call Ed, but felt like he didn't have time. Whatever Bull was planning, Joe was sure he already had it in the works. Bull had trumped him at almost every turn so far. There was no reason to think that he wouldn't do it again if Joe wasn't prepared.

Joe was fairly sure that Bull would have someone at the baseball field in Hollar and Allen Park within twenty minutes of their meeting to stake out the place until midnight. That meant there was no way the drop could be made at the baseball field. But the drop had to be made that night. Joe had to alter his plan.

Joe got out of his car and went back inside to use the phone in the Oval. He called Corra.

"Hi, Corra. It's Joe," he said before she even said "hi." This time there was no joking between the two.

"Are you alright?" she asked

"Yes, I'm fine," Joe said, "but I need another favor. I need the name of another ball field than Babe Ruth Field in town, preferably one with an equipment box

"Well, I don't know about an equipment box, but Chipalot Field has a baseball diamond on it."

"Chipalot?"

"Yeah, it was named after a little boy who was hit by a drunk driver while he was playing in the leaves by the side of the road."

Joe didn't have any more time for the history of the field, but he listened politely anyway. He fleetingly wondered why were baseball fields always named after people who died young?

"Great," Joe said after Corra had finished. "Where is it?"

Corra recognized how much of a rush Joe was in and gave him the directions quickly. Joe scribbled them down furiously in the blank yellow space of an ad from the tattered phone book hanging from a chain in the booth.

"I love you," he said in much the same way he would say it to his own mother or grandmother.

"You just be careful," she admonished him again.

Joe returned to his car. He took out a yellow piece of paper from his legal pad. He took a deep breath and said out loud, "I really hope Chipalot field has an equipment box."

Then he started to write.

*Bull,*

*We thought it safer for all involved to change the drop sight. There is an equipment box at Chipalot field at the middle school. We will leave the bag there by midnight tonight.*

Joe pulled out onto the access road and drove straight to Hollar and Allen Field. He knew he was taking a big risk, but he felt like he had no other choice. The baseball field was on the lower level of Southern Valley High School, but school was in session so no teams were on the field. There was only one group of kids, probably a gym class, Joe thought, on a soccer field clear across the other side of the school.

He pulled around to the north side of the school, not quite sure where the Babe Ruth Field was, and stopped at a locked gate. Not wanting to seem lost and have someone offer to help, Joe stopped his car quickly and got out. Although the gates were closed to car traffic, there was a space for people to walk through. Joe could see in the distance a pristine ball field with an equipment box.

The school was a large school and served the three surrounding towns of Bolster, Johnstown and Gold's Lake. The original building had been added on to several times. Joe hung out near the corner of the building and steeled himself for the long walk across the school grounds when he noticed the cornerstone on what appeared to be the oldest part of the building. It said "Established, 1926."

That was the year his father had been born and this was most likely the school he had attended. Who knows, Joe thought, maybe this is the very spot where Robbie and his father had snuck out of class to smoke. The thought made Joe melancholy for a moment, but he knew there would be time to ruminate on all of this afterward.

At least he hoped there would be.

Joe decided he had to go for it. He started to walk as if he had some purpose other than the one he did have and hoped there would be less of a chance of someone noticing him. He clung to the path that bordered a wooded area. The field was at the bottom of a good size hill and Joe had to stop himself from running. That was more purpose than he wanted to exude.

As he moved along, he heard the slamming of a dumpster lid. He turned his head back uphill to see if he was being watched and saw a janitor who had just dumped a large pile of debris into the dumpster. He wasn't paying attention to Joe, so Joe went on. Once he arrived at the field, he saw an old man walking with his dog along the outside of the left outfield fence. He didn't notice Joe and Joe decided to ignore him.

Joe walked over to the large wooden equipment box, took out the note he had written, and placed it in a lunch bag he found in a nearby garbage can. He stuffed the bag down behind the equipment box.

There was a city street a couple hundred yards away that Joe would have loved to get to rather than walk all the way back across the school campus, but the gate to it was locked and without a pass-through for people. Climbing over the fence would have been too noticeable and could have alerted someone to call the police. That was the last thing Joe needed.

He returned to his car, passing by the janitor who was still emptying trash and was still oblivious to Joe. Once in his car, Joe gripped his steering wheel with both hands trying to get his breathing under control.

By writing the note and leaving it here, Bull couldn't argue or object, Joe reasoned. For once, someone else would be in control, albeit temporarily.

Bull would have to drive to Chipalot field. He would be furious, but by that time, if all went right, neither Ed nor Joe would ever have to see or speak with Bull Junior again.

That afternoon Ed filled a bag with pebbles and gave it to Joe to place behind the equipment box at Chipalot field. The baseball diamond at the middle school was on a large, ten-acre tract of land that was home to the town's athletic department, as well, for use in league baseball, soccer, football or for anything else the town had going on.

Chipalot field itself was completely surrounded by woods. One defunct train track ran along its west side. There was a one-lane road that circled the entire tract, but only one parking area for it on the south side where you entered the area. The ball field with the equipment box was several hundred yards away on the farthest side north from the parking lot.

Bull's gonna love taking this walk, Joe thought.

Joe made the trek from the parking lot across to the field and stayed close to the train track just in case anybody was around. Dusk was falling by now, but there was still plenty of light.

The equipment box was orange and was chained to the backstop behind home plate. There was a green fifty-five gallon drum used as a trash can that Joe had to move out of the way first, though. It hadn't been emptied in weeks so trash was all around the base of it.

Joe stepped back over the trash and tried to lift the equipment box. It wouldn't budge. Joe remembered from his own childhood baseball days that often these equipment boxes were also filled with large bags of lime used for lining the base paths.

Joe repositioned himself for a more mighty lift. If it didn't move, there would be real trouble. There was no way he could leave the bag sitting on top of the box. There was too big a chance that a dog walker or some kids would find it and move it.

Joe pushed up with his legs and pulled with his arms, his back straining. He was able to lift the heavy wooden box half an inch off the ground and move it forward just enough to fit the bag behind it.

There was nothing left to do now but wait.

Joe's days in Gold's Lake were almost over. If all went well, he planned on leaving that night.

He had come seeking answers and clarity, and he had gotten so much more. He had learned about himself. What he was capable of. What was important to him. Why he did some of the things he did. Why his father had done some of the things he had done.

He wondered if he had found answers that would allow him to make peace with his father, and then he decided that thought was disingenuous. He'd made peace with his father long ago. Even as a child, Joe had seen him as he was. A man with challenges, with self doubt, with demons, a man who should have loved, a man who wanted to love, but a man who just didn't know how to love.

Going to Gold's Lake to make peace with his father was a cop out, Joe concluded. It was an excuse for him to misbehave. Cal taught Joe a lot, some good and some bad. Perhaps the best thing he had taught him, though, was to take responsibility for himself.

There were still times that Joe felt that he should hate his father for the way he had abused him and his brother and especially for the way he had abused their mother. But he didn't hate him. He wondered what it would take for him to hate someone if that kind of abuse didn't.

Cal was just a product of his own upbringing, Joe thought. From what Joe had heard, his father was much better than his father was before him. Maybe things would continue to improve through the generations, Joe hoped.

In many ways Joe did feel he was better than his father. In other ways he was only as good, and in some other ways he realized he was not as good.

In the end, Joe decided that it was a bad idea to keep comparing himself with his dad. They were both imperfect men, but both were men who wanted to be better. The jury's still out on me, Joe thought to himself. His children would be the final arbiters of how good a father he was.

He still had time to atone for his sins and be the man he wanted to be.

Joe knew he had trouble showing love. He was trying to address that. He would work harder now to chase his demons away and to enjoy what he did have. He would tell his wife he loved her because deep down, that was the only thing he was sure of. He would have to live with the guilt of what he had done with Melissa. Sure, she had been willing and didn't act like a victim, but how would she feel in a year or two from now?

Joe wondered if years from now, he would feel like the victim of his own crime. He could never again say that he'd always been faithful, and infidelity had destroyed his father.

His mission would be not to let it destroy him.

Cal had looked at his life as a balance sheet. Did he do more good then bad? Joe did the same. Did the mistakes outweigh the good he had done? Did helping Ed and his sister outweigh fooling around with Melissa? Barbara might not think so.

And why was he helping Ed? Was he doing it for his love of mankind or because he wanted to write a book or to find the answers to questions about his father that had bothered him for a long time?

Gold's Lake had become a part of Joe. Perhaps, he thought, it always had been part of him. Maybe what had been imprinted on Cal's DNA had made it through to Joe. He was leaving, but some day he'd be back.

The next time, however, he would bring his wife and kids.

# Chapter Twenty-two

The bag had been placed at Chipalot field and Joe was ready to leave, but he was going to make sure that he said a proper good-bye to everybody and thank them for their help. He knew hanging around was dangerous, but he had to tie up loose ends.

On his way back from the field, he headed over to the library, hoping it was still open. If not, he would leave Corra a note.

The big front door was wide open so Joe walked in. He saw Corra and saw the relief sweep over her.

"You're still in one piece, I'm glad to see," she said.

"I don't have much time, but I wanted to make sure I saw you."

Joe told her what he could without endangering her and told her that he would call her and fill her in on the rest. He asked her not to talk about any of this for a while.

She sat down, apparently astonished by what Joe had told her. For the first time, she looked old to Joe.

"If I told anybody any of this, no one would believe me anyway," she said. "They'd think the final marble had rolled out of my head."

Joe couldn't tell her everything because he wanted to protect her from Bull and his cronies. It was important that she be able to plead complete ignorance to what was going to happen that night. Joe knew of Bull's vindictive side and his willingness to be cruel, and he knew he would be crushed if he found out Bull's venom had been sprayed at her. Joe thought that somehow Corra did appreciate what he was doing for her.

"You're a good boy," she said. "Did you find what you were really looking for?"

Joe knew she was no longer talking about the robbery or the murders.

"Yeah, I think I did."

"Good. Now go home and give that wife and those kids a big kiss for me."

"I will," Joe said, again thinking that he'd underestimated her one more time. She seemed to have known all there was to know about him in the first five minutes they met.

Joe got back in his rental car and headed for Robbie's house, but he couldn't keep his attention off the upcoming night. What if Bull or one of his guys went to Hollar and Allen field early and found the note? They could be looking for me right now, Joe thought.

His pulse quickened.

Maybe I should leave now and send Robbie a note. Well, that might work for Robbie, but it certainly wouldn't work for Melissa.

It really wouldn't work for Robbie either, he decided. She'd waited years to tell him he had a half brother and now he was going to run out without even saying good-bye? Joe didn't think so.

Finding out he had a half brother seemed almost like an afterthought to his adventure, Joe realized, and while Joe wanted to meet him, that would have to wait for another time.

He pulled up to Robbie's house, but there was no answer at

the door. She was Joe's only and Joe's last connection to his father. She had loved Cal and had had a child with him. She and Joe were related. Her age made it likely that Joe would never see her again. Once she passed, his father's chapter would be forever closed. No one who knew Cal Mann as a child would exist.

All that would be left was his book.

# Chapter Twenty-three

Bull arrived at Hollar and Allen field long before midnight just as Joe suspected he would. It was about nine p.m. and darkness had settled over the entire field. Bull pulled his car on to a side street behind the high school about three hundred yards from the fields. He was content to just sit and watch and maybe even surprise Joe or Ed with the high powered spotlight mounted on the side of his squad car.

Around 9:30, though, Bull got out of his car and made his way over to the equipment box. He was giddy with anticipation.

Joe knew Bull would be there early, so he was too. He stood about five feet into the woods off the road that ran along the back side of the school. He could see out, but he knew he couldn't be seen. It was risky, but he thought Bull would never expect him there. Bull would have the loot on his mind and little else.

Joe had been there when Bull had pulled into his hiding space, uncomfortably close to Joe. Joe knew he couldn't leave now even if he had wanted to.

Bull became furious when he found the note. Joe could see the change in the way he walked away from the equipment box from the way he had walked toward it. He was pissed, Joe knew, that was for sure.

He had gone to the field himself rather than send one of his men because he didn't want any questions about what he was going to do with a bag full of antique valuable jewelry, Joe surmised.

It was too dark on the unlit field so Bull had to wait until he got back into his squad car before he could turn on the overhead light and read the note.

"Son of a bitch," he screamed, loud enough for Joe to hear. Joe could picture the large vein about to burst on Bull's forehead.

Bull wasn't used to being told what to do and he didn't like it at all. He thought about not going to Chipalot Field at all, but just going directly to Ed's house and arresting him. He had reasoned that Ed would never be crazy enough to cross him. Ed, of all people, knew the cruel history of Bull and his family. But Bull had been taught at a very early age to always control the situation.

"Have them come to you," his father always said. "Keep them off balance. Know your enemies. Never allow the playing field to be level. Always have it sloped in your favor." And, most importantly, "Never go into a situation blind."

Bull Junior had always done well by listening to Bull Senior's advice. It had saved him and his job many times. The jewelry from the country club heist would be his grand prize. He couldn't run the risk of letting someone else find it.

He turned his car toward Chipalot Field, all the while cursing Ed and Joe, swearing to get even with him for this insult.

It had never occurred to Bull Junior that Chipalot Field might be a set up, but if it did, he felt he could talk his way out of it by saying that he recovered the loot after forty years through his own good police work and that he planned on turning it in as soon as he left the field. He could spin this. No problem.

Joe had already left for Chipalot Field as soon as he had seen Bull read the note.

A little while later, Bull pulled his car into the Chipalot parking area and stopped it, facing the distant equipment box.. The field with the bag was about three hundred yards away. Ordinarily he'd drive right onto the field, not caring about the tire tracks he would leave the maintenance men to repair. But this time he didn't want any tracks left, so he would have to walk.

He opened his car door and shimmied his belly around so it faced the door and then pulled himself up with a grunt and fart. As he made his way across the field, he looked around several times to make sure he wasn't being watched. Everything was completely dark and silent. The only sound was Bull's labored breathing.

He had no idea Joe was watching every move from his hiding place in the woods behind the railroad track.

Bull reached the baseball diamond and headed straight for the equipment box. Having played on this field as a boy, he knew exactly how it sat. As he approached it, he eyed it carefully and then looked behind it to see where the bag was. He shined his flashlight along the back side of the box and saw the bag pushed almost all the way down to the bottom of the space between the box and the backdrop.

He reached behind and down, but couldn't reach the bag. His large girth kept him from getting close enough. Believing this was an additional insult, he muttered a string of obscenities. It should have been stashed by the end of the box instead of in the very middle at the very bottom. Bull saw this indignity as one more thumb in the eye that Ed and Joe would pay for.

"Those sons of bitches are dead," he said into the quiet night air.

The words brought a smile to Joe's face.

Bull stretched and grunted and was still sweating profusely from the walk across the field. Both his feet were now in the air as he stretched to reach the bag and did everything he could to extend his reach the last two inches he needed to get the bag.

Once his fingertips brushed the bag, he knew he was home free. The long sought after prize was his. He finally was able to grab hold of the bag and with great difficulty bring it out from behind the box. The bag was heavier then he expected and he let out a little yell of excitement, but then he covered his mouth with his hand.

Bull hurried across the field back to his car. The walk back seemed endless due to his excitement, and as Joe watched, he seemed even more nervous now that he had the bag.

A car with a broken headlight was approaching the parking lot. Bull paused for a second as the car drove on by. A teenage boy and girl were in the car paying no attention to Bull. They were probably going somewhere to make out, Bull thought with a smile, briefly recounting the times he had staked out the kids' make-out joints for his own enjoyment.

He opened the door to his car quickly and squeezed in and turned on the dome light. He opened the bag and stared inside. At first he wasn't sure if his eyes had adjusted yet to the light. What was he looking at? Could it be? They looked to be ordinary pebbles and rocks, like the ones you'd find on the side of any road, with a cassette tape sitting on top of them.

Bull's mood changed abruptly. It didn't change to rage, though. It changed to the childish disappointment one might witness when a five year old opens a present and it isn't what the child anticipated. Bull seemed to be trying to hold his breath until he got what he really wanted.

He was sad now, and the rage would come, but first the sadness slowly turned to a queasy intrigue. What was on that tape that made Ed and Joe think they could give him a bag of rocks?

Bull removed the tape from the bag, shook off the dust and stuck it in the cassette player on his dashboard. Bull turned on the ignition, listened for a second, and then recognized what it was. His mouth fell open.

He heard the sound of his own intimidating voice. He recognized the conversation immediately. It was the first of a series of conversations that Bull had had with Ed at his house. Bull kept listening to the tape. The final recording was the conversation that Bull had had with Joe in his squad car earlier that day.

In all these conversations, Bull had made it quite clear what he thought the town owed him and what he thought of the town. It was clear he was going to keep the items robbed from the country club for himself. The tape showed a police chief completely out of control, serving not the people of Gold's Lake, but only himself. It showed a policeman willing to use cruelty and torture for his own gains. It showed that he knew that Ed Kutz wasn't dead and that he hadn't reported it.

Despite what Bull had told Joe about consolidating power after the scandal and then getting rid of his enemies, he knew he was still extremely vulnerable. Even a minor incident would bring him tumbling down, and once he was out of power, his real enemies would line up to repay him.

Like the coward Bull had always been, he turned off the dome light and started to cry.

By then Joe was on his way to see Melissa at the Oval. A broad smile already on his face, he flicked on the radio just in time to hear the last two lines of a Bruce Springsteen song.

*It's a town full of losers*
*I'm pulling out of here to win*


This is all too good, Joe thought.


Ed knew from the day he had gotten out of prison that he would have to deal with Bull Junior. That apple had fallen right at the base of the tree, so there was no getting around it.

He had started taping every encounter he had with Bull. He didn't trust him and he was afraid that Bull would fabricate a story to get him locked up again. When Bull came to his house, he turned the tape recorder on in the top drawer of the end table. Afraid that Bull would approach him outside, he started wearing the tape recorder fastened to his leg with medical tape.

In the hotel room, Ed had told Joe that he'd been recording the conversations with Bull since he had gotten out of prison. Jim Switzer, the private dick with extensive knowledge of recording and wiretapping who Ed met in prison, was only too happy to do whatever he could if it meant causing pain to Bull Jr. Jim had been released from prison shortly before Ed was released, and he was one of the first people Ed had looked up when he got out.

If Joe had been wearing a standard tape recorder during his meeting with Bull, Bull would have found it when he hugged him. Ed, with Jim Switzer's guidance, had been shrewd enough to put a small, state of the art device behind Joe's left calf. The microphone ran from Joe's calf up the outer seem of his blue jeans, across the backside of his belt and came out at the buckle. It was so small, even if Bull had run his hands over it, he would have missed it.

Joe wore the bug when he had the meeting with Bull at the Oval in Bull's squad car. Joe had been so nervous, he feared that his sweat would short circuit the device and electrocute him.

By the time Bull had recovered his bag of rocks and the cassette, Ed was in his handicapped van with his sister and a nurse he had hired temporarily. They were heading out of Gold's Lake forever.

There was a high end home for older handicapped adults that Ed had discovered in Scranton, Pennsylvania. Ed's plan was to get himself an apartment right nearby so he could see her every day. With all that cash, he could do it easily.

The last two stops Ed had made before leaving Gold's Lake were at the modest homes of Charlotte Allen and Beth Hollar. He had planned these stops years ago, before he knew if he would ever get out of jail.

They lived within three blocks of each other. Neither had ever married again, according to Corra, who had given Joe a complete rundown on them for Ed. Joe would have liked to meet them himself, but time just didn't allow it.

Ed pulled up to the first house and a few minutes after arrived at the second. At each house he had gotten out of his van while his sister and the nurse looked on, walked up to the porch, and put an envelope in each mailbox. Inside each envelope was a cashier's check for $100,000 and a note that said, "Forgive me."

He hadn't signed the notes.

As Ed would later relate to Joe during one of their phone calls, he had no feelings for Gold's Lake and no plans to ever return. The place had meant nothing but pain and heartache to him. When he needed the town, they abandoned him and his sister, and that was something he couldn't forgive them for.

Joe told him, "I can see why you hate that place."

There was a long pause on the phone and then Ed spoke. "Its not hate that I feel when I think about it. It's apathy. It's just a place to me now, but it wasn't the place that caused all the pain in my family. I don't even hate the people. I'm responsible for what I did. I can't blame anybody else. When I'm not feeling apathy, I'm feeling badly for the policemen's families. That's something I have learned to live with. I can't escape it."

Ed and Joe talked by phone frequently after that and even got together once or twice. On one such visit, Ed confessed that he had hated Joe's father for the way he portrayed him in the book, but had since reconsidered after meeting Joe.

"He couldn't be all bad. He had you for a son," Ed said.

Joe just smiled and said, "Yeah, that's right. He wasn't all bad. Not even close."

After watching Bull at Chipalot Field, Joe no longer felt like he had to leave Gold's Lake so hastily. He was pretty sure he had delivered a mighty blow to Bull and that Bull would want to lay low for awhile. Part of Joe wanted to be visible to Bull to help rub his lesson in his face, but he decided against it. Bull always had the option of shooting him, he reasoned. Maybe it was time to leave.

Joe had to see Melissa. They had shared so much in such a short time that he felt like he'd known her all his life, or maybe that he had known her in another life.

Joe pulled his rental car around the back of the restaurant and slipped it in between the dumpster and the block wall, out of sight from any police cars. His confidence ebbed and flowed. He did and then he didn't want to come face to face with Bull. Only the El Camino remained in the Oval's parking lot.

He entered through the back door, walked through the kitchen and found her in the stock room. She knew he was there without having to turn around.

"I guess you're leaving," she said.

"Yeah."

"Vacation's over? Time to get back to your real life?"

"Yeah."

"Did you find the answers you were looking for?"

Melissa stood up and turned to him. She was starting to tear up. Joe pretended not to notice.

"In some ways I did and in some ways I created more questions."

"Any regrets?"

"Well, I don't regret meeting you, if that's what you mean."

There wasn't a lot to say. They had met, fooled around and now he was leaving and she was staying. To both of them it was more than a physical encounter. If they had both been single, they might have had something.

But Joe was married. He had gone down the path married men were not supposed to explore. He had risked his marriage and his family. Had he thought fooling around would make him understand his father better? The only thing he felt sure of was that his father would be disappointed in him for not learning from his mistakes.

Melissa was sad. She'd lost her husband years ago and Joe had stirred up feelings she'd long since buried. She knew her sadness was more for the husband she lost and the life she should have had than it was for Joe. She'd spend her remaining days smiling at the world and working fourteen hours days to avoid going home to a lonely house. The chances of connecting with another guy like Joe, and that guy being available, were not good. She wasn't a home wrecker and she would have had to cut it off with Joe if it had gone any further.

Now she'd have to be happy serving drinks and flirting with old men.

Joe mumbled something about staying in touch, but Melissa cut him short.

"No. Go home. It's where you belong. Write your book. Make a million dollars. Don't try to contact me and don't come back. Think of me and smile once in awhile. I'll do the same."

"Maybe in another life," Joe said wistfully.

"Yeah, maybe in another life." Melissa smiled back through her tears.

Joe put his arms around her in a hug they both wanted to have last forever. She was crying and he felt he might also if he didn't get out of there quickly. He pulled away, kissed her on the forehead and said good-bye.

Joe walked out the back door slowly and turned for one last look. Melissa had already gone back to work restocking her bar.

Even though it was late at night, Joe had one last stop to make before leaving.

He wanted to go see the place that had started it all, the place he imagined so many times in his childhood dreams. The Wrin house wasn't too far from the highway so he could catch it on the way out.

He returned his rental car to the lot and dropped the keys though the slot in the front door. He had paid for the car for another three days, but that didn't make any difference now. He got into his Explorer and made his way towards the highway.

The town seemed much less strange to him now. He'd come here not knowing anyone and now he was leaving friends and family behind, not to mention an enemy or two. He knew it would be months before everything that had happened sank in and he could truly assimilate it. If then.

He passed Route 100 and wondered if the burnt out Porsche was still there. He passed the library and Strongwaters'. He resisted an urge to wait until morning and tell off Walter Strong. What good would that do?

He saw the police station and stayed clear of it. No need to poke that injured dog.

He had been in town a little over two weeks. It seemed like much less time, and much more. He had a hard time remembering when Gold's Lake wasn't part of his consciousness, even though this was his first real trip there. He had met good people and bad, just as he would anywhere else in the country. He'd helped a man that deserved help and he had participated in the eventual undoing, he hoped, of a tyrannical police dynasty.

The Wrin house was still there. Joe hoped someone would burn it down. Maybe the city would demolish it. What good was it? It had an awful past and a useless future. It should be knocked down, paved over and made into a playground or something else worthwhile.

In its present condition it reminded Joe of a portal to hell. If there was one thing this world doesn't need, Joe thought, it was another portal to hell.

George and Bill were long gone. Ed had served his time. Joe's father was long dead and Robbie would be also in the not too distant future. But she would never burn it down. It represented some strange monument to her history with Cal.

Maybe the wives of George and Bill would use some of their money to get rid of the house, Joe speculated. He knew, though, that the house would probably stand until some developer needed to clear it for a strip mall or condos. They'd plow it down without a thought to what had happened there. The world would move on.

Joe took one last look. The house looked less ominous than it did when he first arrived. Maybe because he was able to discover it's one remaining secret. The jewelry was gone. The story was ended. Now it was just a house.

Joe smiled, put the car in reverse and said aloud, "No. It's not just a house. It's so much more."

The moon was darting in and out between the clouds. The night felt warm one minute and then, when the moon disappeared, it felt cold.

It might rain and it might not, Joe thought.

"Yeah, I guess I got the answers I was looking for," he said to himself. He pulled out onto the Interstate and headed for home.

- SHOW, don't Tell
- Usage
- Verb tense / conditional
- Compound words ??
- Inconsistencies - motel / apt
- Implausibilities — Why would
  no one suspect that jewels
  were hidden in Wren house?
  That's where the murders
  occurred. Duh.
- Authorial Rationalization — no
  basis for murderous conclusions
  (ie Dad, eg) at end

CPSIA information can be obtained at www.ICGtesting.com
227047LV00001B/71/P